Inside
Out

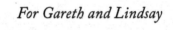

For Gareth and Lindsay

CHRIS RICKETTS

He will kill the woman in his life.
She will welcome her death.

Inside Out

Little Singing Bear Publishing

First published in 2016 by
Little Singing Bear Publishing
Dalkey, Co. Dublin, Ireland

Paperback	ISBN: 978 1 911013 204
eBook – mobi format	ISBN: 978 1 911013 211
eBook – ePub format	ISBN: 978 1 911013 228
CreateSpace paperback	ISBN: 978 1 911013 235

Produced by Kazoo Independent Publishing Services
222 Beech Park, Lucan, Co. Dublin
www.kazoopublishing.com

Kazoo Independent Publishing Services is not the publisher of this work. All rights and responsibilities pertaining to this work remain with Little Singing Bear Publishing.

Kazoo offers independent authors a full range of publishing services. For further details visit www.kazoopublishing.com

Cover design by Andrew Brown
Printed in the EU

ACKNOWLEDGEMENTS

THANK YOU TO ALL THOSE who have helped *Inside Out* reach this stage, especially Vanessa Fox O'Loughlin, Aifric McGlinchy, Chenile Keogh, Andrew Brown and Robert Doran.

Mair, Susan and Sarah Ricketts, Lindsay and Gareth Connolly, your encouragement has been invaluable.

THE END AND THE BEGINNING

'The world as we have created it is a process of our thinking. It cannot be changed without changing our thinking.'

– Albert Einstein

I KNEW THAT WITH EVERY injection I was killing her, but it had to happen.

It was looking in the mirror that brought the grief. I would bring the blade down over the thickening stubble and wonder how I had spent so many years locked in such a painful prison. It didn't help that I vacillated between loving her and loathing her. We'd had good times, many moments to cherish, but I had grown as a person while she had remained in the past, and there was no meeting point to keep us together.

As a child I had read murder mysteries and felt a strange curiosity about the minds of those capable of such a crime. The deviousness, the calculated cruelty, the lack of sympathy for their victim, and yet in each callous deed there was the passion to kill in the first place. I can relate to this passion. I want Rachel removed from me so that I can find what I have always wanted – a woman to love me, because that's what this is all about. It is about the need to be loved and desired for the adult I have become. I have outgrown Rachel.

It hasn't been an easy decision though. The first injection caused nightmares. In my dreams I played out the scenarios of the disbelieving faces, the cold eyes and the venomous words, and yet, when I stood at the foot of the bed, the small needle in my hand, I didn't feel a monster. I felt the time had come to release her from this life. Rachel wasn't happy. The needle was only giving her a sense of relief. She saw things the same way. I know she did.

The needle pricked the skin so softly. No significant loss of blood or searing pain, just a tiny blue mark. She took it as I knew she would, with resignation and a sense of release. That was my persuasiveness. I had talked her into understanding that all this was for the best, that she had suffered so much and that there would be relief in the next life. But there were nights when I lay in our bed and thought of her body slowly dying, the fluid coursing through her veins, and I shrivelled with the thought that I was taking her one step further away from life. Within a year she would cease to exist and I would be left to live my life on my own.

Of course there was the fear of loss. Living with a familiar pain is often easier than bringing about a change that cannot be reversed, and death is irreversible. If she died, I could not bring her back. It would be the end. It would be final. And yet by killing her I would be free to live again. But I would also have to cut myself adrift from all those I know. I could not stay in my home with sacrificial blood upon the carpet. I would have to leave. That was the bold step I was taking. The injections were easy in comparison. Closing this chapter of my life and starting again was the scary part.

How many people out there will sit in judgement of me? Yet they are probably living lives that they don't want and are afraid to make the bold first move to alter their world. There is a piper calling their tune, a weak and feeble tune that their tired legs run behind, tripping and falling on the way, whereas I am now the master of my own destiny. My own parents spent years in a failed marriage, scared to face a future alone. I was not going to perpetuate that tradition. If all it took was a well-placed needle, then I was going to face the consequences of my actions, happy in the certainty that I would not be like them. I would not die from inactivity or passivity.

CHAPTER 1

Mornings in autumn frequently came shrouded in mist, a damp breath that touched every lamp post and door, stone wall and rusted gate. The greyness on these days would lift from the landscape like a heavy dream, slow to release its inhabitants from their darkest thoughts.

I ran a café near the small harbour with its rusty-bottomed boats and overturned fish crates. I had bought it from an English woman who had fallen in love with the village one beautiful summer and then grown despairing of its lonely winters. In summer, Clochan is vibrant and noisy, with tourists trying to find a spare parking space and the ice-cream shop in full swing. Yachts of all sizes sail up and down the narrow inlet, their sails like brightly coloured clothes strung along a line. Irish music fills the air, bodhráns and fiddles a constant reminder of a fast-disappearing Celtic past. But in winter, the circus leaves town – the harbour creaks with a pervading emptiness and the grey clouds consume any colour.

Thus my café was a seasonal business – people passing through on their way to the islands for their dose of culture and solitude; backpackers with woollen socks and tough boots, masochistically content under the weight of their raincoats and heavy jumpers; families wishing they had gone to the sun, dragging kids through puddles, searching for a good pub with a clean toilet.

In some sense I was their last taste of civilization – filtered coffee, croissants and baguettes. Bedraggled and dreary, they would enter the aromatic warmth, faces stinging from the salty wind. Young Fran would take their orders, her voice heavy with the local accent, and I would stay in the small kitchen, uncomfortable being front of house. Although the café was a new beginning, I was not yet ready for the limelight. My insecurities were still attached to a different existence, and until every trace had been removed, I could not entirely begin to live. From the small window behind the sink, I could see across the bay and watch the waves carry across the next ferry of customers.

There is a sense of pride in owning a business. Before moving, I had spent my working days in front of a computer screen in an office. I was well paid but removed from human contact. Faceless clients and overseas employers fed into my machine. I didn't talk to them, I interfaced (a misnomer, if ever I heard one). It was just me, my desk and plastic cups of coffee. My bank balance swelled, but my withdrawal also accelerated. Perhaps isolation is what I wanted.

The woman from Devon was eager to sell and I was eager to buy. She left most of the interior behind, and when the keys were in my hands, I sat quietly and mentally recreated my premises. Where she had pots and knick-knacks, I saw clean stainless-steel surfaces and polished wood. For every plate she had littering the walls, I envisaged paintings from local artists. I only kept one of her pieces. It was so tacky that I couldn't bear to remove it. It was a china representation of a flowerpot, filled with the glossiest of plastic roses. With a flick of a switch, they would twirl and bedazzle the customers with a display of flashing colour. As I redecorated and introduced pastel colours and soothing wood, the little pot remained a constant reminder that life was never just plain or simple. Almost arrogantly, it sat on the counter, next to the till, refusing to be ignored.

I changed the name of the café too. She had called it The Boatman, but I wanted the place to reflect a part of me and my new beginning. So I sat for ages with paper and pen, wondering what to name my new business. In the end the decision was easy. I called it The Bare Bones Café and commissioned a local craftsman to make my new sign.

I was careful not to be seen those first few months. The transaction was done through an estate agent in Galway, in his dingy office off Eyre Square. I sat on his crinkly leather couch and read the *Connacht Tribune* while he argued over sheep on the phone with a farmer. The mustiness of the room reminded me of my exam days, studying in an airless room. No wonder the estate agent was surprised by the speed with which the deal was cemented.

I revelled in the bleakness that first winter. It was as if the landscape and I were stripping our lives for a new beginning. The greys and dismal whites were like new pages on which to add fresh colour. As leaves abandoned the trees, the flaky paint fell around my feet. Slowly and carefully the transformation progressed, and as I painted the ceilings and walls, my own new coat developed. It was one of the happier times of my life, with the winter storms lashing the village, clearing the beaches of the detritus that had accumulated during the year, breathing fresh life into the coming spring.

The café belonged to me. There was no part of my old life that remained. Rachel was never allowed through its doors and she was never even the smallest part of it. Even though she had wanted this move, she was dying and becoming the past.

Rachel had made it clear that if she was to die, she was not to be surrounded by those who knew her. She couldn't face their guilty looks and questioning countenances. She wanted to be in a place where her passing would be ignored, to die in the shadows. She was hidden in my small cottage down the road. In darker moments I allowed my coldness to slip and I cried over the finality of what I was doing. There were tears for all the people she would never see again, those who had been cast adrift by the decision. Although family and friends, they had never really known her, never acknowledged her pain. And now as my life grew, hers shrank.

A village has eyes and ears. I knew they watched me come and go, but the sombre winter mornings and the darker winter evenings hid as much as I needed, and when the café opened its doors for the summer trade, I was partially ready for the revelation.

The café was full those first few weeks. I had every local for miles around sitting on the new wooden seating, staring at my freshly painted walls. They got to know me as Joe White, and I slowly learned their names and their relationships with each other. There is a smaller gene pool in which to swim, down the country. I soon realised that I had chosen a community where not marrying a cousin was a difficult thing to achieve, but I had chosen wisely. These were friendly people who knew the value of a conversation with a passer-by. In Dublin, the streets are full, the noise is deafening, but no one talks to you unless driven to it. I had vowed to create a better existence.

That's why I didn't feel so guilty about my actions. I was only continuing the process that had begun four years previously for Rachel, when part of her died too. She never recovered from the blow. In her mind it had all been her fault, a divine retribution for her failings.

'Mr White, it's 4.30. I've cleared all the tables. Should I peel some potatoes for tomorrow?'

The café was empty and rain was streaming down the window. I suspected we would have no more customers today. Fran looked at me from under her mop of red hair. I had never liked redheads but her hair was a deep auburn that framed the greenest of eyes. She had come to me through a visit to the post office – a small white card, stuck with Sellotape to the door. I realised by the end of her first week that most of the skills the card announced were exaggerated, but she was a good worker and pleasant to the customers.

'No, you're fine. You can head off. I'll manage myself until five.'

'I don't mind staying to help. I could peel the vegetables for tomorrow.'

'Thanks, but I'm sure your dad will be looking forward to seeing you.'

I had discovered that Fran's father was Malachi Joyce, a local fisherman. He had long since given up trying to make a living from the sea and was supplementing his income with a variety of other activities. It was the way of the world down here – extra jobs fixing fences, building walls or plastering houses.

Left widowed at the age of thirty-nine, Malachi had seven children to rear. Fran was the second oldest and the only daughter. She had picked up her kitchen skills from catering for a father and six brothers. Of all the families in the village, hers was the most interesting. I suspected they had skeletons in more closets than most, but Fran wasn't quick to open those doors to me.

It was the same for most of the people down here. They talked, they listened, but they hardly ever gave the details of their lives to a new arrival, and it would be years before I would be anything more than a blow-in. It was one of the reasons I had chosen somewhere so remote and quiet. I thought there would be fewer people to interrogate me, but I soon realised that I was the new curiosity and my circumstances would be a source of great interest. It would have been far easier to have disappeared in a city. In the village I would have to give some history of my life and I would have to think carefully about how much to tell.

Nevertheless, for now I loved the solitary moments in the café, when I could sit in the galley kitchen and watch this new world outside. It was more vibrant than the greys of the city. Wind, sea-scented rain and cold morning dews were the elements that painted most days. My favourite backdrops were the crisp skies of a sunny day, or those dark with an impending downpour; intense green fields, shiny grey stones, scraggy plants and trees.

In the kitchen, the smell of potatoes from large brown sacks brought an earthiness to my existence. Cooking for the community made me feel a part of it, a belonging I never thought I'd experience again.

There was little cordon bleu about the menu. The stainless-steel oven baked deep-crust pies filled with steak and kidney, or hotpots of chicken or minced beef. The potatoes came in wedges, or baked or boiled, but rarely fried and greasy. I changed the salads frequently and developed new flavours for quiches and pasta sauces, but the attempt was to fit in and not confuse. This was a new profession for me. Evening classes in cooking and catering had prepared me well for the preparation of simple food, but I was no Michelin chef.

At night, when I was loathe to go home to the cottage, I would sit in the light of some dwindling candles and pare vegetables into shapes with a thin-bladed knife. These were strange sculptures made to adorn the serving plates that sat behind the glass display case. It was labour-intensive and a solitary comfort. Listening to music and allowing the darkness to slowly surround me, I would think of Rachel. Strangely, her death allowed part of me to love her again, and I mourned her loss. It was only in the darkness of the café that I allowed myself to think of her.

The bell on The Bare Bones door jangled and a cold wind confirmed another presence. Sometimes a person walks through your door and their arrival changes your life forever. Although you have never met them, there is a sense of familiarity, a look about their countenance that echoes of an entanglement yet uncovered. As she turned to face me, I was immediately attracted.

'Hello, anybody there?'

It was a warm enquiry, friendly and confident. Part of me didn't want to answer, to break the spell by entering the frame. There was a voyeuristic pleasure in standing there unseen and watching her as she sat at the table, pushing her hair back from her eyes. She was beautiful, but unconventionally so, with full lips and expressive eyes. I entered the room.

'Hi, what can I get you?'

She smiled, and it was as if everything I had done, all the injections I had administered, had allowed death to become a birth.

'Just a black coffee, please.'

I gave her a smile. In the reflection of the stainless-steel surface, I caught sight of my tired face and realised that this was what she was seeing too. It wasn't the image of myself I had imagined in my head. I poured the coffee, placed it before her and headed back to the security of the kitchen. The art of conversation had long since left me.

I timed my re-entry perfectly. She was just rising from the seat, patting the front of her skirt with long, thin fingers.

'It's good coffee. How much do I owe you?'

'Two euro fifty, please.'

I could never tell brown eyes from green. They all looked dark and deeply mysterious, never as cold or as calculating as blue. I wondered whether she looked into my blue eyes and thought the same.

When the door closed I sighed, looking at her table, hoping that she'd left some book or personal belonging behind, but the coffee cup just sat there mocking my inanity.

INSIDE OUT

I put the money in the till, tidied away the table and locked the door. Outside, the night was cold and windy. A strong westerly wind was making its way across the bay from the Atlantic. The walk home was going to be tiring.

CHAPTER 2

Brian Matthews looked down at his hands. The band on his wedding finger was digging into his skin. No matter how hard he pulled at the thin gold circle, he couldn't budge it. In a strange way it reflected his marriage; there were elements of the relationship digging into him too. He had that horrible knot in his stomach that indicated something was wrong, but he didn't know what it was and he didn't know how to ask her. Or was it that he was afraid to know, so asking her was out of the question? Brian liked certainties. He wasn't built to withstand emotional turbulence or drastic changes, and he was afraid that somehow things might never be the same if he questioned her. Yet not asking left him feeling ineffective, a victim of circumstances rather than a master of his own destiny.

Laura was a good wife. He did love her. But she had stood there again last night, in front of the mirror, doubting her beauty. He had said comforting words but it had made no difference. It was the same emotional pressure that made his fingers swell and his ring bite. But he didn't know what to say; he didn't know how to make her happy.

Laura had frowning down to a fine art. Her eyes narrowed only slightly, her lips pursed gently, but her whole face spoke harshly. It was a harshness that he could forgive because he loved her softness – the long, deep smile when he had just made love to her, their faces almost touching as she lay in his arms, her fingers tracing the outline of his cheek bones and complimenting the strength of his features. 'Brian, as a man, you don't have to worry.'

Sometimes he understood what she meant; he saw things her way. He knew that his worth lay in more than his physical appearance. He didn't worry or care or even have to think about it. A pound of weight gained here or a wrinkle there didn't affect his confidence, which came from his job, his money and having his beautiful wife on his arm. He wanted her to feel the same safety. Didn't having him as a husband give her confidence, give her a feeling of pride? And this is where the nagging ache came from, where his ring became even tighter, so tight that it would prompt him to ask her, 'So what's missing, honey? There must be something, if you're so unhappy.' It seemed a logical question to him. Desire comes from a need, need comes from a lack. What did he fail to give her to leave her so discontented?

But she would just look at him sideways with her dark brown eyes and shake her head. 'It's not that simple, Brian, it's not always you or us.'

Her answer always annoyed him. Surely that was what marriage was all about. It was about the closeness of 'us'. Brian held that thought for a moment as he looked out of his dirt-streaked window. Below him moved all the other relationships that he would never make, potential he had left behind as soon as he had spoken the consenting words. A secretary on her way to work, her high-heeled feet quickly stepping across the pavement; a student in a heavy winter jacket and multicoloured scarf, reciting words from a small book that she held in her hand; a suited executive, pushing her blonde hair from her eyes with long thin fingers. These were some of the countless women, all possibilities for an alternative existence. The city was his oyster but he was no longer a fisherman. He was only allowed to stand on the pier and watch the boats come in for others.

His strange mood this morning puzzled him. He was usually a happy man; at least he thought of himself that way. His cup was mostly half-full, but recently there had been an odd undercurrent sweeping away at his steady attitude and it was irritating him. It was an undercurrent created by Laura. Her moods were spreading dangerously into his thinking.

Contemplating his wife's apparent discontentment led him to wonder why he was contented enough himself, even though somewhere along the line his life had become static – the window, the watching, the inactivity. Below him was noise and movement. Inside him, if he dared admit it to himself, was a growing boredom. Mostly it had been the excitement of his publishing company that had kept him going all these years. But the reams of white paper no longer provided the rush they had once delivered. They had been the lotto tickets of his earlier career, each one promising rags-to-riches success. But he had opened too many brown envelopes and tasted their bitter pills of failure. There was no originality within the pages he read, no Booker Prize winner jumping from the black words into his world. These were all sitting on other publishers' desks, providing them with the fat cigars and smiles.

He wished he could write himself. He knew all the plot lines, knew the type of work that would set the cash registers ringing, but somehow the pages remained large white lakes in which his words drowned. He couldn't find the right frame in which to place his ideas. They were colours without a canvas. He had once read that genius was ten per cent inspiration and ninety per cent perspiration; perhaps he wasn't prepared to perspire enough. If another poor soul could sit and sweat blood and tears, he would be happy to publish their hard work.

But night after night, he had read the rubbish of aspiring authors, each one totally deluded about their ability to write. Last night's manuscript had left him with the same feeling of resignation. The wife, the husband, the lover, the angst; there was nothing new.

The view from the window enticed him again. Dublin lazily lying down in soothing green foliage, too sleepy to notice it was straddled by hundreds of cranes, like a Gulliver under the watchful eye of its industrious Lilliputians. He wanted the thrill of tearing open a large brown envelope and finding the new Dean Swift, standing shoulder to shoulder with him at a book-signing, the press clicking shutters and spilling superlatives.

Looking out at the rain spluttering down, the Irish dampness, he wished he were back in Spain bathed in hot sunshine. The summer had passed too quickly. He couldn't even remember the taste of the wine or the food.

He had expected Spain to be brown, the earth almost baked, but he had stood in the salty water and smiled with disappointment. He had hired a car and driven them off the main track, but instead of fields of olives and vines, they had found fields of plastic, wrapping the earth, binding it into a hothouse of accelerated growth, their hideous modernity matching the greed of the dwarfed coastline.

He had hoped that Laura's attitude would warm with the sun but the bronzed bodies on the beach only made her feel worse.

'Jesus, Brian, they're so bloody thin. Don't they ever eat?'

He had watched her walk away from him back to the hotel, her body covered in a wrap, her legs tanned from the sunbed. She was elegant – tall and demure – but she couldn't see it when she looked in the mirror. She couldn't see it when she sat on the sand, her legs pulled up to her chin, watching the younger women walk past, a never-ending parade of arrogance.

One night they had sat on the balcony watching the day fade into the red horizon and she had held his hand and smiled, momentarily forgetting the insecurities that took her away from him. 'Remember when we were in college and I wore the shirt with the flowers?'

'And I ripped two of the buttons off in the heat of the moment.'

'Actually that's not what I remember. You slagged me for being old-fashioned and I said that one day I'd be everything you wanted.'

'And I told you that you already were.'

'Yes, but you were lying. We both knew that. You wanted me to be more sophisticated and gorgeous. You wanted a woman on your arm that everyone looked at.'

'But I stayed with you. I chose you.'

'That's not the answer, Brian. You're supposed to say I was that girl.'

He had been here before, backed into a corner, sparring until his nose was bloodied and he was driven into submission.

'Look, Laura, you are everything I want.'

'Only because I bought new clothes, dyed my hair, moulded myself into someone else.'

'No, Laura, because you were funny, shy and intelligent.'

'But not beautiful, Brian? Not attractive?'

He had wanted to shake her then, beg her to stop finding fault with 'them'. They were in a good relationship, a positive couple. They were the friends other couples wanted at their dinner table, the couple that fitted together with ease, like Astaire and Rogers or Bogart and Bacall. They laughed at the same jokes, they liked the same food, and at weddings he watched her dance with other men and knew she would come back to him. He trusted her.

He ordered champagne on that Spanish balcony, stood with the red rose between his teeth and tried to win her over. Her smile had temporarily lifted their evening. He had even found her willing to lie beneath him, the lights turned off, the curtains fully closed.

It was strange how watching the day outside had brought it all back – the rain contrasting with that warmth, the city streets instead of the sandy beaches, the cold Dublin sky more accurately reflecting her feelings.

He would take an early lunch. His mind couldn't focus; he would eat in the pub by the canal, a fresh baguette filled with the latest fad food – spicy Cajun chicken. He had always been amused by the addition of the word *spicy*, as he had never eaten anything Cajun that hadn't caused him to break out in a sweat he had to wipe away with his handkerchief. Whether eating the chicken was worth it or not was always debatable. Of course Laura didn't like Cajun chicken. It was cooked in oil, and besides, it was impossible to tell whether the chickens used were free range. It was easier to eat at home, regulate the amount of proteins, fats and carbohydrates. In their house the big C stood for cholesterol. It was amazing that he had managed to gain a middle-age spread at all. His home-cooked meals were free from radicals, free from fat and mostly free from enjoyment.

He blamed the books Laura ordered through the post, the glossy 'put your life in order' books that always featured garlic, nature's cure for all ills.

When he was allowed to cook, Brian gave not one ounce of thought to the fat or carb content of his meals. He cooked with passion. It was pasta dripping with pesto sauce, with pine nuts, parmesan and fresh basil, or a hot curry with coconut milk and fenugreek. Cooking was for pleasure, not for health. An old joke buzzed through his head: I cook with wine, and sometimes I even put it in the dish. Brian smiled. He would savour the greasy chips, creamy mayonnaise and fried chicken for his lunch. Tea was tofu. He had already been warned.

CHAPTER 3

RACHEL FELT ILL. THERE WERE shivers chasing up and down her spine and her head felt warm. With her back against the wall, she saw the patterns of colour flicker across the aisle as the sun broke through the stained-glass window. If she held her hand high, the light touched her too, playing across the back of her wrist, tiny shards of heaven colouring her world. This was wrong. She shouldn't have come. It was not a place Joe would have visited. She had been the religious one, the one who had gone to Mass, the one who had looked for acceptance from the church. She had believed that God would love her exactly as she was and maybe even teach her to love herself. But that hadn't worked. So here she was sitting on the floor of a church, watching shards of light play along her hand.

She wondered what the dictionary definition of simple was. She knew that whatever it was, her life would reflect the exact opposite. She had prayed for normality, longed for the sanity of boredom. Every day her mind had spun in endless circles with the overwhelming awareness of the problem. At least this time there was an escape. There was finality to everything.

Joe had refused at first. He hadn't wanted to carry it out. He had cried and searched for an alternative. They could stay, face the future together. He would always be with her, always be there. Rachel had gone along with this for a while – remained in her job, kept her pain a secret and desired the release that, one day, might be granted to her. But the awareness grew, like a tumour inside her, taking over every waking thought, manifesting itself in eruptions of the skin, terrible cramps and dramatic weight loss.

Rachel knew that her life was a mistake. God would have made her healthy and perfect otherwise. He would also have left her with the one part of her life that she had been proud of. But to rob her of that one perfect element of her world was a robbery she could not understand, unless it was a punishment.

She had expected the men and women at the local Mass to turn and stare at her, their faith giving them an insight into her heart. Only Joe understood her. He knew that she could not make it through life with the cards it had dealt her.

When she was very young, it had all seemed so much easier.

'What does Shakespeare teach us about love, Rachel?' the teacher had asked.

She had known that her reply would be too naïve. Shakespeare demanded a different reflection of love from the one she felt, The English teacher had not wanted to know the ramblings of an adolescent all those years ago.

Today she would be capable of answering that question. Love is the unselfish giving of all you have to another. In her innocence, as a young woman she had given without expecting to receive. She had given because it did not matter what she received in return. For her it was all wrong anyway. And rising, like an echo from a nightmare, she heard Damien's voice, addressing her roughly.

'Go down on me again. It was so good last night.'

She had come close to biting him that night, sinking her teeth deep into his firm flesh. But when it was over, Damien would lie there sleeping and she would watch him, hoping his breath would falter and his lips would turn blue. But it wasn't really him she wanted dead. Damien dying was only a reflection of her own inner state and a desire to escape. He was not the problem, she was. He was simply behaving as expected, being true to their relationship as he saw it.

On other nights, he would explode inside her with such force that she would slowly leak his pleasure when he was done. The bathroom floor was colder than concrete then. Her shoulders barely moving, she would sit quietly and allow the tears to run down her face.

She had found no alternative but to end their relationship. There was no honesty to it. She didn't love him. She couldn't love him. Damien was only a way of hiding the truth. Being with him had all been a way to hide Joe. And Damian hated her for it and hated Joe.

Remembering the day she had told him, she recalled his hand firmly clenching his pint, knuckles white. Five years, Rachel, and for what? To be told this bunch of shit? She had expected his anger but she had also hoped for some understanding. She had not loved Damien but she had liked him. She had enjoyed his company, warmed to his silly jokes and quirky smile. But when she had told him the truth, he had looked at her as if she was a murderer. There had been no compassion at all.

Rachel felt her cheeks now and the moistness

surprised her. These memories would be buried with her, she thought. It was why she was sitting in the church. Her final days were near. She would be gone forever, a woman lost to the world. She deserved to die as she had failed to look after the precious life God had given her.

'You have to mourn,' the psychiatrist had told her. 'Death needs its own space.'

But the psychiatrist had lied. Rachel had wrapped death into a small box and then she watched it lowered into a muddy grave. The earth had fallen on the lid with a harshness that Rachel had never forgotten nor forgiven. It had been the defining moment of her life.

The psychiatrist's passive eyes had shown no signs of emotion. His ink pen had scratched thousands of words onto reams of paper before Rachel had refused to take another hour. He kept saying the same thing, over and over. The death had not been down to her. Nor had it been a punishment from God. But his words fell on deaf ears. She had no right to call herself a woman. She had not even managed to prevent the horror of that moment. She had not kept her child safe.

'Have you thought of having another child?'

How could anyone be so stupid, she had thought, especially a psychiatrist. A child is not replaceable, and the whole act of creating a child was something that she could no longer contemplate.

'You'll still need help. Don't forget others can support you.'

Rachel's only comfort, as she lay alone in the dark, was knowing that one day she would see the small face again.

The door of the church creaked open. Rachel's back tensed in annoyance that her hiding place might be discovered. A gasp of air circled her ankles and a shaft of light momentarily blinded her. A small figure stood under the Romanesque archway, a man dressed in the garments of a priest. He did not seem to notice Rachel; he was concentrating on a sheet of paper he held in his hand.

She should stand up and warn him of her presence. The longer she sat and watched him, the more embarrassing it would be to be discovered. Then there was the fear that the priest might turn around, go back out the wooden door and lock her in the old church. Joe had to be in the café at five. Joe would be late if she was locked in the church.

The priest finished reading, strode down the centre of the aisle and placed the paper on an old-fashioned lectern. He cleared his throat and started speaking, his eyes looking up every now and then to address an imaginary congregation.

She felt a sense of guilt watching him perform. The priest, believing he was alone, practised his sermon with gusto and aplomb. Rachel saw the fragility of this clergyman's confidence and it made her feel sympathetic towards him. There was also the apprehension of discovery. How would she explain her presence at the back of the church? She was not meant to be there. She would bring suspicion on Joe.

The sermon was good. Rachel found solace in its words. It concerned suffering. It reminded her of an old Buddhist story she had once read, sitting in the wardrobe of her bedroom, a small torch her only light. She had often read in that way as a child, hidden from her parents, alone with her main love. She had a stack of novels reaching from the bottom to the top of the wooden closet. *Tales from India* was among her favourites. In this book was her favourite story, the story of the mustard seed. It reminded her of a biblical parable. A poor Hindu woman had lost her only son. It was a story that meant more to Rachel as her own life unfolded. The woman, distraught beyond life, appealed to Brahman to return her son to her. Brahman tells the woman, with all the sympathy of a divine deity whose offspring are immortal, that she must go and find a mustard seed to bring to him and only then will he give back her son. However, there is always a catch. The seed had to come from a household where no one had experienced the loss of a loved one. The woman sets off smiling, thinking her task easy. For weeks and months she travels across the land knocking on every door she passes, looking for that small mustard seed.

Even as a child, in the darkness of her wardrobe, Rachel knew the outcome of this quest. The woman would return to Brahman empty-handed, as of course there were no homes that hadn't experienced the loss of death. In true Hindu fashion, the woman returns with gratitude to Brahman because she has learned a huge lesson – she now understands the nature of life. Death does not have favourites, it touches everyone. Still, Rachel wanted a different God, a god who could right all wrongs and make everything perfect.

The priest cleared his throat again and folded the sheets of paper. He seemed pleased with his performance. Standing down from the steps, he paused to kiss the cross around his neck and then turned and walked towards Rachel. She felt as if the shadows were brighter now and that the priest, his eyes accustomed to the dark, would notice her. But the door was pulled closed and the quietness of solitude soon returned.

It was time for Rachel to leave the church. This going back to the past and dwelling on old wounds was doing no good. The cottage would be filling with the damp autumn air and the fire needed lighting. But her thoughts of leaving came too slowly and, as she rose to her feet, the church door opened for a second time. There was no hiding now.

Rachel felt her pulse quicken as, with a slow deliberate movement, the small figure turned towards her and looked straight through her. Then, with careful steps, this second intruder moved as if counting the distance between the door and the sidewall. It was an old woman. She was wearing mismatched clothing – a brown woollen skirt and a thin pink cardigan; around her neck was a polka-dot scarf. Her hands were small and pale and she held a box of matches. She was heading towards the candles.

'I'll bump into you if you don't move. I can hear you breathing.' The voice of the old woman was scolding but calm. 'I know you're in front of me, but I'm not scared, although I think you are.'

Rachel moved back towards the wall, out of the old woman's path. She wanted to talk but the words were trapped.

Silent breathing filled the church.

'Will I light a candle for you too?'

There might have been comfort in replying, but it was easier for Rachel to leave.

CHAPTER 4

'Are all the boats to the island the same?'

I had answered this question before; the worried tourist was anxious not to board a rusty old vessel that might sink to the bottom of the Atlantic. 'Oh, they're much of a muchness really. Both of them have life jackets and lifeboats.'

He noticed my sardonic smile. 'I'm happy with any boat, you understand. It's just my wife.'

I looked at him sympathetically and nodded. He wasn't the usual American tourist, straight off a bus with a camera and an Aran sweater. Those anodyne travellers never seemed to reach as far west as Clochan.

Clochan wasn't on the whistle-stop tour of Ireland. It was on a small road, too cramped for the big buses. The whole village was strung haphazardly along that one small road. The centre of the village was the oldest part. Here the houses were thick-walled, with small windows and narrow doors. My café was one of these nineteenth-century buildings. It sat proudly on the main street, where a small break in the houses allowed a side road down to the harbour. The harbour was why I had chosen this remote village for my new home. It was everything an old Irish harbour should look like: the boats were barnacled and half-rusted. The pots on the pier had remains of the sea jutting out from their roped edges, and the grass poked through between the cobblestones. There wasn't a rich man's yacht in sight throughout the winter months. I had seen enough of those in Dun Laoghaire, where I would walk the pier after Rachel's group session in the hospital. It was these visits that brought us to Dublin. Still, I was always drawn to harbours.

The intrepid traveller in front of me coughed as if to prompt me from my daydreaming. This American, like me, was happier to see the poorer side of the country. He wanted to return to America to tell his many cousins that he had found the world of his ancestors, from where the Famine boats had left with a cargo of cramped human beings, most of whom did not survive the journey.

He fidgeted in his pockets to pay for his family's lunch as he continued with his questions. 'Where can I buy the boat tickets?'

'Up at the shop, about four hundred yards away. You can buy tickets for either boat there.'

'Not very competitive then?'

'No. They're owned by the same family.'

'And I suppose they own the shop too?' He grinned.

'Now you're catching on.'

He looked out the café window at the two boats resting in the harbour. I could see the worry come back to his face as he saw their dilapidated appearance. 'It's a good day to travel anyway,' he said.

I was sure later that he must have regretted saying those words, because from the corner of the room a rasping voice cut over him. 'Don't be looking at the weather to tell you what kind of day it is.'

The tourist turned around to face the old man sitting at the table behind him. 'I'm sorry?'

'I said the weather isn't your best way of telling.'

My American tourist looked quizzically at Tom Lacey.

'It can be a beautiful day and the storm will come up from nowhere,' Tom continued.

The tourist looked at me for authentication, but I shrugged my shoulders. 'He should know. He's been here far longer than me,' I said.

Tom Lacey pushed the cap to the back of his head and wiped away a trickle of sweat with an old handkerchief. His face was not merely lined but pitted with age. 'I can remember,' he said, his eyes somewhere far away from the rest of us, 'I can remember back to that big day as if it were just happening.'

'How's about a cup of tea, Tom?' I suggested, hoping to break his train of thought, but he had an audience now. A few faces had turned from other tables.

'I remember the sun beating down with no care for man or beast.' Tom spoke with a broad accent, difficult to understand unless he spoke slowly. He was slow now, deliberately resting on each syllable as if he were delivering the oracle. He had told it so often that his rendition was word perfect, like the comic who practised in front of the mirror, except with this story there was no punchline. I looked at his face. The word craggy had been created for him. He was nearer a hundred than ninety, and yet his feet and his mind could travel down any path you showed him.

I placed a cup of tea and a scone on the table but there was no deflecting him from his moment of glory, and it was stupid of me to try – this was good for business. The tourists sat on the edge of their seats and the locals stayed to listen. He was Clochan's answer to the legendary seanachaí of the past.

Tom pushed a crumb from his lips with a veined hand. 'The sea holds our riches but also our graves.'

The café was silent now, except for his voice and the clinking sound of the masts in the harbour. Somewhere out in the backyard, a shed door swung on its hinges, eerily banging against the frame. It all added to the mood as we sat on the wooden seats.

'I remember helping with the pots that Friday morning. We used to stick the sally rods into the earth and weave them into baskets. We were happy, looking forward to the evening and the fishing. The mackerel were running and the nets would be full. My uncle had an old nobby anchored out in the bay. My father and four uncles would row out in the currach and then fish off the coast. They were never more than three miles from the shore. Sometimes they took lobster but they never used more than thirty-three pots, one for each year of Our Lord's existence.' He stared around him to make sure he was still holding everyone's attention. 'I bet few fishermen today would care about that. But that's all they would ever take – thirty-three pots.'

Tom stopped and wiped his eye. 'To think that they all kept the faith and it still befell them. Sure they even used to keep a bottle of Holy Water in the stern for the time when they would lay their nets. It's a wonder that God left them at all.'

I looked at the face of my tourist. He was enthralled.

'As the boats left the harbour, I was standing on a

barrel of salt, waving goodbye to my father. I remember playing with Micilín down on the strand and shouting after them, trying to skim stones towards the black shapes disappearing out into the bay.' Tom looked from one apprehensive face to another.

'The weather was good when they left, no sign of the storm.' It was as if he was trying to convince us, assure us that his father would not have left him on the beach had he known he would not see his son again.

We nodded. Outside the café, a tin can blew against the door and a few half-smiles broke the tension.

'He was only forty-two. The gale came from nowhere, slates were ripped from roofs, doors from sheds. A thick blackness darkened all the sky and left each house fearful for its men. On the wireless, only minutes after they had left, the warning was issued, but none of them had a radio. My mother had been out at the turf. I met her running to the beach, where Micilín and I stood rigid, our eyes fixed on the sea, each roaring wave tossing the boats like matchsticks. And that's all that lay on the beach the next day – matchsticks that had once been boats.'

No one said a word.

'They couldn't swim, you understand. They all believed that a quick drowning was better than trying to cheat the sea.' Tom stopped and looked down into his cup of tea. 'You can never cheat the sea.'

A few chairs turned back to their tables. People knew the story was finished. It always finished as abruptly as it started. A few humbled tourists made it to the door before the old man could see into their faces, their journey to the islands tinged with apprehension. They would be the first on board to check out the lifeboats. They would stand by the jackets.

The American stood and looked at Tom. 'Is it true?' he said, turning to face me.

'Yes, it's true. A violent storm back in the 1920s, but they have radios and jackets and warning systems today.'

'That's comforting,' he replied, handing me the money for his bill.

'Ah, old Tom, you're still scaring the tourists, I see!'

The familiar female voice drew my attention. I hadn't seen her enter the café. I had presumed after the first time that I would never see her again. She exuded a different air than the locals and I had taken her for a tourist. I looked at my reflection in the counter, afraid she would look at me and know everything, as if my life was written on my face.

'Hi. A black coffee, please.'

She really did have a beautiful face. It was as much as I could do to conjure up any kind of reply. 'No problem. Anything to eat?'

'Just a coffee, please. I would have asked for food if I wanted it.'

It was not the answer I had expected. A flush of red started from my collar and moved up my neck.

'Sorry,' she said. 'I didn't mean to sound so rude. I can be a bit abrupt.'

I looked at her, puzzled. 'Oh, don't worry about it. I just need to make sales. I'm not here that long. Call me overeager!'

She smiled. 'Me too, I arrived a few months ago.'

I handed her the coffee and she walked away to a table by the window. I should have asked her something else.

It was a good opening line that she'd given me. If I was quick enough, I could take a serviette down to the table, but before I could move from behind the counter, the door swept open and James O'Connor entered, looking around the café.

'I thought I saw you come this way! How are you settling in?' He didn't wait for an answer, just turned around a chair, straddled it and sat facing her at the table, his elbows resting on the back of the frame.

I strained but I couldn't hear her answer. My imagination was left to fill in the rest. He didn't even order a coffee, just blocked my view of her face with his broad shoulders and dark curly head of hair. It hardly surprised me that she knew James O'Connor, even if she had been in the village only a short time. His parents owned half of Clochan – the local grocery, the petrol pump, the post office and the funeral parlour. There was no part of the community they didn't have a hold over. They had even put a bid in for my little café.

I heard her laughing. I was surprised at the irritation it caused me. As the café had emptied of all the other tables, the tourists heading out for the afternoon boat, I decided the kitchen was the best place to find my sanity. I didn't want to stand behind the counter playing gooseberry to their conversation. There was brown bread baking in the oven and the smell was more than enticing. Every day I filled the three small steel racks with the little round dough balls, each crossed on the top like my grandmother had taught me. When I had asked her why all those years ago, she had laughed at me. 'You're forever asking questions. Life doesn't always have an answer.'

But I had wanted answers. It wasn't enough just to

know things happened. There had to be a purpose for everything under the sun, good or bad. If my family had known how often I had read the Bible, they would have entered me into the church. Thankfully, I had found no answers there either. At the holier-than-thou religious groups, there were only blank faces when I posed my questions. They didn't want their faith shaken with the unknown.

I heard the outer door close. I wondered whether they had left together or if she was still there, sitting by the window. The timer on the oven pinged and I decided not to look into the room. Instead I took the bread from the oven, the aroma of yeast and baked cereal wafting throughout the kitchen. I turned them out onto steel racks where the perfectly round loaves hummed away in the growing darkness. I couldn't resist cutting one open and spreading a warm slice with thick butter and blood-red strawberry jam. Food had always been my comfort. As I sat on the counter stool, eating the product of my hard work, I suddenly thought that all this might work. That I could actually be happy.

Before I realised it, it was ten to seven. I had to be home before eight. There was a syringe waiting for me. It didn't seem right to think about another woman when I was still dealing with Rachel. But my musings were irrelevant anyway. As I left the kitchen for the evening the woman was standing by the till waving at me.

'Do you want me to pay next time or now? I've been here for ages. Thank God for newspapers.'

I had forgotten to take her money. She was wincing and holding a note in her hand.

'Oh, right, sorry. I forgot.'

She looked at me curiously so I blurted out an excuse. 'I'm not used to running a café yet.'

'Well, a presence behind the counter might improve your bank balance.'

She looked around the kitchen while I floundered for words.

'A lovely smell of bread. Can I buy a loaf?'

Minutes later she left with a warm loaf tucked under her arm. I tried not to charge her, but she insisted.

'I can't ask for one again if you don't let me pay.'

It was a strange conversation. I still didn't know her name. I should have asked. I had come across as so dim. She had appeared more confident than earlier, but there was a curious mix of forcefulness and shyness, as if she were trying out a new personality.

I walked back to the cottage under the cover of darkness. The trees were swaying, creaking and cracking under the pressure of the wind. I thought of Tom Lacey's story, of the small boats tossed on the waves with no safe water to save them. It was an easy storm to imagine in the bleakness of an autumn night.

I stopped and looked out towards the islands. The fishermen still didn't know how to swim; their boats still set sail without life jackets or floats. They were content to ignore the past and live in each moment the future gave them. If the sea took them, it was the way of their world. Life was not about cheating God with man's ingenuity but about floating on the wave and coming to rest wherever it ordained.

It was a conservative community. These people did not accept change easily.

CHAPTER 5

STANDING IN THEIR BEDROOM, BRIAN Matthews allowed his clothes to fall to the floor. Inebriation was controlling his actions. He knew she was watching him through closed eyes. She could do that. She could hear him turn the key in the lock when she was sleeping, she could see him lurch from the door to the bed and she could smell his breath even though her shoulders faced him.

He had found the dinner on the table. He had sat and eaten a cold plate of Quorn lasagne. This was becoming a cliché.

'Brian?' Her voice was heavy with sleep as he quietly opened the bedroom door.

'Sorry, did I wake you?' He could almost hear her eyebrows rise.

'Your mum rang. Your dad's back in hospital again with the same thing. But you're not to worry. Ring her in the morning.'

'Okay.'

'Brian?'

Her voice was stronger now and he knew what was coming next.

'Spare room.'

He thought about remonstrating, but then he thought better of it. She was not one to change her mind.

'I'm just not prepared to listen to you snoring again.'

He always snored after a few pints and he always woke up with a throat drier than a desert. He bent forward to kiss her on the cheek but the duvet suddenly grew two inches longer, covering her neck and face.

'Goodnight, then.'

She didn't reply and he hadn't expected her to. It was his own fault. He should have rung her and left a message. But one pint had led to another.

The spare room doubled as his study. Sheets and a duvet were kept in a trunk in the corner, on top of which was a thick pile of brown envelopes. There was huge guilt attached to these. Some had been there for longer than he cared to admit. The unlucky ones at the bottom were always buried by the new deliveries, buried so often that time would pass too quickly for them. Dog-eared, dusty and coffee-stained, they were the faded harbingers of embarrassment. He hadn't thought of that word for a long time – harbinger. There was a Middle English or Old French feel to it. He repeated the word over and over again as he floated the sheet over the makeshift bed. He could feel a rap song developing, a one-thirty-in-the-morning song, fuelled by too many pints.

He was awake now, uninterested in closing his eyes and sleeping alone. A sense of purpose was attaching itself to him. He looked over at the brown envelopes.

Tonight he would release a captive chore from its hiding place. He would open the dustiest envelope and give some poor bastard a late-night/early-morning break.

The postmark on the chosen beneficiary of his magnanimous mood was faded, but Brian could make out the writing with a sideways squint. The place name did not augur well; nothing good had ever come out of Athlone. As a child he had merely passed through it on the way to somewhere more interesting. He could imagine some bored bank manager typing in the corner of his converted garage, the fluorescent light flickering irritatingly as he fumbled for the right words. His wife would stand pathetically in the doorway, a new dress expressing her hopes for the evening, but he would hit the keys with a boring monotony unable to see the futility.

Brian smiled. Are you my horrible bank manager, he thought, holding the envelope up in the air, or are you someone exciting and promising?

The writing was double-spaced and in a clear font. He was grateful for that. He loathed the handwritten productions, a hundred thousand words scrawled with no respect for his eyesight. He read the title out loud. The title – *The Olive Tree* – neither thrilled him nor annoyed him, it just sat there, simple and humble, and the words that followed it were slow, enticing and enveloping. Without much fanfare or pretension, the book slowly dragged him in, wrapped him in its world where the people were flesh without faces and the countryside a land without a name. He had read over a hundred pages before he noticed that his hands felt cold. When morning came, he was still on the sofa bed turning over the pages, afraid to relinquish his grasp on the characters.

'Jesus, Brian, you have to drink less. You look awful.'

He kissed Laura on the cheek and smiled.

'I mean it, Brian.'

Even though she was scolding him, he liked the small

flick of his hair she did with her hand. 'I know, honey, I'm sorry.' His attempt at a smile was pathetic. 'But look, I've found it.'

He held up the wad of paper. His smile was growing by the second.

'What's that – a really good novel?' She was no longer frowning.

'Yep. This is the new car you wanted, the trip to Rome, the new kitchen, maybe. This, after all the years of crap, my love, is it!'

The kiss was good. The hug was better.

'Good morning, Dublin. The weather is a cool ten degrees, but dry.'

The radio didn't annoy him. The traffic didn't annoy him. The Rock Road was bumper to bumper and the exhaust fumes hung in the dry air. He usually was in work before the rush, sitting at his desk while others swore at the jammed lanes, but this morning had been different. This morning he had gone back to bed, and not alone.

'Jack, come into the office. I need a word.'

Jack was sitting at his desk, coffee cup in his hand. It was 9.40 a.m. and he was relaxing in the absence of authority. He stood up immediately, the crumbs of a doughnut falling to the floor. Brian thought about making a comment but his brain was responding too slowly.

'Shut the door and take a seat.'

He felt more purposeful than he had for a long time, as if being the boss actually meant something.

'Do you know who wrote this?' he said, holding out the manuscript.

'*The Olive Tree*. No, I've never heard of it. Where did you get it?'

'I had it at home.'

Jack shrugged his shoulders. 'Well, the cover letter should have been inside. Wasn't it there?'

'No, it wasn't.'

'Then, I'm not sure there's anything we can do to find out, but I will go and look through our files. Maybe the book title will pop up.'

Brian had one of those moments then, one of those moments when you see your life passing you by and you know that you're missing the boat. The author was going to remain a mystery. It would be his punishment for the tall pile of envelopes on the trunk. They shouldn't have been gathering dust for so long. He thought about lighting a cigarette but he didn't have any. He wasn't supposed to smoke any more. Laura had seen to that. This was what Brian had most feared. At five o'clock in the morning he had searched the brown envelope for a letter and failed to find one. There wasn't even a return address on the back of the envelope. Why did people do that – send a manuscript that they had slaved over for two years without the precaution of a return address?

He really wanted a cigarette now. He felt angry, cheated. When his phone rang, he was not as pleasant as usual. It was all he could do to prevent a growl.

The voice at the other end seemed slightly perturbed. 'Hi, am I ringing at a bad time?'

'God, no. I'm just tired after last night.'

'And this morning!' Laura said.

The crumpled sheets, her body arching, his feet pushing into the frame of the bed, those moments seemed years behind him now.

'Will I ring back later?'

'No, there's nothing that can't wait.' He picked up a pencil from the desk and stabbed it into the wooden frame.

'Good because I was wondering if you'd come to lunch today?'

'Really?' The stabbing continued.

'Yes, I want to talk to you about something.'

Even in the middle of his new-found crisis, he hoped she meant children. He had always expected her to push the pace in those conversations, but Laura seemed content to aim for an immaculate conception. It's not that they were never together, just that she was always protected.

'Yeah, lunch would be great.' With the blunted pencil, he struck a line through the name in his diary and hoped he would be forgiven. 'I'll pick you up, darling.'

He returned the phone to the receiver and wondered when there would be a silver lining to his clouds. When the door to his office reopened, he knew that keeping his fingers crossed was at best a childish response.

'I've found your author.' Jack was beaming. 'They actually wrote a letter to us asking had we read *The Olive Tree* yet, as they hadn't received a reply. I'm surprised Casey kept it, but then she finds it difficult to throw anything out.'

The letter was neatly handwritten and there was no indication of his boring bank manager. In fact, it was difficult to tell who was behind the writing. The letter was a simple request for the work to be read and as soon as possible. He looked at the date. The letter was exactly a year old, but there was a name, an address and a telephone number and that was all he needed to make contact and arrange a meeting.

He picked up the receiver to dial the number but an obvious thought disturbed him. It could already be on someone else's desk. It could already be at the printer. He might have missed his chance to publish the one book that would have raised his company from small-time player to the big time. He laughed at his own naivety. Obviously R.J. O'Loughlin wouldn't have let such a good book lie unread at a single publishing firm. It would have been sent around all the houses. They probably had an agent by now and a deal well and truly cemented.

He read the letter again. There was something about it that made him feel the phone call was worthwhile. *I apologise for writing back to your company, as I'm sure you get so many manuscripts to read through, but I wonder have you received mine by post. I sent it over six months ago. It's my first book, possibly a bit raw, and so it may need some editing.* But last night, Brian had read the whole book and unleashed its emotion. Cold and tired on the sofa bed, he had allowed the story to flow over him and he knew it needed very little editing at all.

He dialled the number.

A small voice answered. 'Hello?'

'Can I speak to R. J. McLoughlin, please?'

He heard muffled voices and then the phone went dead. He dialled again, irritated to be cut off. It rang for longer this time.

Come on, R. J. McLoughlin, answer, damn it.

It wasn't a good name for a writer. He would have to

negotiate a change. This time the ring tone stopped but there was no voice at the other end.

'Hello, I'm looking for R. J. McLoughlin.'

Again the phone went dead. Brian was rapidly losing patience now. It was approaching lunchtime and his blood-sugar levels were low. Third time lucky. He decided not to speak when the phone was answered this time. Two could play at that game.

A gruff voice spoke. 'Hello, who's there?'

Good, he had reached an adult. 'Hello, I'm looking to speak with R. J. McLoughlin.'

Brian cursed loudly when the phone went dead again. It was more than a matter of a book now, it was him against the rudeness of this person. He was determined to get a civil response. He hit the redial button, drumming his fingers on the desk as he sat waiting. Three calls later, he was still waiting. The phone was off the hook.

A reclusive fruitcake hammering away brilliant novels in Athlone, it would be just his luck to discover the Salinger of writing.

He placed the letter and synopsis into the top drawer of his desk. Mr R. J. McLoughlin would keep until later. There was more than one way to skin a cat.

CHAPTER 6

THE CHURCH WAS DARKER THAN on her previous visit. There was no dust dancing in the sun's rays, like angel breath in the air. There was just a pervasive coldness.

Rachel looked quickly around the echoing building. No other person was seeking refuge there this Monday evening. She would be able to sit undisturbed, but the tiled floor looked dusty and unwelcoming this time and there were no flickering colours to wash over her. The stained-glass window was dark due to a large black cloud.

She walked up the polished aisle. Many feet had worn a path to the altar – the feet of those mourning and of those rejoicing a wedding or a birth. It was a cruel irony that even at the birth of a child, the only thing you could guarantee for them was death.

Stopping at a pew, she knelt down and genuflected. It was something she hadn't done for a long time. There was a strange comfort in the act. It seemed to drag her further into the spiritual essence of her surroundings. All across the world millions of people were connecting in the same symbolic gesture of faith. In the past she had gone through the ritual in a hollow, meaningless fashion, but she was here to make peace now. She knew there wasn't much time left and she needed to feel accepted.

Kneeling down to pray, she noticed the corner of a

white sheet of paper under the raffia matting. It was a wedding programme. The happy couple were probably on their honeymoon now. The date on the crumpled page was for a week past.

She had never wanted a wedding. She couldn't have married him. She couldn't have taken Damien's name or cooked his meals or washed his clothes or slept beneath his sheets. All she had wanted was to keep the baby, and even that was fraught with fear at first. Initially there had been no pleasure in the knowledge that some small human being was forming inside her, just sheer panic that she was incapable of having a baby, becoming a mother.

She had wanted it removed at first, from the moment the stick went blue. She knew the test was not mistaken. She felt different that month. She was bloated, her breasts tingled and she was anxious about the smallest things. No, she had known it was an accurate result.

The bedroom shrank to the size of a phone box as she sat despairing on the patchwork quilt, her eyes focused on the little blue lines. Who would she tell? Her parents wouldn't want to know. They would disapprove of the unmarried state. So she decided to tell no one until her problem became obvious.

There were endless nights of tossing, waking in the morning to look at the bedroom door and wish it would open into another world. Opening doors had always been easier than conversations. There had been an escape from other problems, but this time the problem came with her.

She had sat at the table of an old friend and cried. This was not meant to happen to her, this was not a joy or a blessing; this was a painful expression of something she had wanted to ignore.

Now those repugnant thoughts came back to haunt her. The consultancy room had been cream, the curtains in neat folds in front of a closed blind that kept her hidden from the outside world. The grey blob had swirled around the monitor as the jelly squelched across her flesh, the doctor's eyes showing more than the routine examination. She could see from the beginning that there was trouble ahead, and he was calm in his delivery of her penance. There was always a chance with a first conception for something to go wrong, he had said, but in this case there was an unusual occurrence. The words hadn't surprised her. Of course she was an oddity. What else could she have been? His advice had been simple – go home and wait. It would happen spontaneously.

Crowds clapped spontaneously, balloons burst spontaneously, but there seemed nothing spontaneous about sitting on a chair for a week, afraid to move in case her unborn baby fell out between her legs.

Of course, now that there was the fear of losing her baby, she wanted to keep it, so badly.

It had been one of the longest weeks of her life, a week where she had learned to pray, to appeal to God. If only he would save her child, then she would live in a way that honoured him.

Then the miracle happened. The egg did not evacuate its warm surroundings. Instead it became a medical wonder and grew inside her with a healthiness the monitor loved. She heard the tiny heartbeat, saw the bubble-like fingers flex and realised that she was looking at the son she had never expected to have.

But if conception had been a struggle, the birth was her darkest hour. Her body was the wrong shape to release her son into the world. The knife was the only way to give him life, a Caesarean birth, an epidural, everything screaming to her the shallowness of her skills as a woman.

The carefully placed needle had not been enough to stop her screaming. The pain had still been unbearable, and she had gone through it all alone. There was no partner or family by her side. The hospital was empty of support.

And afterwards there was her mother with the endless cups of tea, served with a slice of humble pie.

'Rachel, if you had married the father and done things properly, you wouldn't have had to go through this alone. And who's going to help you bring up the baby now? I suppose your dad and I will have to help. If your father forgives you, then you can move back in with us. I know you won't manage alone.'

What kind of warped, unchristian attitude was that? You wouldn't be with me for the birth of my beautiful baby because I was an embarrassment to you but you want to have my son to mould into another uncharitable person. Rachel was angry with the pious, punitive attitude of her parents and their God. She knew God had already punished her with the pain she had endured during the birth and he would soon punish her for so much more than not marrying the father of her baby.

'Rachel, are you listening? You shouldn't have even got like this. What were you thinking?'

But did her mother really want to know what she was thinking? Rachel doubted it. It was partly why she now had the urge to tell her the whole rotten story, to watch the teacup fall from her mother's hand and break into pieces on the polished floor. In her mind Rachel saw the porcelain pieces looking up at her from the sanitised floor, mocking her decision to keep her child and be a mother. It will end in tears. You can't do this. It will end in tears.

How prophetic those memories now seemed. As she knelt in the pew and listened to the drops of rain hitting the stained-glass panes, Rachel knew she had failed to be a good mother. She had tried her best, but there was no living with some types of pain.

Standing up, she placed a hand on her abdomen. The scar was still there: the place where her baby had been snatched briefly from the jaws of death, only to be cruelly taken from her two years later.

'Aren't you cold?'

The voice came from nowhere. Rachel hadn't realised that her eyes had been closed or that tears were running down her cheeks. As her eyes adjusted to the light, she saw a figure stand before her: small feet covered in a pair of wet slippers, dusky stockings up to the hem of a skirt. Rachel didn't need to look any further.

'I hope you'll talk to me this time.'

There was a strange lilt to the accent, which wasn't local.

'How do you know it's the same person?'

The old woman's laugh echoed round the wooden rafters.

'Is there more than one of you, then?'

'No, I suppose not.'

'I may be blind but my other senses compensate. I can smell the fart from a mouse.' She laughed. 'Do you have a name, or are you just strange like me?'

'Why strange?'

'A question with a question. You are a difficult fish to catch.'

A drop of rain fell from the roof and died on the stone floor beneath them.

'I'd like a name to put with your face.' She winked a blind eye and revealed an open smile.

'R.J.' Rachel surprised herself.

'Ah, the enigma of initials. What do they stand for?'

'Does it matter? A name's a name. There's no significance. It's just a label.' Rachel stood up from the pew and looked the woman in the eyes. There was no hint of movement, no expression on the face, just a quiet resigned attitude to the world and its shortcomings.

'A name is more than a name. It's an expression of your identity.'

'I can't see why,' Rachel answered. 'I didn't pick my name. My parents did. So how can it express anything about me?'

'Oh, I'm sure your parents didn't call you R.J. Those initials you have given to yourself to hide behind. That alone says a lot about you.'

'Maybe.'

'So what do you see when you look at me, R.J.?' The old lady sat on the end of a pew and waited for a response.

Rachel was unsure of what to answer.

'What do you see, tell me?'

'I see an old woman.'

'Is that all?'

'Why do you want to know?'

She smiled. 'It's a long time since I've seen myself. I don't know how I've changed with age. I can only imagine what I'm like. And we always imagine something better. The mind does curious things. My mind can keep me young because I can't see myself getting old. I can't see the wrinkles on my face or the liver spots on my hands. I have no wrinkles in my mind's eye. Do you know what I mean? Do you understand? I'm sure, even with your eyesight, you have imagined yourself to be something different than you really are. Although I think some people's imagination finds something worse to see about themselves. I suppose it depends on whether you are a half-full or half-empty person. I'm sorry, I'm rambling. That is one way I know I've aged, that and my aching bones.'

The old lady coughed quietly and then frowned. 'I don't know how the villagers see me. I'm sure it's not as the young woman they met before my blindness set in. They see me as Blind Marta, that's all I am to them now. I have become my label of imperfection. Why do we do that, my initialled friend? Why do we just look at someone and judge them by their appearance? I can't do that anymore, so to me R.J. you're not beautiful or ugly, you are just like Schrödinger's cat, you are both possibilities at the same time, until someone else looks into the box and informs me.' She laughed at herself. 'I think I've become more of a philosopher since I've lost my eyes.'

'I don't know what to say to you.'

'Well, just make it nice, then we can both hide inside this church.'

There was a thought forming in Rachel's mind but she

didn't want to give it shape. 'I have to go, I'm sorry. But if you really want to know, you've a kind face.'

Marta's smile was longer this time.

'Even with the scar that breaks my cheek in two? It still stings in the wind.'

Rachel looked at the woman's pink scar and suddenly felt cold. Outside the sky had darkened and the rain was spattering the windows.

'Your scar looks painful.'

The old woman nodded. 'It's more painful when it's cold outside. But I'm sorry, I have upset your peaceful thoughts here today.'

'No, it's alright, but I'm really going to be late if I don't leave soon. You'll have to excuse me.'

It was windy outside. The trees overhanging the church grounds were bent in submission to the small bell tower. Wet leaves glistened on the path, making each step perilous.

Rachel had taken too much time in the church. This was the night of her last injection. She could imagine the filled needle sitting on top of the bathroom cabinet, right in front of the mirror where he washed himself. She had started the process and now Joe was finishing it. He was doing what she had wanted, but sometimes that deep part of her felt like shouting at him, 'I deserve more dignity than this.' But she knew Joe had suffered too much, that she had cost him dearly.

It was Joe's turn now. And I love Joe enough to release him, she thought.

CHAPTER 7

THE COTTAGE WAS ALL I had ever wanted. I suppose you think it odd to want something so small and unexciting, but it overlooked the sea and the jagged rocks, giving them a softness they didn't deserve, the softness of a home. And the thick, yellow thatch stretched like warm fingers across the bare stone walls and changed colour with the seasons, as if it were still alive.

From my bedroom I could see across the sound and out to the white waves. For hours I would sit in the window and watch the landscape change with each passing cloud that dipped its head to the shore. The sheer physical beauty of this place was inspiring.

I had always been happiest in nature, in the solitude of the countryside. Nature threw up inconsistencies. Natural selection, survival of the fittest, the runt of the litter – nature presented myriad alternatives born in the certainty that life would either make or break them. Nature allowed variety but man desired a norm.

On cold evenings I always lit the fire. It was a large hearth, dominating the main room, sending flickering light across the bare stone walls, here and there catching in a crevice or hanging off a wooden beam. The rugs on the floor were the slippers for my feet and the throw-covered chairs were my comfort zone.

This evening was like every other – I had my music in the background, the papers spread out on the old oak table and the glass of red wine in my hand. Things were starting to adopt a pattern. My life was, for once, stabilising in a positive way. I felt that maybe I could be happy here.

She had come into my world again, the woman from the café. I had spotted her in the corner shop, a plastic bag tucked under her arm and a carton of orange juice in her hand. I didn't need to go into the shop for the box of matches, but there was no harm in them sitting on the fireplace keeping the others company.

It was while I was standing beside her at the checkout, unable to speak, that I realised how much I needed even the limited conversational ability of Rachel. She would have introduced me to everyone; she would have eased me into their world, smiling, chatting, holding court. Then, little by little, they would come to know me and realise that Rachel and I were not really together at all. She was my partner for life but I hadn't chosen her.

But now that I was nearly rid of her, I had to make my own introductions. It wasn't as easy for Joe White – square-jawed, broad-shouldered but a complete novice with women.

'Hello again. Would you like to go for a drink?'

In what half-assed film had I heard those lines and stupidly committed them to memory? In what state of ignorant dementia had I now thrown them out onto the poor unsuspecting woman before me?

The bemused look I received by return was completely deserved. Her eyes were even laughing at me. 'What? A cup of coffee?' she said. 'Now?'

It was a horrible trapped moment, the shutter speed was slowing and the air was thickening with overexposure.

'Well, I'm not too sure about a coffee. I think I might need a pint after that miss-timed invitation.'

I could have hugged her.

Danagher's was empty except for a practice card game, the card sharks sitting in the middle of the room around a baize-covered table, the onlookers seated in a surrounding circle.

'I'm Joe,' I said. 'Joe White.'

'I know, I asked the other day.'

I had expected her to reciprocate with her own name but I was pleased with her response. 'Oh, that's comforting,' I replied. 'You're not local, I remember you saying.'

'And I know you definitely aren't, Mr White.'

'No, but one day I will be.'

I liked her laugh; it was honest and came from deep within her.

'My mother's lived here for over forty-five years and she's still an outsider. So you might have to reassess your chances.'

'So you *were* brought up here, then?'

She nodded. 'Yes, I know the village. I've seen its good side and its bad, but I've been away for ten years. Nothing has changed. I don't know why I thought it would. Change is a foreign word in these parts. They still think they are fighting a rebellion against the British and the Catholic church is infallible.'

I wasn't interested in what the village thought. I wanted

to know where she'd been. I wanted to know about every moment of her life from her birth onwards. It was as if each strand of her existence was suddenly important to me. I was worried by my feelings. 'Where did you go?' I asked.

'Oh, I don't know if I actually want to tell you my life story yet, Mr White. Why don't you tell me your story first?'

I lifted my beer from the table and, for a moment, contemplated answering her. It would have been a wonderful relief to have had someone to share my secret with. It would have been comforting to allow someone to get that close. I was lonely coping with the wound that was Rachel. But she had called me Mr White twice now. She was keeping me at arm's length. 'There's nothing much to tell. And anyway, I don't tell my story to just anyone either. I don't even know your name.'

'I was wondering when you'd ask.'

'Well, I'm asking now.'

'Sophia,' she said almost apologetically. 'It's Sophia.'

It's funny how a name conjures up an image. I saw a beautiful Italian film star, her wide smile. The image swiftly moved to early days on my mother's knee, the black-and-white television acting up as my father turned the rabbit's ears this way and that, hoping to recapture the reception. Then I remembered my father motioning me towards the stairs while my mother pulled down the hem of her skirt, pushed her hair behind her ears and patiently waited. They had a secret life that I was never privy to, a life as a couple and not just as parents.

'Pleased to meet you, Sophia. So, now that we're introduced, will you tell me about your life?'

'Buy me another drink, Joe, and I'll think about it.'

I stood at the bar and ordered her a glass of Guinness. If I had been asked earlier, I would have said that she was a rum drinker, a short snappy drink lengthened by a Coke, but everything about Sophia was an enigma.

'So, to start with, where did your mother come from to be such an outsider?'

She looked less than forthcoming with the answer. 'Oh, maybe we'll deal with that another time.'

'A drink for answers, that was the deal,' I chastised her.

She gently put her hand on mine in a natural, open way. 'Rule No. 1, Joe White, never trust a woman you don't know.'

'Rule No. 2, Sophia, never expect to cheat me out of the truth.'

She looked down at her watch and sighed.

'Oh, it's later than I thought. I really should be going. Anyway, Mr White, what is the truth? Do any of us really know?'

'The truth is inside us,' I said stoically.

She laughed again. Not at me or with me, but a laugh that was all for herself. And she should have laughed at me; it was a ridiculously pompous answer for the middle of a Thursday afternoon. It sounded like an answer from a bad B-movie or, even worse, an evangelical outburst. The truth shall set you free.

But I didn't really believe that any more. The truth could bury you in acrimony. Rachel knew that. It was why I had to keep her a secret. It was one truth I was soon to bury. And although it was my decision, I hated that my new life sprang from Rachel's death. The world was big enough for both of us. But a stronger personality always invaded my thoughts with its domineering voice. 'Come on, Joe, you know you hate me. Anyway, you know the needle doesn't hurt and it takes me one step closer. You don't need me holding you back, weighing you down.'

Sophia left to go and meet her mother; I sat and finished my pint and watched the boats drift into the harbour, their rusted hulls a sad reflection of the hardships of most of the community. When the tourists were gone, the money was slow – the B&Bs emptied, the restaurants closed, the pool tables were brought out of storage to replace the extra chairs used to seat summer diners. I had contemplated closing the café for the winter – my meagre sales barely covering the overheads – but I had found an alternative use for the café, one I had overlooked at first because of my desire to be alone. Although, how I ever thought I'd be alone running a café I don't know.

It was slow to catch the imagination at first. Most women in the community were too busy to take the time out to learn a new skill, and most of their husbands were too conservative to let them go. It was young Fran who had clinched the whole deal by providing the obvious answers. I would teach the mothers to prepare more exotic dishes in the warmth and cosiness of the kitchen and she would provide a crèche facility in the café for all the young children they couldn't leave at home. It was manic at first, neither of us prepared for the problems that both children and mothers brought with them. But eventually the crayons and felt-tips produced the necessary quietness, and the welcoming glass of sangria eased the nervous women into good humour.

Business increased through word of mouth. From a single Thursday afternoon class, it escalated into three nights a week, with many making the trip from ten or fifteen miles away in cars of three or four. It was more than a creative cookery class; it was a night out without their husbands, a time to talk and meet and do something just for themselves. It was also upskilling for me. I was on a steep learning curve to teach these classes. Every spare night at home I would stand in front of a cookery book and reproduce the prettiest dishes I could find. It kept me occupied.

My cottage kitchen was always littered with the debris of my practising – warm strudels in one corner, meringues cooling in another and lamb tajine baking in the oven. Tajine was one of my favourite dishes. The exotic aroma of ras el hanout frying in a thick-based pot always pleased me. It was a marvellous blend of so many spices – cloves, cardamom, cumin, cinnamon, nutmeg and mace. It was difficult to find a spice that wasn't contained in the pungent blend. Heated gently in olive oil, it unleashed a wonderful, evocative smell. Ras el hanout is Arabic for *head of the shop* or *something from the top shelf*, something expensive and worthy of a high position. It definitely was held in high esteem in my kitchen and became a new product in the supermarket in Clifden, following requests from my students.

The most popular evenings were the baking nights. I would pretend to be Paul Hollywood and squeeze their crusted loaves looking for a soggy bottom or heavy dough, and it all became very flirtatious. The demonstration nights gave me far more than I expected. I was finding myself happily flirting with the group. It was comforting to have a definite topic of conversation. It was comforting that it was all about the ingredients and not about me. I felt in control. I was the teacher and they were my students. Shy, awkward Joe was coming out of his shell.

Having to keep one step ahead of them, I soon became a very competent baker, producing crème anglaise, choux pastry, macarons and delicious, shortcrust pastry tarts. My café even branched out and became a kind of artisan bakery. The classes evolved into selling baked goods to the whole western seaboard. I was amazed at how far customers came for homemade birthday cakes with a professional appearance.

The women in my classes loved the evenings. Once a month, the demonstration in the kitchen would be followed by a meal in the café, with music and wine. My café was quickly becoming a rival to the Irish Countrywomen's Association. The idea even spread to Clifden and Roundwood, where similar small businesses saw the opportunity to play a bigger part in their community, rather than shutting their doors for the winter. But it was a development that was as worrying to the men folk as the early years of the suffragettes. They didn't like change. Their women were meant to be at home at night with the kids, especially if they wanted to go down the local for their few daily pints.

CHAPTER 8

LAURA WAS SITTING BY THE window, the midday sunlight casting a flattering shaft of light across her face. Brian was proud of his wife. In spite of her self-image, she was the type of wife other men wanted when they saw her. Brian knew his sense of pride was chauvinistic, proprietary, due to the fact that when other men saw Laura, they would hold their wives closer to them and convince themselves that beauty wasn't all that important, that their wives had a charm of their own and not everybody could be married to a head-turner. If only she could see what he saw. But she never noticed the glances other men gave her.

He kissed her on the cheek. She was reciprocating today. He could feel her warmth towards him.

'Hi, sorry I'm late. Problems at work.'

'It's all right. I ordered us wine. White.'

'Great. So how come lunch today? I thought Thursday was your day with your mum.'

'Oh, no reason, honey, I just thought it would be nice.'

He should have seen the conversation coming. The alarm bells should have been ringing, but he still had the taste of this morning on his tongue. And then there was always the chance that she was back, the girl he had married, the one who had fallen for his charms and humour, because that's what she had told him on their first night in the four-poster bed. He had almost strangled himself with his bow tie in the rush to remove his shirt, the dance-band still thumping in the reception below, drowning the noise of their passion. She would have stood up from that bed and walked away had the moment not been charged with all the elements of seduction tied up with the right ribbon. It was so easy to burst Laura's bubble, to send her spiralling into her fear of failure. There was always a thin line between good and bad for her.

He had tried to seduce her before the wedding night, taken her to a country house hotel with log fires and crust-free sandwiches, but she had sat on the corner of the bed and told him it was better to wait, that her life was not meant to be as sordidly prearranged as this. Love-making was not to be arranged at all. She had a romantic image of spontaneity that was only to be found in films. A room couldn't be pre-booked – that was assuming that sex would be on offer and the night would go as planned.

She had talked nineteen to the dozen that night, while he had tried to undo the buttons of her shirt, his fingers fumbling awkwardly. He had nearly achieved something, too, when the door was loudly knocked upon.

It was a pattern of frustration constantly repeated. He had tried romance, wine, dinners and soft music, but her overwhelming desire to be the princess in her own Disney movie created a longing for a wedding night that included being a virgin.

'Brian, what are you thinking about? You weren't listening to me at all!'

Laura's voice was less than scolding but he could tell that she was unhappy that her planned lunch wasn't receiving the respect it deserved.

'I've been talking, Brian, and you've been staring into space.'

'Sorry, I'm all yours, my love.'

This would be the point at which she would usually refuse to forgive him and drive home her point, but today she smiled at him and placed her hand over his.

He looked at her worriedly. He had been good in bed this morning but not that good. Something was about to hit him and it couldn't be what he had earlier hoped for. She knew that he wanted children but she was preparing him for a blow. Whatever punch was going to land on him was being softened by purring tones and comforting touches.

'Did you ring your mum about your dad?' Another thoughtful question.

'No, I forgot.' He felt guilty now.

'Never mind, you can ring after lunch. I'm sure your father will understand, my love.'

The bells were ringing now but it was too late to evacuate the building. He was trapped. She was even showing concern about his father and yet she disliked him as much as he did.

'Do you really think the manuscript you showed me this morning is going to be a bestseller?'

'Oh, yeah, I'm a hundred per cent sure, but I've run into a bit of difficulty.'

'Nothing you can't overcome, surely?'

She seemed perturbed. She obviously had the money spent already. He knew she would have a list – a better kitchen, a new wardrobe. He would have to persuade her to add a new car for him to the list. It didn't have to be sporty. Even he realised he was too old to crouch into a low-slung model. But there was something about a sleek Jaguar that announced success. BMWs were for the best of the rest, too common now to be of any social value.

'What problem, Brian? It's just that I have some of the money spent in my mind already.'

'Yeah, I thought you would.'

She looked hurt. 'Well, do you mind? My salary has paid enough of the bills over the years. This would be a lovely bonus for us both.'

'No, it's okay. I've been doing it myself, spending it mentally. It's natural. But we've got to think of chickens and hatching first. I'm having trouble reaching the author. The book might even be published by now.'

She looked crestfallen.

'Look, I'm sure I'll get hold of them, Laura. What were you planning anyway?'

She folded her napkin and placed it on the table. 'It's something that will make me happy, make me feel good about myself.'

He knew what made him feel happy. It was so much simpler for him. It was her body pressed into the crumpled sheets by the firmness of his weight, completely accepting of his desire for her.

'I know you're going to think it unnecessary, but we have to respect each other's different needs, Brian.'

She always used his name when she was starting to get tetchy. He countered with the same. 'Laura, just tell me what it is? I don't need any more preparation.'

She took a sip of wine. 'I want to get some surgery done. I know it's a bit expensive but I need this for me. I need it, Brian.'

It was difficult to know how to react. Why did she need to change the body he loved? Was his love not good enough for her? With surgery there was always a risk, no matter how minimal. Besides, he had some old-fashioned notion that what God had created no man should alter. Every existence was perfect in its own uniqueness. He wanted to grow old gracefully with her, not have her the unnatural product of a surgeon's knife. The plastic mannequin-type looks of reconfigured faces frightened him. There was nothing real about them. Smiles were fixed permanently, eyebrows stuck quizzically. He preferred the lines of honest ageing. Everyone could still see the appeal of women who had aged naturally. He often fantasised about Helen Mirren or Meryl Streep. Their sheer confidence was alluring.

'Brian, say something, don't just go all quiet on me.'

'I don't know what to say.'

'Say what you feel, what you think.'

'Okay. I don't like it, Laura. I don't see why you need to.'

'Brian, inside I still feel twenty-five, young and healthy, but I look in the mirror and I can see lines, wrinkles, bags. I don't see me anymore.'

'But that's because you aren't twenty-five any more. Do you know how much I love you, Laura? How beautiful I think you are, just as you are?'

'This is not about you, Brian.'

It was his turn to feel hurt now. He took a drink from his glass and looked away from her.

'Brian, I know you love me, but it's about whether *I* love me.'

'And do you really think that changing your face will

make you love yourself any more? It's what's on the inside that counts, Laura.'

'Not in today's world, Brian. I will become as disposable as everything else that gets older. I've seen you looking at pretty young girls with that wistful smile on your face. Wouldn't you prefer to make love to a tight ass and a firm pair of breasts? Jesus, Brian, you have to hold mine up to put them to your mouth.'

'Stop it, Laura. I don't need a different you. And every red-blooded man looks at a pretty girl. That's just natural. I've seen you staring at young men when you think I'm not looking.'

'Brian, I really want this. It will still be me, just a better version.'

He didn't know what to say now. He could feel himself getting angry. His mind gave him the option of reminiscing rather than staying in the destructive moment.

He'd met a girl once when he was in school. She'd had a strawberry swelling covering the whole of one cheek. She was one of the most beautiful girls he had ever met. And even as a young boy he had known why. It was her eyes. They didn't avoid the looks of others for fear of being rejected, they challenged the world with a firm stare. That girl had allowed what was inside her to flow out through her face, and it was beautiful. Life had become too visual.

And so he understood Laura. He knew it was a lack of confidence that plagued her. It was the little girl inside of her that was damaged by someone else's perceptions. Someone, somewhere in her past, had told her that she wasn't good enough and she had believed it. In contrast, the girl with the birthmark had obviously been nurtured like a precious rose, and that became her reality.

'Who disfigured you, Laura?' he asked without thinking.

'What are you talking about, Brian?' She sounded furious now.

'Forget about that. But if I was disfigured in an accident, would you stop loving me?'

'It's not about that, Brian. I love you for who you are. You've put on a few pounds and lost a bit of hair but it changes nothing for me.'

'To be honest I don't agree with you on that. You'll judge me and others with the same critical eye that you judge yourself with. You probably do have an issue with my lack of rippling muscles and my paunch. But I don't mind ageing, Laura.'

'Well, bully for you, Brian.' She had no option but to go on the attack. He knew he had cornered her. 'I'm not as simplistic as you, Brian, so I need this.'

'Look, I have to go back to work soon. Can we leave this until later? I really was hoping we'd be discussing something else.'

There would be no conversation about children. He understood that more than ever. She wasn't going to let nine months of pregnancy alter her appearance. She would stop being a person in her own right if she went down that road. She would just become someone's mother. She had experienced that with her own mother, and Brian knew it haunted her. He had always assumed that all women wanted babies. The picture of his mother with her arms outstretched for their hugs filled his head. Her warmth was always the perfect antidote to the troubles of the day. He had never expected to marry someone so loathe to accept that most creative of female experiences.

Every now and then, his own mother would look at him and the obvious question would cross her eyes. But after ten years of marriage, it had almost become a lost look. Up in the attic, he knew his mother kept his old books and toys, his cradle and his christening outfit. They were nestled between his college folders and black suitcases from old package holidays. She was keeping them for her grandchildren. The only negative thing Brian saw about having children was his own father. He didn't want to give him the chance to be a grandparent to any poor kid.

'Look, I do love you, Laura. If it's what you want, then we'll look into the best doctors around. I don't want any backstreet stuff. But let's just drop it right now and talk about something else.'

CHAPTER 9

THE RAIN WAS POURING AGAINST her office window. Laura had looked at the piece of paper ten times but the figures weren't changing. She knew she had made one mistake in her calculations but she couldn't see where. Her mind was elsewhere. It had been elsewhere for a while and this was irritating her. Brian was irritating her. He always saw things as black or white, and things were never that way. Where was the grey?

She knew where it was. It was in the roots of her hair, where last month's colouring had grown out. It was in the lines under her eyes that kept appearing when she smiled. She didn't want to grow old and she didn't want to feel ashamed of thinking that way.

'Do you have the stats on the Laois site, Laura?'

It was Cal. The new recruit to their happy team. He was four years out of university and still full of the joys of spring. He worked hard but also partied hard. He was often out late on a work night, which was a thing of the past for Laura.

'They're on the third shelf in the red folder.'

'Thanks. Are you coming out tonight? A few of us are thinking about some pints and then up to the Indian. You haven't come lately.'

Laura looked at his slim waist and muscular physique

and wondered why she had refused on so many occasions to go out with them. It was fun watching the unmarried girls flirt with him and vie for his attention. But he wasn't interested in their advances. He seemed happier talking with the married women, although she had noticed that she wasn't on his radar. In the pub on a Friday he usually avoided her.

'I'm fine, thanks, Cal. I need to go home this evening.'

'No problem. The others told me to ask you since I was coming up to your office.'

The others told me to ask you. Why couldn't you have just asked me anyway, she thought. She was being ridiculous. What difference did it make who asked her? She wasn't going to go anyway. She needed to talk to Brian. She needed to make him see that her need for plastic surgery wasn't foolish. It was just like having braces on your teeth; it was about tweaking the image not altering it. What was wrong with emphasising the positive aspects of your body? And her face was one of her best features. Even she knew that.

Her phone rang, disturbing her thoughts. It was her mother. 'Hi, Mum, I was going to ring you later. Are you okay?'

The voice on the other side was warm. 'Yes, Laura, everything's fine. I was just wondering did you get to see your grandmother yesterday?'

'Yes, I visited her at lunchtime. She's okay and said that she hopes you and Dad are having a lovely holiday.'

'Oh you know us, we're just haunting the same old places here and doing the same things as usual. But my hands are hurting me less in the heat. I do think it's great for the old arthritis. Did you tell Brian that you were having pain in your joints? You should you know. It's hereditary, so it may be the onset.'

Laura didn't want to sound frustrated with her mother but they'd had this conversation before. She didn't want to tell her husband that she may have early-onset arthritis and end up looking wizened and gnarled before her time. She was quite happy leaving him out of that loop as he was too prone to being over-protective and he would want to look into all the new treatments and make a complete fuss of everything.

'There's nothing to tell him about yet, Mum. It's just a bit of pain. I'm fine. Really, I am.'

'You're as stubborn as your dad, love. Although he's shaking his head at me and saying that I'm the stubborn one.'

Laura looked at her reflection in the window of her office and saw a younger version of her mother.

'Tell him, I agree. I'm more like you.'

'Well, it's up to you what you tell that poor husband of yours. You could be right, maybe it's nothing. Maybe it's not anything at all, but you should at least go and find out for yourself.'

Laura tried not to sound frustrated.

'There's no point, Mum. There's nothing they can really do. You know that better than anyone. I'd just prefer to get on with things and hope for the best.'

'Okay, darling, it's your decision of course, so we'll leave it there. Maybe you'd pop into your grandmother again before we get back. I do worry about her when I'm away.'

'Of course I will. Now go and enjoy your holiday and stop fretting about things here.'

Laura finished the call with the usual pleasantries and then thought about the connection she felt to her grandmother and mother. Both women gave her such wonderful support. They were strong and caring. She wished she was more like them but she was frightened sometimes about having children. There was so much that could go wrong, so much responsibility. She knew Brian wanted children. He was so eager to have a small person to play with and influence. But she had burst his bubble and told him that she loved her career too much to even think of having children. The truth was that she was scared. She was scared of bringing up children in a world where the prospects were so grim.

Her thesis in university had been about environmental problems and how to alleviate them. The deteriorating issues had not made her feel safe concerning the future of mankind. Also there were already so many children out there, unwanted and unloved, living in foster homes and orphanages. What need did the world have for more children? She felt that those already born needed more consideration.

But she had thought about having children. She loved Brian and she knew that he would be a good father – he was so cheerful and childlike. He often made sandcastles on their holidays, even though he looked like a dad whose child had wondered off to leave him building alone. She would watch him from the shade of her umbrella and love the fact that he could be so lost in such a simple thing. It was one of his attractive qualities – he was able to enjoy the little things in life.

Maybe she had lost her childlike qualities. It was the worries she had taken on after college. She worried about money. Brian's business wasn't always thriving and she felt that she had to keep working to make sure mortgage repayments were met and bills paid. She was worried about death and the people in her life that she might lose. She had already lost her grandfather, and her grandmother was now suffering from Alzheimer's and living in a care facility. She had once loved spending time with Nana Joan but now their time together was fraught with episodic shouting and anger. The frail woman didn't even know who she was or where she was most of the time. She hardly ever looked up when Laura wiped her face or held her hand. But every now and again the old woman's face would light up when Laura visited. That made the visits worth it.

Where was the room for a child among all her worries? What if she carried it for nine months and then it died of cot death? What if she brought it successfully through childhood and then it became a drug addict or was killed in a motorbike accident? Having a child was too fraught with fears and these fears were too ridiculous to tell Brian. But if he knew her real reasons for not wanting children, he might understand her more and not think her selfish. Maybe she should tell him.

CHAPTER 10

I WAS BECOMING BETTER AT my new life. Every morning I would take the path that led from the house down the hill to the road. I had even given my home a name. It was something I had always found pretentious in the past but that was because I had never really understood the concept of a home. I called it Chimera.

From the hill on which my house was built, I could see the surrounding islands, but the one that drew me towards it the most was the one I nicknamed the Sleeping Monster. The locals had a Gaelic name for it, which left me cold as I had no understanding of the unpronounceable word. To me this island was the guardian of the inlet, proudly arching its back against the marauding Atlantic waves. At the tip of the island was a series of jagged peaks, hard metamorphic rock refusing to be ground down by the battering tides, the same tides that had created the horns and snout of my monster. I wanted to take the hazardous journey out to its green flanks and see my home from there, but there was no jetty on which to land.

It had taken me nine months to clear the front of my house and create a small garden. The ground in this part of Connemara was hard and unforgiving, the rocks scattered across tufted grass. I didn't want to plant flowers and create a misplaced oasis among the barren land. I just had the need for somewhere to put my bench and rug, somewhere to sit and listen to the waves.

I had no need to drive to work unless I had a delivery to pick up from Galway. I could walk the distance easily and I loved the feeling of my body becoming more muscular – the tightness of my calves, the firmness of my glutes. For the first time in my life I was developing a positive body image. I had even put a small mirror in the bathroom, a thing I would never have done in the past. I had always hated my own reflection.

My beard was thickening also. Before, I had always shaved, taken every hint of hair from my face, but this was a new life. I wanted to hide my past existence so that no one could ask me what had happened to poor Rachel. In some ways her gradual demise was easier than I had expected. She was happily filling the needles for me these days, standing there in the bathroom staring at the mirror, her eyes filling with tears of relief.

She had wanted this ever since Paul's death. It had been a shock to us both at first. She had almost died with our baby, her hands clawing at the coffin as they lowered him into the grave. He had been my son too, but she had given birth to him. I had just wanted to be a father to him. Fate had robbed me of that and I gradually came to understand that I could never live with the despair that Rachel had fallen into. It was an abyss. Rachel felt her life was over with the death of Paul, so it was difficult to feel guilty for what I was doing. I was bringing release.

'Hi, Mr White. I've washed the floor already and put the milk in the fridge.'

'Fran, at this stage you really should be calling me Joe.'

'Yes, Mr White. Sorry, Joe.'

'I think we'll change some of the menu again this week. There are very few tourists out there.'

'Oh, not too much, though. My dad loves the chicken and ham pie.'

She was an endearing person. I was becoming very fond of her.

'Oh, Jesus, I nearly forgot to tell you. Did you hear about the woman killed last night, down the road from O'Malley's? Hit by a car, she was. Walking on her own, out at night. Sure we all do it. It could have been any of us.'

I don't know why, but my thoughts went immediately to Sophia.

'Who was it? Were they local?'

'A tourist, I think they said. An American. You feel sorry for their family, don't you? Dying abroad and all. I suppose it'll take ages to get the body home.'

I didn't really empathise with the poor American relatives. I was just relieved that it wasn't Sophia, but I made some sort of sympathetic reply and Fran continued.

'They don't know who hit her yet. No one stopped and no one came forward. Alfie, the second oldest, was telling me all the news. His friend Gerry is a guard in Clifden, graduated from Templemore last year. Good-looking guy too.' She was talking and grating carrot at the same time, never coming up for air or looking for much of a response. 'Makes you wonder who it was. God, I hope it's not someone I know. Can you imagine them sitting at home this morning scared to leave their house, wondering did they get all the blood off their car bumper.'

'Jesus, Fran, your imagination is frightening.'

She stopped peeling and looked me straight in the eye. 'Do you think so? My daddy's always telling me that. I'm thinking of writing kids' books. What do you think?'

'I'm wondering where you'll find the time, what with working for me and running the crèche and cooking for your family. And they would have to be less gory!'

She gave a broad smile and poked me in the ribs with the handle of the peeler.

'Sure I can always leave you on your own, although I doubt it would be for long. You're becoming very popular around here, Mr White. I mean Joe.'

I gave her an inquisitive look.

'Ah, don't look so innocent. Daddy was telling me there was talk in the pub about you.'

'I don't think I want to know.'

'Sure you do.'

She was absolutely right. I had to know.

'They were saying that you're cooking up a right problem with the women. You're too flipping good at entertaining them.'

It was a strange thing to hear. Me, Joe, a threat to the local men. It was something I hadn't even considered. I had been too busy with my own thoughts.

'Well, you and I know, Fran, it's a load of rubbish.'

She picked up another carrot and waved it mockingly in my face.

'It might have been when you first came here, but not anymore.'

'I beg your pardon?'

Fran dropped the carrot and looked flustered. She

had obviously taken my umbrage seriously. 'Oh, I'm sorry. I wasn't trying to be rude.'

'Fran, I'm only joking. It's okay.' I smiled and she smiled back. 'So I've changed, have I?'

She was still slightly nervous. 'Well, you never came out from the kitchen when I first worked here. You used to just cook and I served.'

'That's because I'm quite shy.'

She laughed. 'I used to think that too, but then you started teasing me and talking to the customers and running those evening classes, so we all changed our opinion of you.'

'Oh, yeah, and what was that?'

A look of embarrassment crossed her face. 'Oh, I can't say.'

'You may as well, seeing as how I like a laugh and have learned to smile.'

She picked up a carrot and started scrapping furiously.

'Oh please, I really couldn't say.'

'Ah come on, don't be a chicken.'

She looked at me. I wondered whether she was worrying about her future in the café or whether her apprehension had anything to do with a fear of hurting my feelings.

'Don't worry about me. I'm tough-skinned.' It was a lie but it worked.

'They thought you were, you know, a man who liked men,' she muttered.

I had heard her but I wanted to make sure. 'A what?'

'You know, Mr White, you heard me clear enough. A gay, a gay man.'

I don't think she expected me to burst out laughing. I

don't know what response she had expected. To me, it was the ultimate irony. Jesus, if they only knew. 'So, in God's name, why did they look at me and think, gay?'

'Do I have to say, Joe?'

'Go on, tell me. It won't change a thing.'

She looked extremely doubtful.

'I promise you that you'll still have a job.'

'Okay, if you're sure?'

I nodded.

'It's just that you had no wife, no girlfriend and you never chatted the women up on a Friday evening. Things like that. Oh and you were way too good at cooking!'

It was a harmless list. 'But has any of that changed? I still don't sit at the bar in the pub.'

'Ah, it has changed all right. You look at women now. I've seen you. Especially Sophia Warner.'

Her perception startled me. 'Do you know her?'

'Oh, yes, she lives down in the cottage on Murrisk Bay. She's just returned from Dublin. She's the new history teacher in Clifden. Daddy said that she was born here but left for Dublin years ago. I wouldn't remember her from back then.'

'Does she live alone?'

'Ha! I knew you fancied her.'

I suppose I had made that too obvious, but I didn't care.

'Well, if I do, you're not to go telling the whole village.'

She smiled. She was warming to me as I was warming to her. Rachel would have been proud of me. I was making new friends, albeit a girl nearly young enough to be my daughter.

'Don't worry, Joe, she lives with her mother. You must

know her to see. She's as odd as two left feet.'

She was going to tell me more but the conversation was disturbed by the jangling of the bell in the café.

'Good morning, Joe.'

'Hi, Brendan, how are you?'

I poured him a cup from the pot and placed it on the counter. 'How about a couple of croissants with that?' I suggested.

Brendan Morrissey nodded and took out a blue biro and a notebook. I always thought it was lucky for Brendan that he lived and worked in a rural community, where the work wasn't too strenuous. His ample body would have made it difficult to chase criminals through the streets of Galway or Limerick. He was the stereotypical village garda. He knew all the locals, knew all their houses and had warmed his backside by all their fires. At closing time, he was tucked safely in his bed or at the station in Clifden, sitting behind the desk reading a paper, a cup of coffee and a biscuit in his hand. Life as a village guard was blissfully slow.

'I'm afraid this is not a social visit, Joe.'

His smile had dropped and I suddenly felt nervous, a myriad of horrible possibilities flashing through my mind. Strangely, the hit and run was not one of them.

'I suppose you've heard about the sad death last night?'

'Yeah, Fran, just told me.' I knew she was behind the door listening to our conversation but she wouldn't have come out. Brendan wasn't one of her favourite people. He had given her a lecture once about riding her bike without lights.

'Well, we've found red paint at the scene and we're examining all red cars in the area, you understand?'

'And I have a red car.' I was relieved. It wasn't the dreaded visit about Rachel.

'Yes, Joe, you do. Not that we think it's you, but we have to rule out everyone before we continue with the investigation and you are not that familiar to us really.'

'I understand.'

Part of me knew that as an outsider I was always going to be held in some suspicion. I also worried that Brendan was probably one of the men who had a certain opinion of me. It wouldn't have surprised me. He had the look of a man who rarely tolerated anything outside his comprehension, and his comprehension didn't seem to stretch that far.

Rachel had met Brendan on the first day we had come to the area, a corpulent figure waving at her from a distance. She had stopped the car as requested. He was manning a roadblock, looking for tax offenders. Rachel had panicked. There weren't meant to be any meetings with the locals. We had planned a straight journey to the cottage, where she would remain hidden from view for months. So she had frozen in fear when he had smiled at her from in front of the windscreen. She had just sat staring straight ahead as he had checked her details.

I changed the car after that encounter. Rachel was right. It was stupid to take unnecessary risks. It was early days. I didn't wish to ruin years of planning through careless behaviour at that stage.

CHAPTER 11

BRIAN SAT IN HIS CAR and drummed his fingers on the steering wheel. He hated the partly finished M50 and hate wasn't a word he used lightly. He found the whole Irish road network a complete conundrum – tunnels built too small for trucks, motorways that led to single-lane bridges and signposts that never seemed to point in the right direction. And with all the road-building and cones, there were the inevitable 30 kph speed limits and bumper-to-bumper traffic. He was sitting in that now, staring into space. He couldn't look at the car in front of him as two young boys were leering out the back window at him, making grotesque faces and inventing a whole new language with their fingers. Maybe he was better off with Laura not wanting children.

He glanced up at the signpost for the West. It was a complete mystery why more tourists didn't get lost. There was no mention of Galway as the final destination of the motorway. According to the sign, the road to the West only led to Sligo. Maybe Sligo needed the business, maybe Galway needed less traffic, maybe there was some sort of twisted logic behind their thinking, but he couldn't work it out.

He had published a book once about Second World War, an interesting little piece on Ireland's response as a neutral country. Blacking out road signs had been one of our counter-invasion strategies. It was comforting to know that if the Germans or Brits had invaded, our grandparents would have been safe in their houses because the dreaded enemy would have been standing at the crossroads looking in puzzlement at the useless signs.

But at least the new road to Athlone was an improvement. There were bypasses now – strange bypasses that took longer than driving through the towns because they were littered with traffic lights, new roads wide enough to overtake on but with speed limits that rendered it impossible to achieve the manoeuvre. This was why he was trapped behind an articulated lorry, unable to see the road ahead. He could feel his patience dwindling; he needed to think of something else besides driving.

Brian wondered if his journey would be successful, if the mysterious R. J. McLoughlin would be at home. He had tried on three consecutive days to make contact but the result was always the same. The phone call was always cut dead at the mention of the name.

It was Laura who had suggested the trip, nervous that her new nose, lifted breasts and wrinkle-free face were slipping out of her reach.

'They can't avoid you, Brian, when you're standing on their doorstep.'

But he thought they could. They could slam the door in his face and he would be left to find a sandwich and a coffee before he made the hour-and-a-half journey home.

His mind had created various reasons as to why R. J. McLoughlin had proven such a difficult person to reach, and none of them gave him much hope. The obvious one was death: he had suffered a major coronary and pegged it out before seeing his work published. Or he had run off to the south of Spain with the tight-assed secretary from Administration. This version made him laugh as it was such a ridiculously laddish explanation. Another notion was that this wonderful writer was a seventy-eight-year-old Alzheimer's patient and couldn't even remember that he had written the book.

He looked at the car seat beside him. On it sat the address and a copy of the contract. It didn't hurt to be hopeful. Maybe R. J. McLoughlin of 18 Fintan Lawlor Terrace would be sitting there having his tea, happy to sign all his rights away. Maybe Brian would be able to dream again of a new car and a happy wife.

The houses were cramped together, some pebble-dashed, others stone-clad, all groaning with the desire to grow up into bigger houses. Number 18 had a Morris Minor in the driveway.

Brian looked in his mirror and flashed a smile to see if his teeth were clean. There was a small smudge on his tie but otherwise he looked as good as usual. He had always been confident in his appearance. He was no male model but he knew he could win a person over if he gave them his full attention.

The appearance of the house gave him a horrible feeling in the pit of his stomach, even though it was neat and well kept. There was a row of well-pruned rose bushes lining the driveway, very attractive but prickly. Brian realised why his stomach was upset. It reminded him of the house of his old schoolmaster, Mr Reynolds, who had spent years after his retirement pottering about his garden in corduroy trousers, pruning his roses while reciting poetry, as if he was stuck in a loop. Brian had found the deterioration of Mr Reynolds' mind disturbing as it was he who had given Brian his love of English. So much did the idea of old Reynolds implant itself in his mind that he was mildly surprised when an elderly lady answered the door in a flour-stained apron.

'Hello, can I help you?'

'Yes, I'm looking for R. J. McLoughlin.'

The old woman's face dropped and her eyes fell to the floor. The silence was palpable. Although her response was disappointing, Brian felt this was not the angry person who had been responsible for slamming down the phone. This woman appeared warm and approachable.

'Look, I'm sorry to disturb you but is Mr McLoughlin here?'

The woman's face melted into a relieved sigh.

'Oh, for a minute there I thought you'd asked something else,' she said, wiping her floured hands on her apron. 'My hearing's not what it used to be. My husband's just gone out. He'll be home in half an hour.'

Brian Matthews looked at his watch, more for effect than anything else. He had already decided to wait outside in his car.

'Is it important you see him today?'

'Well, I've travelled up from Dublin, so I'd like to see him if possible.'

The old lady raised her eyebrows. 'All the way from Dublin? I hope he wasn't expecting you. My husband's usually very careful about things. He's a meticulous man. There's nothing wrong, is there?' Her face had become anxious again.

'No, it's good news, I hope. Actually, I should have introduced myself. I'm Brian Matthews. I'm a publisher, not a taxman or anything awful like that.'

She looked puzzled now but had obviously decided he wasn't a threat to her or the house. 'Would you like to come in and have a cup of tea while you wait?'

'Yes, thank you, that would be very nice.'

Mrs McLoughlin stood back from the doorway and he walked past her into the narrow hall. The wallpaper was covered in primroses that were no longer yellow but a pale lemon. In places a torn piece had been replaced with an odd remnant, leaving sections of headless flowers or stemless heads. The old lady ushered him into a small sitting room and showed him to a leather armchair, incongruous among the other pieces of furniture.

'I'll just be a few minutes,' she said closing the door behind her.

He could hear her out in the kitchen – the tap running, the rattle of cups on saucers. Looking around the room, he thought again of his old teacher. Bookshelves groaned under the weight of hundreds of well-thumbed novels. But there were also holiday mementos in the corner over a wooden shelf that housed a full set of car maintenance magazines and around thirty copies of the *Reader's Digest*. These people read, but not the kind of books that gave him any hope that he was in the right place.

Mrs McLoughlin came back into the room holding a wooden tray. She poured the tea out of a lime-green teapot and presented a plate of plain biscuits. 'So, you're a publisher. That must be interesting work. How do you know my husband?'

Brian put two sugar lumps into his cup and stirred

while he answered. 'Actually, I don't know him. He sent me his book, *The Olive Tree*, and I liked it.'

The old woman closed her eyes and said nothing, but he could see her chest rise and fall with a heavy sigh. It was a strange response, and worrying. He thought it best to continue the conversation as if her odd behaviour was understandable and expected.

'It really is an excellent book. Your husband's very talented.'

Her eyes opened and she shook her head emphatically.

'So,' she said, her hands working the hem of her skirt, 'I did hear you right the first time. I think we've both made a mistake. I think you'd better leave.'

Brian was confused.

'I'm sorry, but what do you mean? It's on my desk. R. J. McLoughlin, *The Olive Tree*. This is the address on the letter.'

She didn't seem to be registering his reply. She had become flustered and upset. She was up from the seat and heading for a picture on the mantelpiece.

'Look at my little Rachel. She was such a lovely girl.'

The photograph was thrust into his hands. Brian looked at the young woman in her cap and gown, clutching her degree to her bosom. She had the same sad eyes as her mother. He didn't know what to say but he felt obliged to give some sort of reply. 'She looks like you.'

'Not anymore.'

She took the photograph from him and cleaned the glass with the sleeve of her cardigan. Then she placed it carefully back in its place and sat on a chair opposite him. Her eyes were glazed with tears.

'I loved her so much, you know. She was my only

daughter. I named her after my mother. She was christened in my old white gown. It seems so tainted now. I hate him. I really do. I hate him for killing my little girl. How dare you come here and bring all this up again. We were moving on, at least we were trying. Do you have children yourself? Do you know what it's like to lose one? She left us, you know. I don't know why she didn't want her life here with us. I don't understand it. As far as I'm concerned, he may as well have murdered her when he first told us. I'm sure she's well dead to the world by now.'

She was becoming more and more agitated and Brian was becoming more and more confused.

'I'm really sorry if my coming here has upset you. I was hoping to bring good news.'

She screwed up her eyes and peered at him. 'Are you a friend of his? Does he want something from us? If Maurice knew you were here, he'd kill you, Mr Matthews. My husband is still very angry about this. He is a proud man. He doesn't like that our family is the talk of the neighbourhood.'

Brian felt as though he had stepped onto the set of *Eastenders*.

'No, I'm not a friend, and I'm sorry but I don't know what you mean. I really just wanted to publish the book.' But really he just wanted to go home, away from this upset woman with her *Reader's Digest* and beheaded primroses. He didn't like drama, especially when it involved him.

'What did you really come for?' she asked, her eyes now filled with an angrier sadness. 'Do you want a story for your magazine? Are you that kind of publisher? One who feeds on other people's misery?

Brian shook his head. 'Not at all. That's not me. Just

tell me what R. J. stands for, so that I can find the author myself.'

'Rachel, obviously. The J stands for Joanna. That's my second name too.'

'So R. J. is your daughter?' He wished that he hadn't delivered his thoughts so clumsily.

The old woman turned to the window and tears ran down her face. 'Not any more, not any more. Didn't you listen to me or did you think I was just an old fool?'

He rose to his feet. This was becoming too bizarre. All he was doing was upsetting an old lady.

'What the hell is going on here?'

Brian hadn't heard the door opening amidst all the confusion. The man standing before him in the centre of the room was tall, old enough to be the woman's husband and gruff enough to be the voice on the phone.

'He's asking for Rachel, but I told him that she's gone. He won't listen.'

'How dare you come in here and upset my wife like this. What do you want with us?'

'Look, I'm sorry, but I think there's been some misunderstanding. I was sent a manuscript by an R. J. McLoughlin and I just wanted to talk to him or her as the case may be.'

The man's eyes darkened. 'As my wife says, there's no point in coming here. My daughter's dead. Leave us be. Now!'

'Of course, I'm very sorry.'

The man put his arm around his wife and sat her on the couch. 'Aggie, don't worry, this man's going now. He won't bother us again. You sit there quietly and I'll be back in a minute.'

Brian knew he was expected to see himself out. He felt horrible. As he turned for the door, the man spoke slowly and deliberately.

'I don't know why you've come here and I don't care. Rachel hasn't lived with us for a long time. I presume she no longer exists. I once loved my daughter but she chose to do what she did and I'll never be able to forgive her for that.'

'As I said, Mr McLoughlin, I'm sorry for disturbing you.'

'My wife, as you see, is devastated. She has lost her only daughter and in the worst circumstances for a mother. It is him you should be searching for. Ask him to explain to you why he killed her off. He's a godless freak of nature.'

'I'm sorry, I don't know who he is. I don't know what you mean.'

'He wanted to be my son. But he's no son of mine. He's a cold person with no heart. He has robbed me and my wife of so much joy.'

'Look, I'm sorry for bringing all this back to you, but your daughter was a good writer. Something could still be salvaged from your pain. She could be remembered in her book if you wanted it published.'

It was Brian's second mistake that afternoon. The old man's face turned to thunder and he pulled the front door open angrily.

'Are you trying to make me lose control? Get out and don't you dare publish one word of anything she has sent to you or you'll regret it.'

It seemed a long walk to the car. Brian felt the old man's eyes burning into the back of his head.

When he reached the outskirts of Dublin, he couldn't

even remember leaving the motorway for the old national road. His mind had been working overtime trying to piece together all the bits of information. Why would a son kill his own sister and where was he living that he had got away with murder? Somewhere in the back of his mind there was a thought growing. The thought had to do with the book called *The Olive Tree*.

CHAPTER 12

It was six-thirty and Laura was wondering how Brian's day had gone in Athlone. He had left so eagerly that morning. She had suggested the trip, not wanting him to lose this chance of publishing a bestseller. She knew he thought it was because she wanted him to make the money for her surgery but in reality she believed he needed the excitement of a bestseller in his career. He had been bored with his job lately. He had failed to find anything among the submissions to make him sit up and feel alive and he had started to look for excitement elsewhere. He was having too many drinks on a Friday and noticing too many women when they were out at parties. He had always been a flirt and she had always felt flattered that he had chosen her, but there was also that worry that he might leave her for someone younger. It was another of her fears, to add to the fears of penury and death.

Publishing this novel might not only give them a slightly better bank balance but it might also reignite his passion for his job and stop him reflecting on other areas of his life. She knew Brian didn't do reflection well. He looked at things far too simplistically. If he was a happy person by nature, his unhappiness had to come from outside of himself. She knew he thought that way. He was always cracking jokes and making light of things, and yet he never really bothered to look at where the cracks actually were in his life. He never looked beneath the veneer.

One of his issues was definitely starting to make itself known in their marriage. He was coming home grumpier all the time and trying to hide the real reason with an attack on her cooking or her choice of TV show. It was what she referred to as his sandcastle syndrome. He found pleasure in little things so he presumed that little things were the things that irked him and drove him to temper. But she knew his issues ran much deeper than these easily surmountable problems. He was a product of his father's parenting.

Laura disliked Richard Matthews. He was a bully of a man, a self-important, self-made millionaire who had no idea on how to raise his children. He believed good parenting demanded high standards from children, and his boys were to learn early that success was the key to happiness. Success could buy you cars and houses and women. Brian knew his father had been unfaithful to his mother; his father had told him. Brian had left home as soon as he could, to avoid the embarrassment of living with such a man, but he was still driven by his father's opinions on success, and he still felt a failure when the money wasn't rolling in, no matter how much he tried to convince himself that it was fine to live an average life. And he still visited his father in hospital every now and again to please his mother.

Laura peeled another carrot and wondered how her husband had managed to become such a loving man. It was one of the sad things about her marriage. She hated being in the company of Brian's father and Brian knew it. But he never wanted to talk about it as he was sure it had no bearing on him as a person or his relationship with her. Laura would have loved to have informed him differently but she knew he wouldn't entertain such a conversation. He was unable to deal rationally with anything about his family.

Marriage was a strange beast. They could talk about so many things so openly and honestly, but there were layers of truth that sometimes neither of them could get to as they were created in a whole mucky area of life before marriage. Brian didn't even want to know about her past boyfriends. He seemed threatened by those old relationships that had been dead and buried before they had ever met. And yet Laura knew the past was important to their future. It was where their fears and insecurities were born and where their personalities were moulded. Before they had dated each other, they were already a complicated mass of emotional baggage. The tough part of marriage was working on all that baggage while trying to maintain a relationship. Maybe that was why so many first-time marriages failed. People were still working through their shit. Maybe, she thought, people shouldn't marry until they had been through therapy to sort out the flaws in their personalities.

Three of Laura's friends were already divorced or separated. Laura didn't want to go the same route. She loved Brian, and when she had said until death us do part, she had meant it. Her parents had gone through many issues in their marriage, and what hadn't killed them as a couple did make them stronger. She knew Brian had his faults, as did she, but she always presumed that they would work through anything that came along to disturb their equilibrium.

A car was pulling into the driveway. Hopefully, the news would be good and he would be the happy husband she had married, buoyed by the hope of success. Otherwise it would be her healthy meals and her plastic surgery that would come under fire for ruining his day.

CHAPTER 13

THE HARBOUR WAS QUIETER THAN usual. The ferries had left for the island and all that was left on the quayside were the empty crates that had once held lobsters. Sophia stood on top of the harbour wall and watched the waves roll onto the rocks. There was no ferocity in their motion; it was a gentle lapping, like a lover playfully licking toes.

Jerry. It wasn't a name that conjured up an image of strength or power but it had been her best attempt at a successful relationship, her first real bite of the cherry. She didn't like that phrase. She wondered why she had used it; probably something absorbed from conversations with her mother, or maybe just something that had floated into her mind and taken root there. Teaching did that to you. It filled you with superfluous phrases because everything had to be repeated and reinforced.

Jerry's vocabulary had been very limited. His favourite stock phrase had been 'one way or another'. 'I'll work out this jigsaw one way or another,' he used to say, holding a small piece up to the light for further inspection. Two thousand pieces of tedious brain-ache was how she saw the boxes he used to bring home every month from the toyshop. It was one of the reasons she had turned down his proposal of marriage, well, that and the veins that used to stick out in his temple when he was angry or stressed. It might have been a simple physical quirk to a more patient individual, but for her it created a mental block to holding him with the passion that marriage deserved. It was also why she kept her eyes open during their moments together, watching his face contort and his neck pulse with racing blood. She always thought he looked ridiculous then, not sensual or sexual or exciting, but absurdly grotesque, ignorant of her feelings. Until one day the realisation dawned on her that it was she who was ignorant of her own feelings – she was nowhere near to loving this man. He was just a comforting presence, a sop for her loneliness.

So she didn't miss Jerry. She could look out at the Atlantic, alone with her thoughts and conclude that there was no emptiness or aching for Jerry. But there was a space that she couldn't fill, a space she felt as she walked around the city streets, watching women pushing their prams and dragging their small children behind them. She had always told herself she would never become that sort of woman, the type who stared at buggies and cots with regret or, even worse, envy.

It was why she had left Dublin. There had to be the push factors as well as the pull of being with her elderly mother. She needed to escape from her circle of friends who had married and had children and were waiting for her to do the same. At least in the small village of Clochan she was accepted as unusual because of her eccentric mother. She didn't have the friends looking sorrowfully at her. But as she looked out to sea, she could hear the ominous ticking inside, the desperate clock relentlessly moving towards infertility. It would just have to wait a bit longer until the right man walked into her life, and she hadn't met anyone who had stimulated her even slightly.

A familiar voice broke her thoughts. 'Hi. Aren't you cold out here?'

'Shouldn't you be in your café pouring cups of coffee?'

He didn't seem perturbed by her answer. He simply stood and looked out to sea. She looked at him curiously. He wasn't her type. He was short and stocky. His hands were small and his fingers squat and he had a habit of pulling at his earlobes and then rubbing his chin as if his face was a mask that didn't fit. His presence annoyed her. This was her quiet moment. She didn't want this stranger standing beside her and pressurising her into a conversation.

'I was just about to leave. It *is* getting cold.'

He didn't answer her. His eyes were following a small boat across the bay, chugging towards an island.

'I said it's cold.'

He turned and smiled at her. His mouth rose unexpectedly high when he smiled, playful like a child.

'I'm sorry, what did you say? I was looking out at that boat, envying the people on it.'

He really was a difficult character to fathom. He never responded the way she expected. He was paying no attention to her.

'Why do you envy them?'

'I'd love to go to that island, to the old monastery. But I suppose there are some journeys we are slow to make.'

She was amazed that he knew about the ruins; very few people took an interest, not even the villagers. They loved the old Famine houses where they could connect the passing tourist to a turbulent past to extract some sympathy for their harsh lives. But early-Christian ruins were of no interest to them. They were just remnants of a forgotten past that had been plundered by Vikings and trampled by the Normans. It was only in the museums of Dublin, where the people had more disposable income, that an interest in such culture existed.

Sophia knew she was being condescending again. She had left the village to find a better life and had failed; her coming home had left her cold and critical of the people who had once swum in the summer sun with her and her brother as innocent children.

'I've been there,' she said. 'I went there as a child with my grandfather. He would fish off the rocks and I would walk among the ruins'

Joe turned to look at her and his smile was even broader. 'Now I envy you,' he said. 'Did you appreciate it or was it just one of those childhood trips that meant more to the person who brought you?'

'No, I fell in love with the old walls and carved crosses, so much so that it actually became my career.'

'A history teacher?'

'Yes. You guessed too quickly. You must have known.'

'Fran told me, the young girl who works for me.'

'But strangely, Mr White, you're not wincing. Most people wince when they find out I'm a history teacher.'

His lips rose higher. 'Why?'

'Because most people hated the subject in school. All the dates and the facts to remember. It just bores some people. And I think others just find it irrelevant to their lives.'

He nodded in agreement. 'But others love it.'

'Oh, go on, tell me if you liked it or not.'

He frowned and rubbed a hand thoughtfully across

his chin. 'Like every child, I was too young to appreciate nearly everything in school. I was more interested in the lunch menu than classes; and then there was the battle of adolescence.'

'Was it a battle?'

He was now playing with the stubble that had become a beard.

'Oh, all life's a battle, or as the Hindus would say, "All life is suffering. Dukhta."'

She wondered whether he had read that in a magazine or seen it in some documentary. He wasn't finished using it in any case.

'It's a great word *dukhta*. It actually sounds like a word that would bring suffering, a bit like hellfire and brimstone. Unfortunately, I found all my schooldays to be dukhta, one long stream of suffering and penance.'

She looked at him curiously. What was he talking about? Was it really necessary to go rambling on about some Eastern religion and its relevance to his schooldays? It was difficult to make him out. He was either really boring or painfully shy. She didn't really care; she just wanted him off her pier. She felt a threat of rudeness coming on again and hoped that he would either shut up soon or just move away. She didn't want an awkward moment. But he seemed to be in full flow.

'I suppose suffering depends on the way you view your life and your expectations.'

'I wouldn't know,' she said, her voice rising tetchily, 'but I do think most people hate their schooldays.'

'Must be hard to work in a job where your work is never appreciated.'

'Every job has its drawbacks.'

He was staring out to sea again.

'I would hate to live my schooldays over again. But I would love to know some history. I feel ashamed knowing so little.'

She could see a faint hope of an escape from the subject of suffering and school.

'Well, Mr White, there's lots around here to see. The place is groaning with antiquities. There's a tenth-century church on the island off the back of the peninsula. It was covered by sand and earth, totally buried from view until some locals discovered it and dug it out. You could walk along the shoreline and miss it altogether. It's sitting in this large crater of a hole, not signposted or even protected. It's got an embrasure window above the altar and large pink granite stones as lintels. When I was very young, I used to play in it as my castle and fire stick arrows out the windows at aggressors.'

Falling into her own childhood memories, she almost forgot how irritating his company was, but then he broke the image with a ridiculous comment.

'And as a teenager you used to go out there with young lads and make up different stories.'

She was not used to blushing in front of people. His comment took her by surprise. It was a tacky invasion of her past. She was sure he could see her discomfort, as his blue eyes met her gaze.

'I really am getting cold now,' she blurted out impatiently. 'I think I should be heading home.'

'Do you have your car or can I give you a lift?'

'No, I'm fine thanks.'

She left him standing at the quayside. She could feel his eyes following her footsteps down the concrete pier.

It was awkward in the half-light, trying to avoid the thick ropes lying on the ground, like giant tentacles searching for the water. She was sidestepping discarded crates and overturned pots, crusty in their lack of use. They reminded her how, as a child, she would stand on the harbour wall waiting for her father to come home from the island. It was always an emergency if he was called out in winter, and there was always an excitement with his safe return.

CHAPTER 14

'I'm scared, Joe.'

'You don't have to be. Everything's fine.'

'If Sophia gets too close?'

'Well, I really wouldn't worry about that. I behaved like a right prat this evening. I'll be lucky if she ever talks to me again.'

'Because you've jumped the gun! I couldn't cope if anyone found out about me now. We've come so far to get here, gone through so much.'

'I can handle it.'

'You can't handle anything, just like you couldn't handle Dad when he threw me out. You should have stopped him, thrown a punch his way. You could have fought back. I could have persuaded Mum. I could have still had her support.'

'Why are you talking this way? Anyway, I don't even know if Sophia likes me yet, so my handling of anything is irrelevant.'

'She likes you. I can sense it. Call it female intuition.'

'Very funny.'

'Joe, please be careful.'

'Rachel, I'm trying. But I lie awake at night and think of her.'

'I know, I lie there with you, wishing you'd go to sleep.'

'I think of her body next to mine, the fullness of her breasts, the hardness of her nipples, the touch of her skin, soft and velvety.'

'I'm glad you have her to think of. But it's too soon. You have to remember the reality, Joe. We have to finish this first.'

'It's not easy. I forget. It all feels so good when I wake up and look in the mirror. I shave, I dress and I go to work. I have this new life, and maybe she can be a part of it.'

'But you have to remember, I'm still here, along with your past.'

'True, but not for much longer, Rachel.'

CHAPTER 15

THE WORDS ON THE PAGE were the same ones he had looked at half an hour previously. It was a waste of time pretending he was reading the paper. Brian knew he had to burst his wife's bubble and there was no point putting off the inevitable.

She was sitting on the couch, curled up with a book. It seemed a shame to disturb her tranquillity. He had thought about how to tell her his news but there didn't seem to be any good way. He had expected to be quizzed about the trip as soon as he had arrived home but she had asked him nothing, as if she had forgotten the words she had left him with that morning. And he couldn't believe she had forgotten. She must have been playing some game with him, one that he couldn't understand. She played games with him often, toyed with his mind so that he didn't know which way was up and which down. After arguments, he would reel, punch-drunk from the blows that had landed on his ears. He was never the winner in a war of words.

He looked over at her reading. She looked so innocent, so much the woman he wanted to spend the rest of his life with. He couldn't see her physical flaws the way she did, but he knew there was an inner monster that could chew him up.

'Aren't you going to ask me about Athlone?' It seemed a fairly innocuous introduction, a means of lulling her into the conversation.

'You were so quiet when you came home that I presumed it hadn't gone well.'

She wasn't looking at him; her eyes were scanning the pages of the novel.

'No, you're right, it didn't go well. In fact, it went bloody peculiarly.'

The book was placed ceremoniously on the floor.

'Tell me what happened, honey.'

He was now more worried, waiting for the sideways blow. She had used the word *honey* and yet she must have known that he was going to disappoint her. Was she really just going to be sympathetic?

'Laura, honest to God, I've had the strangest afternoon of my life.'

'He didn't sign, did he, Brian?'

'Not a he, Laura. It was a she. R. J. McLoughlin is, or was, a woman, and there was no signing along any dotted line. Not unless you can sign with a ghost.' He thought it better to be quick than to beat around the bush.

'Good God, Brian, the author's dead? What happened to her?'

'The mother talked of murder but I don't know. I only met her parents for a short time. Her mother got into a state when I mentioned the name. Showed me old photographs and everything. I felt really bad for opening it all up for her.'

Laura was sitting up now, her hands folded across her knees, her eyes wide with interest. 'Jesus, are you serious,

Brian? If this is one of your practical jokes, I'll kill you.'

Brian puffed out his cheeks and blew out a breath. 'No, at this stage, R. J. McLoughlin would be a genuine ghost writer.'

'Yeah, but murdered, Brian?'

'Oh, it gets worse. The father, who I had the displeasure of meeting, seemed to think it was the son who was responsible.'

'Oh my God! And did you see the son?'

'No, of course I didn't see the son. The father alluded to the fact that he might be living elsewhere.'

Laura looked at him in disbelief. At least she wasn't blaming him. Perhaps he could escape rebuke on the strength of this story.

'All the way back in the car, I was wondering how the poor girl had died. The whole thing is a book in itself, I'd say. An author who writes one brilliant novel and then mysteriously dies.'

'And you say the father blamed the brother?'

'Yes, he was really angry and bitter.'

Laura had a look on her face that he had seen often before. It was her Miss Marple face, born out of reading too many detective novels.

'I bet I know how she died, Brian.'

She always had the answer, especially if the problem involved people and their lives. She had a better instinct for people than he did.

'Okay, how?'

'Suicide, Brian. Their daughter killed herself and they're blaming the brother because he drove her to it in some way. Down the country it's unmentionable, suicide.'

'Okay, I'll buy that, but how was the brother to blame?'

'Oh, come on, Brian, there are endless ways he could have been responsible.'

Brian had already pondered on the part the brother had played. In the car on the way home, he had spent hours killing off his writer with fanciful notions: a drug overdose, a horrific bleeding from an unwanted pregnancy, a fatal fall down the stairs, pushed by her brother. But the truth could be that R. J. McLoughlin had killed herself. The mother had said it was her own fault.

Brian had encountered suicide before, on the street where he lived as a boy. A middle-aged man had blown his head off with a shotgun. He still remembered the ambulance arriving at the house, the man's wife being taken away, sobbing into her hands, the body being brought out covered in an ambulance blanket. Only one arm had been visible. It had fallen out from the side of the stretcher and was lolling to and fro like a charmed snake before his eyes.

No one in the street knew why he had taken his own life. There were far too many theories and not enough evidence. He had left no note. He had not seemed any different in the days before the tragedy. Something inside him had just snapped. Suicide had to be a weakness, a selfishness born of the inability to see the suffering it would create. His children and his unborn grandchildren would reflect on his death and wonder what weakness was ticking inside them like an inherited time bomb. But then there must have been so much pain for him to end it all, so much anguish blocking his senses. A person must have to be consumed by self-loathing to be able to pull the trigger or cut their wrists and, before that trigger is pulled or the blade is brought down, what runs through their minds? Doubt, fear, a sense of release, a hope of rebirth?

'What are you thinking, Brian?'

'I was wondering what would make someone hate their life so much that they would end it.'

'A pretty miserable thought, isn't it? In a way it makes me feel silly worrying about the wrinkles and the bags, looking for my plastic surgery and Botox.'

'That's what I keep saying. For me you're perfect anyway. It's just the culture of our society to try and stay young, cheat age and its virtues.'

'Brian, there's nothing virtuous about old age, sitting in a wheelchair, being fed with a spoon and wearing a nappy, waiting for your relatives to come once a week to relieve the monotony of looking out the window at the grass.'

'Jesus, Laura, not all old age is as morbid as that.'

'Yeah, and not all plastic surgery is to cheat age. What I want is personal, Brian. It's about my own vision of myself. I need to see on the outside the person who I believe I am on the inside. I've never stopped being twenty-five. I never see myself as older than that. Maybe I was secure back then. Maybe I had hopes and dreams back then that haven't been fulfilled and I don't like looking in the mirror and feeling that time has passed me by. Maybe, Brian, by changing how I look, I feel I can buy back those years and achieve something.'

This was difficult to hear. He didn't want her to think that her life with him had led to unfulfilled dreams, dreams that could only be achieved when she stood up for her second performance. Was this a mid-life crisis?

Would she want to leave him for a younger man once the wrinkles were gone? Then again, could he bear to live with her if she didn't get what she wanted?

'Look Laura, we'll find a way to pay for what you want. R. J. McLoughlin isn't the only way.'

He liked her hugs: her hands on his shoulders, his hands around her slim waist. He wondered whether she would sleep with him tonight, but he wouldn't ask. He didn't want to hear her refuse.

CHAPTER 16

'THEY CAN'T FIND ANY NEXT of kin, you know.' Fran was leaning over the table with a cloth in her hand, wiping crumbs off onto the floor.

'Sorry, Fran, I'm not with you. What do you mean?'

'That American woman who was killed, they haven't been able to chase down any relatives. Sad, isn't it?'

'I suppose so.'

'Oh, it is, Joe. After all, who'll be there to bury her, or claim her body and fly it home?'

'Yeah, I didn't think of that.' I was far too preoccupied trying to force the filling into homemade éclairs to worry about a tourist I had never met. I had over-whipped the cream and now it was difficult to coax it through the piping bag. I knew I had to throw it out and start again.

'It would be horrible to lie in a morgue in a foreign country and no one knowing you're there. Alfie was telling Daddy last night that, according to Gerry, if they didn't find anyone soon they'd have to bury her here. I think that's so sad, I really do. I'd hate not to have family. Family are so important. They're everything to me. Sure I wouldn't know what to do without my brothers, even though they're always teasing me.'

'Well you love families because you come from a rather large one; some families are more hassle than they're worth.'

'Oh, that's so negative. I hope you don't mean yours by that.'

It was time to change the subject. My own family was at the forefront of my thoughts. They had kicked me out as soon as I had told them my secret. Twenty-eight years I had kept it bottled up, afraid they would reject me if I told them, and it turned out that my fears were completely justified. But I didn't want to reflect on the past now. I was creating a future. I jabbed another éclair with the sharp end of a knife and pumped cream into its empty pocket.

'Oh, by the way, Fran, did I see you last night with Dan Summerville down by Danagher's? I knew this would work. She blushed immediately and took some napkins over to the tables.

'It can't have been me. Sure Daddy doesn't like me out late with the boys.'

'It wasn't a whole pile of lads. It was just one and he was being very attentive.'

'Oh, promise me, Joe, that you won't tell my father. He'd go ballistic if he knew. Dan is six years older than me but I really like him.'

I smiled at her and waved a wooden spoon in her direction. 'Only if you promise not to be doing anything you shouldn't be doing.'

She smiled back. I had played her well in changing the conversation; but she was capable of turning the tables on me.

'I've heard that there's an old-fashioned dance in the school tonight. Are you going?'

I looked at her, amused. 'It's not my scene. Anyway, I'd have thought the school was too small for anything like that.'

'No, not the primary school down here silly, the college in Clifden. I've heard Sophia Warner is selling tickets, but you can also buy at the door. I'm surprised you didn't know. There's posters up in the village.'

'No, I've been caught up in the cottage lately. I didn't know anything about it.'

She had turned from the tables now and was staring at me as I washed the counter down with a cloth. 'I think you should go. She's bound to be there.'

'And I think you should mind your own business if you want to keep your job.'

Fran laughed and I was pleased that she knew me enough not to take the comment seriously. I was also pleased that she had told me about the dance. It would be the perfect place to get on better terms with some of my new neighbours and it would be a good thing to be seen to support a local charity. Rachel was over and I needed to ignore her incessant ghostly tapping on my shoulder. She was in no position to stop me from living now.

I would buy the ticket to the dance. Besides, I had to be more involved in my new community.

The air outside was cold. The sky was untouched by clouds and the stars were out in profusion. I decided to take the long road into town; I wanted to enjoy the moonlight on the dark blue water. I was probably also nervous, trying to delay my arrival as long as I could. Inside my head I could hear Rachel with her worried thoughts. 'Don't let her know. Keep her at arm's length, Joe. Most people wouldn't understand.'

But my thoughts were also on the dancing. I had never

learned any of the old-time waltzes. I would probably stand all over Sophia's feet if I was lucky enough to dance with her. Maybe it would be better just to turn round and go home.

I had always been plagued by the voices in my head, the voices that wanted an alternative existence. I had never been a good sleeper, lying awake at night replaying every element of the day and looking to see if I could have survived it better. Most of my problems centred around trying to impress my father. Sitting with him, watching him fix a plug or mend a puncture, holding out the tools and asking him if I could learn. But he had always looked at me as if I would be useless. All I had ever wanted was for him to be proud of me. But he didn't need me in that way; after all, he had the perfect Kenneth, the muscular football player, the keen golfer, more than capable of filling any father's need for a son. How I had hated poor Kenneth. And he had never shown anything but patience towards me.

I missed my mother. She had tried to understand why it had to happen. My father had just shouted, shaken his large fists and thrown me out. I think she would have let me stay but he was so racked by the shame of it all. He had even burned the sheets off my bed. I found that difficult to believe. It was Kenneth who told me. 'Dad loved Rachel. He can't stand the fact that you've done this, Joe. There's no coming home. Everything's tainted with it all, nothing will be the same again.'

Tainted? Didn't they understand that I loved her too? I loved her more than they did.

My mother wanted to go back to my childhood. She wanted to find a safe place in past memories. So she sat down on the couch and pleaded. 'Don't go. We can work this out. It's just losing the little one that's left you feeling this way. It would hurt any woman. I loved Paulie too, you know. We all used to be happy together and we can be again. I'll talk to your father. He's just shocked by it all. You can understand that, can't you? It's come as a huge blow. He never saw it coming.'

But my father would never have accepted it, even if he had seen it coming. Rachel was his little girl and I had snatched her away from him and stupidly stood there hoping that he would understand. 'You're no son. Leave my house.'

The school was bedecked in fairy lights, and a huge banner announced the event. It was obviously a popular night as the cars were parked down the road as far as you could see. I was tempted to drive past and make the long journey home again, but I saw Sophia standing at the door smiling. It wasn't me she was smiling at but it really made no difference. The car seemed to park automatically and I ended up in the queue hoping to receive that same smile.

'Hi, Joe. I didn't know you were interested in dancing.'

'I'm not really, just thought I'd like a night out.'

'Well, there's always the bridge night in O'Mahoney's on a Thursday if you want to change your mind.'

I managed a half smile. It was all I ever seemed capable of with her. Maybe Rachel was right. I wasn't ready to meet people in a romantic way yet.

'Mary will show you a few steps later if you want to learn.' She elbowed a shy looking girl beside her, who was blushing profusely.

'Thanks, Sophia, but I think I'm a prop-up-the-bar type.'

As I moved on, the embarrassed girl dug Sophia sharply in the ribs.

The dance music came courtesy of four local men. They sat in a semicircle smiling broadly at the crowd. Two played guitars, one was on the keyboard and the fourth worked the accordion. The keyboard was the centrepiece of all the bands, only rarely was it replaced with a bodhrán. And the keyboard player was king; the rest took their lead from him.

The women danced. While the men fetched pints from a temporary bar, a beer keg on a classroom table, or talked about the weather, their wives partnered each other, twirling around the wooden floor in endless spirals. I didn't care about the weather and I couldn't dance and, even if I could, it would not have been acceptable for me to ask another man's woman. I was too much of a blow-in. They didn't trust me, and tonight the unattached women seemed few and far between. I felt in limbo.

'Are you sure you don't dance?'

I was surprised by the question. I hadn't put Sophia down as a woman who asked anything twice.

'Actually, I think I'd better learn fast if I want to socialise down here.'

'Oh, I don't know. A lot of men don't bother. They just stand at the bar and drink pints.'

Sophia nodded towards a customer sitting on a chair next to the makeshift bar. 'You see him. That's Seamus Madden. His wife, Issie, loves to dance but he doesn't, so she always dances with John Duff. They're over there doing a waltz. You'd think they were husband and wife if you didn't know, they dance that close. But Seamus doesn't mind. It gives him a chance to drink his pint in peace and quiet.'

'I think I'd prefer to dance with my wife than take the risk of losing her.'

'You can't lose a woman if she really loves you. Seamus is obviously sure of their relationship.'

'Or he doesn't care.'

'A cynic. I thought I was the worst in the room.'

I decided to be brave as she was actually talking to me unsolicited. 'Will you teach me to dance so that I can be prepared for any eventuality?' I was shocked when she agreed.

Sophia's hands were so soft, her fingers long and thin. I felt awkward as she led me step by step through the dance. Either I couldn't tell my left from my right or I couldn't count to three, because I constantly stood on her feet and left her wincing.

'Don't you think you should give me up as a useless cause?'

'I'm a teacher, I don't recognise failure. If it takes me all night, I'll get you to waltz properly.'

I thus decided that I was going to be the slowest learner. It wasn't just the touch of her hand on my shoulder but also the gentleness of her voice as she counted out the steps. One, two, three, one, two, three, one, two, three. I was dizzy with the whirl of it all and I found myself holding her closer with each song. Strangely, I could also see that she was enjoying herself. She was letting down those walls she usually put up around her. One song turned to two, two became three and suddenly the hours were passing quickly.

'I think I need a break now!' She laughed. 'You have the hang of it and my poor toes are sore.'

'I'm sorry. I know I'm a bit clumsy. Can I get you a drink to thank you?'

'Yes, sure, I'll have a gin and tonic.'

'No pint of Guinness?'

'No, that's purely an afternoon drink.'

When I got to the bar I realised she was standing beside me smiling.

'Well, now you wouldn't lose your wife to any other man, would you, Joe?'

'Why do you say that?'

She looked down at my hand and gently pulled hers away.

'Am I red or just pinkish?' I asked.

She smiled and ran the same hot hand across my cheek.

'Oh, I'd say you're hot with embarrassment.'

The night got even better from there.

The schoolteacher and the café owner went to sea in a beautiful pea-green boat. The sea was the dance floor and the boat swayed and rose, bringing them closer to each other. This was the life I had waited for. There was no tragedy now to remember, the past had become history and the present was making the future look rosy.

We sat on small stools around a table. We watched the revellers pushing forward singers from among their friends. Men crooned with their hands behind their backs, women hit high notes on the subject of love, beer gave others licence to entertain on the most meagre talent. And when the waltzes were replaced with slow sets, we danced closer than I could have imagined, and I knew I was going to invite her home.

CHAPTER 17

'COME ON, BRIAN, YOU'RE NOT really going to give up on this one?'

She had been at him all night like a flea in his ear.

'Laura, I don't know what you want me to do. The poor girl's dead.'

'Brian, that's my point. There's a book in your study that hasn't got a publisher and you could publish it. Her death shouldn't stop it from being a success. It might add to it. This R. J. McLoughlin could be the Eva Cassidy of the literary world.'

She prodded him. 'Brian, you could go back to the house and ask them again. You could be more sympathetic with her family this time, now that you know the full story.'

'But I don't know the full story and I was sympathetic last time.' He thought of Laura lying behind him and chastised himself sternly. Don't let her do this to you, think blonde, think long legs, think happy thoughts, think *Baywatch*, just stop letting her rile you.

'Brian, are you listening? I don't want you passing up on the opportunity to have something good happen in your work.'

The feel-good moment was fading fast. He couldn't keep the picture in his head; all he could see was the little old woman handing him the photograph of her daughter.

'If you loved me ...'

'Oh, good God, Laura, don't try that one. You know I love you. I just can't go back to that poor woman.'

'Don't then. I will.'

Maybe he was half asleep and not taking things in properly.

'I'll go, Brian.'

'Laura, you can't go. It would be ridiculous.'

'A woman might seem more empathetic. They might listen to me.'

'No.'

He wasn't going to have his wife interfering with his work. It would set an ugly precedent.

'Oh come on, it might work. Besides which, I'm really curious to know the full story on this one. Aren't you?' She propped herself up on one elbow. 'Brian, come on, let me go and see them. You might have lost your passion for your work but I'm going to help you get it back.'

'Look, I might go back again myself. If I could talk to the old woman, I might get somewhere.'

'Okay, I'll live with that.'

'I'm not saying for definite but I'll think about it.'

Brian wasn't sure whether he wanted Laura to snuggle up to him. He had been slightly unfaithful in his thoughts and was now feeling guilty as she nibbled his ear. But Laura was making her presence felt. He had never been able to resist the soft biting. He had always thought it strange that his most erogenous zone was in such an unattractive place. It was not that he had big ears; in fact she had often called him a hippo as they were so small compared to the rest of him. It was just that he could hardly see them as sexy.

She always kissed him there if she was really serious. It made the heat spread from his groin until he was unable to contain the pressure it was creating. He knew he would come; it was just a matter of time.

'I love you,' she said.

'Why? Because you can twist me around your little finger?'

'Yes.'

She was resting in his arms now, her head leaning on his shoulder, her breath warm against his skin.

'No, I'm telling a lie. I love you Brian because you always want me. You want me and I love that.'

'You're easy to want.'

'Oh, I'm not so sure about that. And maybe it wouldn't make any difference which woman was lying here with you if they pressed the right buttons.'

Her mood was changing now. Her lack of confidence had a way of doing that. It always robbed the good moments of their final glow. What would begin in warmth and pleasure would end in self-doubt and recrimination, and it was always his fault for not loving her enough. But he thought he should try anyway.

'I've always just wanted you, Laura.'

She turned over in his arms then, allowing herself to be wrapped in his body, like a small creature nestling in for warmth and security.

'I'll go to Athlone, Laura. I'll get the contract.'

She snuggled into him. 'I was only being so pushy because I know how good the book is, Brian. I read it yesterday. I couldn't put it down all day.'

'You never said.'

'You never asked,' she smiled.

'It's difficult to ignore isn't it? It's raw and old-fashioned, not like today's manufactured novels.'

'Brian, didn't you see the parallel?'

'What do you mean?'

'Do I always have to be quicker to see the hidden message? You're so black and white sometimes.'

Brian was too tired to work out riddles; he was still cooling down and waiting for his senses to return. She was always faster to bounce back. It was as if she hadn't let herself go at all.

'What do you mean?'

'In the book the main character kills his brother. He's responsible for his sibling's death. Don't you think that's spooky? He has to leave home because of the guilt and shame he feels.'

He was annoyed with himself then. It hadn't crossed his mind. Why hadn't it? It must have been because he was inebriated that night he had first read it. He hadn't thought back to the storyline since he had visited Athlone. Surely it was a coincidence, or was the story autobiographical? He wasn't going to give Laura the victory of being right.

'It means nothing, Laura.'

She turned back to face him and raised herself on one elbow so that she could look at him properly.

'Do you know, Brian, you are so unimaginative for a man who publishes books.'

'Thanks.' Maybe he should have agreed with her in her earlier hypothesis. Now she thought he was a simpleton.

'Don't you think there might be a reason for all that happened, hidden in those pages? The secret of her death to be found amongst the pages of her book, hidden in the relationship of warring siblings, the trauma of her past there for everyone to read.'

'What trauma? We don't know that there was any trauma. All we know is that she died and the parents blame the brother. It could have been a drunk-driving thing. And secondly, she could have written the book years before her death and her life might have been perfectly rosy then.'

He was tired beyond fantasising now. He didn't want to speculate on anything else except how much sleep he could get before his alarm went off.

'I'm telling you, Brian, the clue's in *The Olive Tree* somewhere.'

'And I'm telling you to turn around and go to sleep.'

He heard her mutter something and then she was quiet. A few minutes later it annoyed him to hear her softly snoring. It meant that she had yet again fallen asleep and he was yet again wide awake. If he had been left alone half an hour ago, he could have fallen into the deep contented sleep of the lover, but she had disturbed that tranquil place and left him tired but not calm.

He tried to count sheep. He had never found that to work. They always ended up refusing to go over the fence or bonking one another in a faraway field while he waited for them to return. He was sure a psychiatrist would have raised an eyebrow if he had reported that he couldn't get his errant sheep to behave.

It didn't seem to be an autobiographical book. He didn't want Laura to be right. It always annoyed him that she was one step ahead of him. He would travel down to Athlone tomorrow and lay the ghost to rest.

CHAPTER 18

Sophia didn't know why she had agreed. Maybe it was the gin and tonics, maybe it was the slow dancing or maybe it was that she hadn't had a man touch her so intimately for a long while. She secretly ached for it. He had good skin, soft, and it seemed young for his age. And his eyes were blue with flecks of green running through them, making them mottled like those multi-coloured marbles her brother used to play with as a kid.

He had offered to drive, but she had taken her own car. She needed to know that she could leave if things didn't work out, although she wasn't really sure what that meant. Did it mean if the coffee was only instant? If she had been one of her own students she would have laughed at herself for being so naïve. There was only one reason for her to follow him home in her car and that was to take their night to a more physical level. It was about being able to do things that weren't possible under the watchful eyes of the dancers, and also about going somewhere more attractive than the backseat of a car. She was too old for that – steamed windows, cramped limbs and awkward fumbling.

Now, as she thought about the reason for her journey, it seemed lacking in emotion or intimacy. She was not being whisked away in a carriage; she was taking the matter into her own hands.

Angry with herself, she turned on the radio. The late-night music might lull her back into the mood; after all, he had been very sweet at the dance. Not as forceful as the men she usually went out with but more polite than most; he had held the door open for her and seemed to anticipate her every need. Although, that was strangely irritating too, as if he was trying too hard to make her like him. He didn't seem at ease with himself. She really couldn't bear another unconfident man. She wanted to be dominated sometimes. Maybe this was a mistake; maybe it was better to turn around and go home.

It was too late for second thoughts. His car turned into a driveway and the headlights went out. She knew he wouldn't leave her in the dark. He stood by the side of her car as she parked, and he opened her door and smiled.

'This is what I love about this place, Sophia. Look at those stars.'

'Yes, they're lovely.'

He was holding her hand again, gently pulling her from the car, holding her around the waist and pointing to the sky.

'No, look properly. The longer you look the more you see. A glance doesn't give them enough time.'

That's all that she needed – a bloody stargazer who probably did jigsaws in his spare time. She just wanted a cup of coffee and, at this stage, very little else. Even the coffee was becoming unattractive. What had she been thinking? She didn't even know whether she liked him. He had the strangest idea of good conversation and he wasn't that easy to understand. She didn't really know anything about him, except that he ran a bistro-cum-coffee shop and held evening classes. And what kind of man moves to the country and starts cookery classes for women? He seemed the oddest Casanova. Maybe the rumours were true.

'I'm being too enthusiastic, aren't I?'

He was looking at her intently with a sad smile.

'No, I like the stars. I do.'

He laughed. 'That sounds so untrue.'

'Look, I'm just tired after a long day. I'm probably not being the easiest.'

'And I'm probably showing my rustiness with women.'

She couldn't bear a confession. She didn't like inadequacies.

'No. I've enjoyed your company this evening.'

'Let me make you some coffee.'

'I think I'll just go home.'

'Are you sure? I haven't managed any visitors yet. You'd be my first. Stay for one small cup.'

She wished he were different. It wasn't the way he looked. There was something strangely attractive about that. It was more his approach. It gave her too much leeway to dominate him. It was there in front of her as he waited for her to answer; she was looking at a boy and not a man.

'One cup, then.'

The interior of the cottage was not what she had expected. There were no clothes on the chairs or papers on the floor. The front door opened into a large living room with rugs and leather couches, soft lighting and vases of flowers. In the corners bookshelves heaved with recent titles, and in the centre of the room a large bog oak sculpture sat on a glass coffee table.

'The room's lovely.' She had to raise her voice. He had disappeared through a door into the kitchen.

'Yeah, I like it. But then I would, wouldn't I? Make yourself at home and put on some music.'

She hated being asked. It was not something she knew much about. Her taste in music had always been a source of amusement to her work colleagues. She knew no titles, no artists and no differences between the songs she heard on the radio. It was all background music to her; she was tone deaf. Scanning the CD rack for an interesting title, she grew bored.

'Is there anything in particular you'd like me to put on?'

'Oh, it doesn't matter. Something bluesy.'

Typical. If it didn't matter, why give her an answer, especially one she didn't know. What the hell was bluesy? She didn't know any blues performers. She was still staring at the CDs when he came back into the room with a tray of coffee.

'Do you really like the room?'

'Yes, it's really warm and homely.'

'It's the first home I've had.'

It wasn't something she wanted to hear. He must have been in his thirties. She could imagine a mother and father still keeping his belongings in a bedroom, dusting around the picture of him with a splatter of freckles across his nose and a school tie under his chin; storing his old jumpers in a suitcase under the bed along with a ragged old teddy bear.

'Where were you before now?'

'I lived where I worked.'

'And where was that?'

He gave her a disparaging look. 'Your coffee's going cold.'

'Is that "Don't ask me", Joe? Is that a "Mind your own business"?'

'No, it's just boring, that's all. If you really want to know, it's no problem.'

He stood up from the couch and crossed the room to the large open hearth. On the chimney breast was a picture of three people crossing a beach. He took it from the wall and brought it back to her.

'That's my family – my mother and my father and my sister.'

She thought she recognised the beach, but it wasn't a buckets-and-spades snapshot. It was a beach empty of people except for the three small figures and a sky that looked cold and grey.

'Your sister's pretty. She looks a lot like you. In fact you both look like your mum.'

He took the photograph back from her and wiped the glass with the sleeve of his shirt. 'Do you really think she's pretty?'

Didn't he know? Those were just words that you said when someone showed you a photograph – you made a pleasant comment, feigned interest. Now she felt that she really had to look at the girl and think of something honest to say. 'She's pretty but she looks a bit sad.'

In fact they all looked sad, trooping down a beach, scarves wrapped around their necks, hands thrust into their coat pockets. There had to be a better photograph somewhere that he could have framed and put on view.

'It was a cloudy day, not much going on.'

'What's her name?'

'Rachel.'

'Is she married, kids or anything?'

'No, she lost her child, a baby boy called Paul.'

'Oh, I'm sorry. What happened?'

There were always minefields in a person's past and Sophia knew that she was adept at standing on them.

He took the picture back and she looked at him apologetically.

'Look, I shouldn't have started this, Joe. That's the problem with getting-to-know-you sessions. They can become tedious – revelations of family history and all that. Much better left untouched usually.'

'It's good to know a person, though. It's good to understand their past. In the past you can find the person who forms the future.'

Sophia knew that she had pushed Joe too far. He was flinching awkwardly in front of her. Her mother had always warned her that her curiosity would kill her one day, but this background history was an aspect of Joe that she found less boring. She wanted to know more about him, even if it meant some awkward silences.

'Is there just the four of you then?'

'No, there's Kenneth, my older brother.'

'What's he do?'

'An electrician like my dad.'

'Is he married?'

'Yes, to Ruth.'

'Do they have children?'

Maybe she was being too pushy. She really should have consumed far less gin. It was time to show more sympathy towards his feelings. But he had already started with his reply and he seemed less defensive.

'No, they have no children, and my mother hates the fact. She always wanted to be a grandmother.'

'Oh, they're all like that. I have one at home exactly the same. She thinks I should be finding an honest man and doing something urgent about it.'

He didn't offer to be the honest man. He just sat there and looked ashen.

'It was why my mother was so upset when I lost Paul.'

Sophia looked at Joe closely. '*You* lost Paul? I thought he was your sister's child.'

Sophia noticed the anguish crossing Joe's face.

'Well, it was my fault. I was the one to blame. Why do you think I'm here? My life ended when he died. Do you mind if we don't talk any more about this? It's a very painful topic.'

Sophia felt terrible. The man in front of her looked pale and suddenly very tired.

'I think it's time for me to go,' she said.

'You don't have to.'

She wanted to hug him then, and apologise, but she was also now slightly wary of him. What had he done to lose his sister's kid? And why should she hug him? He had not shown any inclination to kiss her or make any romantic move past the holding of hands. The mood from the dance hall had completely melted away. The whole silly situation was the story of her life. She always picked the wrong man. She felt stupid. Joe was sitting on the couch, looking at her. She had come expecting something that he had now obviously no intention of giving and she was left feeling like a real slut.

'Sophia?'

She turned to face him. She hadn't realised that she

had turned away. 'What?'

'Thanks for the dance lessons tonight. I enjoyed them.'

It was the sentiment of closure, not a request to stay and turn things around. Joe wanted her out of there as much as she wanted to leave.

She wanted to be home in her bed with a good book and a glass of wine. At least they were reliable. She was in no mood to sleep. Her mind was racing.

Joe didn't say anything as she left. He was irritatingly quiet. And when he stood at the doorway and waved goodbye to her, she felt she hated him.

CHAPTER 19

'WHAT WAS ALL THAT FOR? You're pathetic.'

'I did what you asked. I didn't rush things.'

'But you did rush things. Don't you understand? You shouldn't have invited her over; you weren't ready. You've just made yourself look disinterested. You'll be lucky if she ever comes near you again. I wouldn't if I was in her position. Do you really think she came back for just a coffee?'

'No.'

'Look, you have to make this work, Joe. You have to stand on your own two feet. We've always been together, you and I, through good and bad times. But now it's your time. I won't be in your way ever again. Jesus, Joe, this has all been so hard. It has to work.'

'I always thought my life would be easier without you. I imagined the perfect scenario – a wife, a house, even children – but the truth is I don't know whether I'm going to be any better on my own. There will still be something missing. And that something will be you, and that is the ridiculous truth about us. Maybe we belong together, like yin and yang, and neither of us are whole without the other.'

'I don't want to hear this, Joe. I really don't. It's too late to stop it now. The injections were irreversible, Joe.'

'We should have stayed together, Rachel, and just managed to get along somehow. How will I cope without you?'

'You're just nervous, Joe. You're trying to run before you can walk. You'll be all right.'

CHAPTER 20

IT WAS TIME FOR HER to die.

The wind had finally abated and the hummocks of grass were able to stand tall again. The road to the beach was wet and muddy. It was too early in the morning for many people to be out of their houses, and she knew the beach would be empty. It was a fitting backdrop for her final resting place, the place where she wanted the memories buried. She didn't want a tombstone where the flowers would wilt and the plot would look untended.

The box under her arm felt heavy and yet she knew that its contents were light. She had left the cottage with the significance of her task clear, but now as she stood on the damp sand with the water seeping into her shoes, she wondered whether she was losing a grip on the thin reality that she had created for herself.

Joe wouldn't be doing this. He would be far too sensible to take such a sentimental journey. He was a typical man, not given to wallowing in his emotions. He always had to find the rational path. And she loved that about him. He was becoming more of a man everyday – more certain and more physically developed.

She placed the box on the ground and took the small shovel from her coat. The handle was shiny and red, the metal blade clean and unused. Digging into the sand, she could hear the words rolling around her head, waiting for her tongue to find them. 'Dearly beloved, we are gathered here today to mourn the passing of Rachel Joanna McLoughlin. She was a strange woman. It is why so few of you have turned up for this ceremony. You never really understood her, and sometimes she hardly understood herself. I know she would have liked her parents here today but they have chosen to ignore her passing. She will miss them greatly.

'So, seashore, shells and sky, as there is no family here to make a short speech, I hope you will not mind if I address the congregation. Life is precious. There is no knowing how precious it is until we face losing it. For each life that exists there are millions of waves crossing the surface, touching on that single solitary path. Rachel touched many people. They may not have known the full extent of her impact on them, but she pushed the boundaries of their thinking. She forced them to see outside the narrow boxes of their own world, in such a way that their own existence became less perfect and more of an occasion of random success in the amazing diversity of creation. For creation is diverse. It throws up anomalies, gives us mutations and demands a further order of specification. We may have started with Adam and Eve in that biblical garden of life, but when we left that garden, we flourished in our own search for evolution.

'In short, the world may now be ready for the change of order that Rachel and others like her have brought. As with all change, it has not been easy. In fact among some it has been violently opposed, as they fear it. These people look down at the chimeras of expanding creation and believe that they are attempting to topple their security.

They strengthen the barricades and arm their castles, hoping that their fragile existence does not become an archaic system, unable to survive the liberalism of awakening mankind. And liberalism does scare them because it means opening up their minds to change and they are terrified of change. And in order to exist in their world, Rachel Joanna could not have been allowed to change. So she killed herself.

'And where does the lack of understanding of Rachel come from? Would her existence really have undermined the lives of the multitude?'

Rachel Joanna McLoughlin dug the hole in the sand and sat back on her haunches. These were good words coming from her head. She liked them. There was more for her priest to say but she also knew that Joe had to go out tonight, and she was aware of the time passing. Besides, she was alone now on the beach and that situation might change if she waited any longer.

She made sure that the hole was deep enough. The sand was gritty and thick, slow to release the small spade from its grasp. She hoped it would be equally as slow to release her secrets. It was difficult not to open the box one more time. She had packed the contents with reverence and solemnity but she had a yearning to see them once more before the earth covered them. Carefully she opened the clasp.

It was the photographs that moved her most. The young girl sitting on her father's knee, looking up at him for guidance, hoping for understanding and always wanting him to be her role model. The teenager wearing clothes too big and baggy, hiding from the world any sign of maturity, wishing to create a protective bubble in which to exist. In every picture she recognised the sad eyes, the lost look, the hint of unhappiness. She could feel herself filling with anger. The photographs in her hand were the sum of her life. And there, staring back at her, she also saw Joe, equally morose.

The rest of the box seemed ugly, and it tainted her thoughts. As she replaced the lid, she wanted to scream and give vent to all the years of pent-up emotions, lost relationships and shattered dreams. But the priest was still there, shaking his head and waiting to speak.

'Rachel's life was no doubt a hard journey, but every life is hard and there is no monopoly on pain. Self-indulgence, self-pity – they're not nice traits. And what about the mustard seed? No life is without suffering; there are only levels of suffering, no absence of it. It is why some people believe in reincarnation, every soul living through a cycle of growth and learning until they understand what life is truly about. And it's always about suffering, no matter how we package it. Rachel may be dead to us now, but we must worry whether in her next life, which she so eagerly awaits, she will suffer too. Maybe, as with our Hindu friends, she will carry the stains of this life with her. For her sake, I hope not.'

She did not want to hear her priest's words now. It had to be over. Joe had helped her. If she was to be reborn, it had to be into a more perfect existence.

She placed the box into the hole, the contents of her life in its dark chamber. The grains spattered the lid, until the beach that she had carefully disturbed was returned to the way she had found it. She stood there looking down at her work. She was stunned by the stupidity of it all, the sheer ridiculousness of her own actions. She had made her life a trivial game, reduced it to a sentimental scene. She had also, in some unthinkable way, sullied the memory of the last time she had watched earth splatter over a tiny box.

It had been warm that day. The sullen November skies had disappeared and the sun shone in a blinding display of warmth and affection for life. Her clothes were black, her shoes were black and the people standing around were looking into her blackness and invading her private misery. She wanted them all to go away so that she could pull the coffin from the ground, rip the lid open and retrieve her son.

If his birth had been hard to bear and accept, then his death had seemed a vindictive act. She had worked on being the perfect mother – breastfeeding, spending every waking hour meeting his constant demands, giving up her life for his, hoping that she could find happiness in his perfection. And Joe had loved him too. He was as much his son. It was his boy who would one day grow up to be a man and reflect his dreams.

It had been a malicious death – tiny grotesque creatures thoughtlessly robbing her of all she cared for. She had kissed his forehead, wrapped him in the blanket and pulled away from the little fingers holding her thumb so tightly. His eyes had remained open, watching her leave the room, listening to her making the low placatory sounds to comfort him. And all the time, they had been there, hiding under the cot, laying low, waiting until she left.

Paul had cried. She recognised the difference in tone as she sat downstairs. She took the stairs three steps at a time, but it made no difference. The room was full of noise – their angry buzzing as they circled around her head, his loud cries as she picked up his small body and clutched him to her chest. Her baby's cry stung her as she tried to hear his breathing and found none. The swarm showed their indifference as her screams pierced the air.

And then she wasn't alone. Her father and mother were there with her, pulling her from the room, waving their arms frantically, saying words that lost their meaning as soon as they left their lips. The world was upside down and nothing made sense any more.

She remembered lying on her bed, her grandmother's quilt wrapped around her, the room full of people whom she now hated – her father talking to the doctor about sedation, her mother crying on her brother's arm, her aunt pacing about wanting to make tea and hand out tissues, and all of them blaming her for the unseen nest of wasps outside his open window. And Joe, numb and speechless, feeling it was all his fault and that he had never deserved to be the father in the first place.

At least that's what she saw. It was in his eyes. Just like when she had become pregnant. It was his fault for not stopping it. He could have come clean; he could have saved her from the pain of sex and the horror of pregnancy. All he had to do was come forward and talk, tell the truth.

And it was her fault too. She had brought about her own downfall. All she had wanted was Joe and she couldn't have him in her life.

So many things had changed since then, so much talking and listening and misunderstanding. The beach was the only place to be now. The past had to be buried.

INSIDE OUT

She didn't want to face it again, and she didn't have to. This was her final day.

CHAPTER 21

I BOUGHT MYSELF A FULL-length mirror.

I had to go to Galway to purchase it; the local shops didn't stock such infrequently bought items. I chose to go before seven in the morning as the roads would be empty and I could enjoy the drive without sitting behind tractors or trucks. The only negative factor would be the darkness. There were few catseyes and the corners were sharp. I thought of the American woman. She had been walking on a dark road. It made me more careful. I didn't want another death on my conscience.

Rosemary Frances Benson. They had held the funeral last Thursday. Fran had been accurate in her gossip. There had been no family located, no one to pay for her flight home. The whole village had been affected by her death. They still had no idea who was responsible and so the rumour mongers went to work, causing chaos among the families of the mentioned young men. But at least I had been taken off the list of suspects. My car had been examined and the bodywork found free of any bumps or indentations.

Fran and I went to the funeral. Fran said it was the least that we could do, as the woman had no loved ones to cry for her. She was even more pleased that she had attended when she heard the woman's full name. There was a bond between them she assured me, a bond due to their names, and she would take it upon herself to put flowers upon her lonely grave.

We weren't the only two sentimental mourners. Most of the village appeared, including Sophia. She stood at the back, paid no attention to me and left without a word. I knew I had ruined her evening by starting something that I hadn't been prepared to finish. But I wanted to see her again. I had to know her better to make her understand. Although maybe all that was impossible; maybe I was too naïve about it all.

Galway was not one of my favourite cities. It was too buried in roads and roundabouts, as if its heart had been squeezed out. And I couldn't find any trees, just an over-abundance of cement and brick. Galway simply appeared like a shabby drunk, spilling his way to the sea, dirty and old, rambling and incoherent.

I parked outside the centre, needing the long walk after an hour in the car. The last person I expected to see as I made my way through the streets was Sophia. She was walking ahead of me, tall and elegant. She was not alone. A small woman walked stiffly by her side, her arm resting on Sophia's for support. The old woman looked vaguely familiar, although I couldn't see her face as she had her back to me and wore a headscarf. I presumed that I had seen her in the village. I also presumed that she was Sophia's mother as there was a closeness between them. I had no definite place to be and I followed slowly behind them, feeling rather ridiculous.

It was strange watching Sophia. I knew she was angry with me but I also knew that it was because I had made her feel rejected and, ironically, to me that meant that she had wanted me, even in some small, strange way. For my part, I had thought of her often since the dance. I had longed to experience our first kiss, and much more.

The objects of my fascination walked into an ophthalmologist's and I felt even more ridiculous standing in a street, far from any shops, with nothing to do and nowhere to go.

'Joe, what are you doing here?'

Sophia had come back out of the building, but without the old woman. I didn't know what to say. The truth would have been too embarrassing. I knew she was waiting for an answer but I couldn't think of one.

'Joe?'

'I'm up in Galway to buy a mirror.'

She gave me a quizzical look. 'Well, you're a long way from the shops.'

'Yeah, I know. I parked the car outside town and sort of got lost.'

She eyed me suspiciously so I thought it best to continue.

'But now that I'm here, can I buy you a coffee?'

'I think we've been down that route before, and it wasn't that successful.'

It was difficult to argue with her. I had tried to sleep that frustrating night, with her body waltzing around in my mind. I had gone to bed angry with myself for pushing things too quickly. I should have left her at the dance with a kiss on her cheek. That would have been enough. I could have built it from there. Rachel had been right – I had wanted to run before I could walk. But as I stood there in the street looking back at Sophia, I knew there was no Rachel to help me now and never would be again.

'Look, I'd like a chance to explain. I don't want to leave things on a bad note.' I tried to give her my most imploring look.

'Okay, but I can only be half an hour. My mum will be finished by then.'

'Great. I think we passed a coffee shop back there by the corner.'

'We?'

A liar had to have a better memory. It was time to deflect. 'So that was your Mum?'

'Yeah, I came back to the area to look after her. There's only me, and my brother in America. Mum really can't cope on her own any more. She has arthritis as well as the blindness. It's difficult for her. It's why we're here today. They think they might be able to operate on one of her eyes and give her some sight. Things have changed so much since it happened.'

It was good to hear her news and move away from the problem between us.

The coffee shop was small but they made a good coffee and the seat by the window was empty.

'How long has your father been dead?' I thought it better to find out as much as I could before she became disillusioned with me again.

'A long time, about ten years. It was fine at first. Martin was still at home and working in Galway, but he left for Boston over three years ago. She misses him dreadfully. He was always the closest. Irish boys and their mammies! I'm sure your sister thinks the same way about you and your brother.'

It was going to be a problem now. I had to decide whether to lie or not, and which lie would be the best. In some respect the closer the truth was to my creation, the less chance there was of losing her completely.

But she was happy to continue her story and I was given a reprieve.

'Martin was always given the last slice of cake or the best seat by the fire or the warmest jumper she knitted. Nothing was too good for him. He could do no wrong. But where is he now while I'm bringing her to the doctor?'

She laughed at her own unforgiving nature. 'Siblings, eh? I don't know how we got started on this. I just have a problem with him at the moment. He hasn't written since the summer and my mother's very upset, although not admitting it, of course.'

She was talking and I was listening. But not just listening – I was watching her too, noticing the way she moved her hands as she spoke, understanding why I found her face so pleasing. It was all to do with femininity. She exuded it. She made my manhood respond.

'I hope you're not the same, Joe. I hope you contact your parents. Too many men don't bother.'

I didn't know how to reply. I had drifted from her words. I had somehow lost myself in her face. So I said nothing and shrugged my shoulders.

'I suppose your sister is there for them?'

It was time for a revelation but one that would engage her sympathy. 'Sophia, I didn't get the chance to tell you the other day, but Rachel's dead.'

'Oh God, Joe, I'm so sorry. There's me rambling on. What happened to her?'

'It was suicide.' A part of me felt sad when I said the words. I liked the touch of her hand across the table. I liked the warmth.

'It must have been so difficult for you all. Do you know why she did it?'

'I suppose you never really know the full reason. You just know bits of what she said and did.'

She was holding my hand tighter now and I felt sick that I was cheating her of the whole truth, making her feel sorry for the wrong reasons.

'Was it because she lost her child?'

'It definitely was a huge factor. Paul meant everything to her. She'd gone through a torrid pregnancy, and the birth was difficult. Rachel thought Paul was her miracle, something right in her life for a change.' I looked down at her hand, still holding mine. I pulled it away gently.

'How did she do it?'

I didn't think she'd ask, most people didn't. But then Sophia had the knack of being blunt about things. This was where the truth became almost impossible to reveal, but for some reason I plunged straight into the abyss. 'She injected herself, and I helped her.'

Her eyes never flickered. They just stared at me coldly. 'What do you mean?'

If she had shown any other emotion but coldness I might have continued with the truth but I couldn't face a blank heart.

'She told me she was desperate. She'd been ill for some time, slashing at her wrists, not eating. I told her she was hurting our parents. She said she'd be better out of their lives.' I stopped and Sophia waited for more. 'She needed help, and I should have stopped her.'

'You can't blame yourself. It was her choice.'

'I know, but I wasn't discouraging her either.'

'What did she inject herself with?'

'Does it matter? She's gone and that's really it.'

She gave a sigh and I couldn't tell what she was thinking. I had blown it again. To make matters worse, she looked at her watch and made her excuses to leave and meet her mother.

I was left at the table with the half-empty coffee cups and my foolishness.

The mirror looked good in the hall. It bounced the light from the window through the narrow room and it gave me the chance to look at myself properly. I looked so much better. The muscles in my arms were more defined and my chest looked broader, stronger. However, it was the mat of hair on my legs that always surprised me the most, as even my brother wasn't that hirsute. As I looked at myself, I was proud of who I had become. I might have let myself down with Sophia again in the coffee shop, but physically I was starting to feel that I was someone whom she could find attractive. I was seeing my inside reflected on the outside.

CHAPTER 22

18 FINTAN LAWLOR TERRACE WAS seemingly quiet. The Morris Minor had just left the tiny driveway and headed into town. Brian felt like a shady gumshoe sitting in his car, hiding behind a newspaper, watching for movement. He was waiting for Ronald McLoughlin to leave the house. There was no way he wanted to face the anger of that man again. All the way down in the car, he had wondered about the sanity of his mission. There were eighty-four new manuscripts sitting on his desk; a blockbuster could be among them. Perhaps there was no need to chase this particular rainbow.

Such was his lack of enthusiasm for the trip that he had stopped twice along the route. He had found the fridge empty of any decent breakfast ingredients and thus had the perfect excuse for a pause at a truck-stop café. The large plate of bacon, sausage, egg and beans was packed full of Laura's most dreaded enemies. He ate happily, knowing that his cholesterol was rising with each mouthful. He would gladly eat muesli with low-fat milk if it tasted as delicious.

But for now, he sat in Fintan Lawlor Terrace wondering whether he was more afraid to face his wife or the people in No. 18. He hadn't even worked out how he was going to start the conversation. He thought he might simply ring the doorbell and wait for the old lady's response.

It was a longer wait than he had anticipated. She answered the door on the third ring. He had nearly turned away in relief.

'Oh, hello. You're early.'

It was not quite what he had expected.

'Hello, Mrs McLoughlin, can I come in?'

She had an open smile. 'Oh, where's my manners! Of course you can. Sure you can't do anything out there.'

She stood aside and held the door open. He had to be honest. It didn't seem right to start on the wrong footing. He had presumed she would recognise him from the last time. He had assumed it would have taken some clever words to gain entry. This didn't seem right.

'Mrs McLoughlin, I'm Brian Matthews.' His name didn't seem to register. 'The publisher from Dublin.'

She smiled at him. 'I'm sorry. I thought you were Doctor McKenna. He always comes on a Thursday to check me out. You look like him. He's tall and broad-shouldered too. Mind you, he's never usually this early. Ronald's usually here to let him in. I'm so forgetful these days. So are you here to see Ronald, then? What did you say you do?'

This really wasn't right.

She showed him into the small living room. He would have preferred the kitchen or anywhere else. The same photograph she had handed him last time was sitting on the mantelpiece. It was flanked by two other larger ones of a son and his parents; he wondered whether this was the killer son. But it would have been strange to have left those photographs either side of the beloved daughter. He would have thought that they would have been thrown out.

'Ronald's gone to the bowls. He always goes there on

a Thursday. Would you like a cup of tea?'

'No thanks. I stopped along the way. I just wanted to ask if you knew where your son was?' He didn't know why he had asked that particular question. It just popped into his head; maybe it was because of the photographs.

'Oh, it's Kenneth you want.' The tone of her voice didn't register disapproval. 'He's down at the shop, most likely. You'll catch him there.'

'Oh, that's great, do you have the address?'

She stood up from the chair and looked around her as if the address was hiding in the corner of the room. 'It's just off the main street. M. C. Electrics it's called. Ronald bought it from Corrie, the butcher, who moved to a bigger shop, but he leaves it all to Kenneth now. Ronald's retired a long time. Who did you say you were?'

'A friend of Kenneth's,' I lied. 'Look, that's great. I'm sure I'll find it.'

He wanted to get out of there, out of the house in case the father returned. He stood up and put his hand out to shake hers. He felt guilty for the intrusion and lies. What was he going to do now? Call in to ask questions of a murderer at his workplace?

At least this time he wasn't going to leave the woman in tears. She smiled at him as she led him back to the front door, past the primroses. Her hand was cold and small when he shook it. She seemed pleased with his gesture.

'I can't remember your name,' she said, her face clenched in a puzzled look.

'Brian.'

'Oh I hope I remember it to tell them when they get home. Kenneth will be sorry that he missed you.'

*

As he drove away from Fintan Lawlor Terrace, Brian was more confused than when he had arrived. He had no idea of what to make of the facts. All he knew was that Mrs McLoughlin did not portray her son as a murderer. There had to be some other explanation for the father's words. Maybe there was a second son?

M.C. Electrics was a ramshackle shop down a laneway off the main street. It had one of those window fronts that looked like a spare-parts factory with pieces of vacuum piping, elements of kettles and motors from lawn mowers all enmeshed in multicoloured wiring. The door was bright yellow, with a grubby window that allowed no light into the interior. Stuck on the front with yellowing Sellotape was a hand-drawn notice that said NO CREDIT.

A little bell jangled when Brian entered. A tall man with an open face looked up from his work on the counter, a pencil behind one ear and a screwdriver in his hand. He didn't look like a murderer. Brian felt more relaxed.

'Hi, can I help you?'

Brian realised that he hadn't thought about what he was going to say. It would be so easy to offend this man standing in front of him and lose any chance he had of publishing the book. Although, strangely, that aspect had dwindled in significance. In some ways it was the mystery of the writer that interested him now.

'I'm hoping you can help me. I'm looking for your sister, R. J. McLoughlin.'

The man didn't respond immediately. He simply stood behind the counter, staring back, his face blank, although Brian noticed that he was holding the screwdriver tighter.

'And you are?'

'Brian Matthews. I'm a publisher from Dublin. Your sister sent me a manuscript and it's good.'

'So little sis' could write after all, then.'

'Yes, she's a very good writer. In fact, I want to publish her book.'

He smiled then, a large, broad smile like his mother's. 'Well there's irony for you. Have you talked to my parents? Do they know that you're here?' His voice was accusatory for the first time.

'Your mother gave me this address. She's a nice woman.'

'Yeah, but not as all there as she used to be. The thing with Rachel really got to her, especially so soon after everything else.'

'So your sister is dead?'

'Is that what they told you?' He smiled again but with a touch of regret.

'They told me that she was dead, and your dad said it was his son's fault.'

He was taking a risk now but he was tired of being in the dark. The face opposite him darkened slightly.

'He said what?' It wasn't really anger that he displayed, just disbelief.

'He said that you were no son of his and that you were responsible for his daughter's death.' Brian knew that he had to say the words but he didn't know how to soften their blow. 'I can honestly say though that I don't think I have the full story in all this.'

The man rubbed his hands through his hair, knocking the pencil from its perch. He deftly caught it with his left hand.

'He meant Joe, not me. As they see it, he killed Rachel.

It's the only way that they can live with it. And you don't have a clue, do you?'

'I'm sorry if I've come in here and accused you of something that you didn't do. I just want to publish your sister's book and, if she is sadly dead, I would like you to persuade your parents to sign a contract, as her next of kin, and let me publish it in memory of her. There would be money in it for them.'

The man shook his head. 'I can't do that. You really don't understand. It's not that simple and I can't explain it to you. It's not my story to tell.'

'Well who can explain it to me?'

'You need to see Joe. He has all the answers for you and for the book.'

'Do you know where he is?'

'No, and I don't really care. But my mother would know. Joe wrote to her about six months ago, but my father wouldn't let her reply. He's a very straight man. He can't cope with what's happened. He loved Rachel like any father would love his daughter, took care of her, kept her away from harm. Do you have any children, Mr Matthews?'

'No.'

'Well, I do. A baby girl, in fact, born three months ago, and I can promise you that it would be awful to lose a child. Just like it's awful to have lost a sister. Because that's what it is. I used to play out on the road with Rachel. We used to share a room when we were really young. There's only two years between us. I don't have that sister anymore and it's Joe's fault. He's just a selfish little shit. I don't like him any more than my dad does. He's not my brother.'

Kenneth paused and sighed.

'I bet you're sorry you asked now?'

'No, I'm just sorry for your loss.'

'No loss to me anymore. I'm over it all. You move on.'

Brian felt sorry for this mild-mannered electrician. He seemed a good man. He had taken the time to talk to him. He could have shown him the door or been aggressive.

'Actually, do you know, I would like you to find Joe, Mr Matthews. Maybe you could ask him if he's really happy now, and if he knows what he's left behind. Tell him Kenneth will never forgive him for hurting our parents so much. I know he has problems too, but you have to think of how your actions will affect your loved ones first, don't you?'

It wasn't really a question demanding an answer. Brian really had no answers for him. All he had was one final question.

'Could you get your brother's address from your mum for me? I don't want to upset her.'

'I'd prefer if you didn't call him my brother. He's just Joe.'

'Sorry.'

Kenneth McLoughlin took the small pencil from the counter and held it out over a piece of paper.

'Put your phone number on that, I will text you. I'll warn you, though, I don't think Joe will want to see you. That's one of the reasons why I'm helping you.'

The day was cold by the time Brian Matthews got back to his car. The sun had faded and the roads were starting to clog with workers returning home. He wasn't sure what to make of his afternoon. Two brothers, a dead sister and a family divided – there was a novel in there somewhere, possibly an even better one than *The Olive Tree*. Maybe if he could find Joe McLoughlin, he could persuade him to write a memoir.

CHAPTER 23

I WAS NOSTALGIC SOMETIMES. IT wasn't just the photographs, the recollections or the lack of cards on my birthday, it was the impact of other people's lives on mine: Sophia with her frustration over her brother, Fran and her constant talk of her family, and Rosemary Frances Benson lying in a fresh grave in the plot next to the wall. I visited her and left behind more than a flower. She was thirty-five years of age, only a year younger than me. Someone had paid for an inscription on her small headstone: GOD HAS CLAIMED HIS CHILD.

Family or no family, I was going to make a life for myself where people would turn up at my funeral. The problem was that I had no idea of how to make these relationships. I had never kept friends in the past. There was always the problem of Rachel. She had come between me and all the friends I made. Things would start out well enough but then they would get too close and everything would disintegrate. So I kept people at arm's length and paid the price. I almost withdrew.

Rachel wrote to purge herself of her anger. She committed to paper all her feelings. It was the ultimate escape for her – a place where the world could be exactly as she wanted it to be. She had dreams of being published, sat for days in her room, tapping away at the keys. It was the perfect hobby for her – no interaction, no expense and no reality. She could sit for hours, one eye on the cradle in the corner and one eye on her story. She had even sent it to a publisher, but there was no reply and she didn't take the rejection well. I held the same rejected pages in front of me now, three hundred and twenty-two pages of her love for writing. It was a good book. Rachel would have loved walking through a bookshop and seeing her novel on display. It would have been something she could have been proud of.

I hadn't taken it from the large brown envelope for a long time. It seemed to belong with her, yet another part of her life that had not worked out, yet another rejection of the person she was.

Well, we were both rejected now.

And yet the reason for my rejection was ironic. It had happened because I had merely asked others to accept me, and my need for acceptance had led to those people feeling extremely angry. They had wanted everything to appear as they perceived it. They didn't want an alternative reality that made them feel less secure in the world. I had learned that I was only there to fit into their reality and not to belong in my own. In wanting my own identity I had no alternative but to leave.

The reality in my home had been Dad, Mum, Kenneth and Rachel. There had been no space for Joe. There never had been. They had rejected me from birth. They wanted Kenneth, they wanted Rachel, but they didn't want me. And now I didn't want them either. I couldn't even talk to them.

*

I nearly didn't hear the knock on the door the music was so loud.

'Hi, I hope you don't mind me calling over, but I just didn't want to leave things as abruptly as I did in the café today.' She was wearing a heavy coat and the rain was dripping from her shoes into a puddle in the porch. Sophia was drenched.

'No, not at all. Not a night to be out, though. Come in and take your coat off. I have a fire lit.'

'Did you stay in Galway long after I left?'

'No, not long. I managed to find the shops and buy my mirror.' I gestured to the wall behind the door.

'You have it hung and all. It's lovely.'

'I'm not one to change my mind when I want something.'

She walked towards the fire, running her fingers through her damp hair, putting it back in place from where the wind had blown it. 'I'm sorry about earlier, Joe.'

'It's all right. I shouldn't have blurted it out at ten o'clock in the morning in a coffee shop. It's not really the place for home truths.'

She said nothing but held out her hands to warm them in the heat from the burning turf.

'Would you like a glass of wine? I think there's nothing nicer than a glass of red wine and a fire.'

'That's typical of you, Joe, asking me do I want something and telling me what to have at the same time. Just like the music that night. I don't have a clue what "bluesy" is!'

She was smiling but I felt that I was under the microscope. 'Okay then, would you like a beer or a gin or white wine?'

'I'd love a glass of red, please.' At least she was smiling now and teasing me.

'You're as bloody difficult as me, aren't you?' I said as she took a seat by the fire.

'I don't know, Joe. Maybe I'm just trying to gain back some of the ground I lost since the last time I was here.'

'I'll get you the wine.'

When I returned with the glasses, she was up on her feet again, leaning over the table, reading the first page of Rachel's book.

'Is this yours? It's really good.'

I flinched slightly from the intrusion but I decided to be honest. 'No, Rachel wrote it.' I thought I'd be more annoyed, even angry with her for interrogating me again, but it was my own fault. I had left it sitting out on the table.

'Have you read it all?' she asked.

'I've read every word of it. It means a great deal to me.'

'Tell me what it's about.'

'What it's about or what's it really about?'

'Both.'

I handed her the glass of wine and sat down on the couch. To my surprise she sat down beside me, kicking off her wet shoes and curling her feet under her slender body.

'You don't mind do you?' She had noticed me looking down at her wet feet. 'It's ages since someone has told me a story. I'd like to be comfortable.'

'What makes you think I'm going to tell you the story?' I asked.

She smiled and took a small sip of wine. 'Because you like me.'

She looked at me with a different expression than I had seen before. It was warm and affectionate. 'Also because, Joe White, you're not the only one who always gets what he wants.'

There was a danger now. It was all too comfortable, too easy. I hadn't killed off Rachel only to be uncovered by Sophia. But there was also a warmth in her being there, a warmth that I hadn't felt in a long time.

'So go on, what's the story about?'

'It's about the relationships within a family, like most stories. It's about a boy not being appreciated for who he wants to be and the hurt that it causes in his life. It's set in Greece.'

'That's exotic! Had your sister ever travelled there?'

'For a short holiday.'

Sophia was not to be dissuaded from her course of questioning with a quick answer. 'Well, that's the theme. What's the plot?'

'The central character is responsible for his brother's death. He leaves home to find a new life and by doing so rediscovers his past and who he really is.'

'So it's a coming of age novel then?'

'I suppose it is.'

Sophia put her hand on mine and held it tight. 'Are you living out Rachel's book, Joe? Are you coming of age, maybe a late developer?'

I had never thought of it that way before. 'It seems that way, doesn't it?'

We were both quiet then. The fire crackled, the windows rattled but the room was eerily empty of our voices. I wondered what she was thinking. I knew what was crossing my mind. She was too close to everything.

Could I keep her in my life? She could be a danger to everything I had chosen.

'Would it be wrong to ask for more wine? It's pouring outside. I'd prefer to stay here a little longer.'

I couldn't refuse her another glass of wine. I didn't want to refuse her anything.

'What about you, Sophia, what's your story really about?'

'Nothing out of the ordinary really. A few failed relationships, a job that takes up most of my time and a biological clock that is ticking relentlessly.'

I thought Sophia was unusual in that respect. Her blatant honesty was always there, making me wonder if it was one of the factors that had left her on her own. Her honesty looked for a considered reply but I had none, so I just squeezed her hand tighter and then took the conversation off in a different direction.

'Sophia, I'd like to spend more time with you. I know we've had a few ups and downs already but I think there's something there.'

She didn't avert her gaze from the fire.

'That's so unromantic, Joe.'

'Okay, well how about I find you really attractive and I'd like to get to know you better. Is that more appealing?'

She turned to face me and gave me a gentle kiss on the cheek.

'Actually, Joe, that's just fine.'

'There's only one thing, which in this day and age may sound strange. I'd like us to take it slowly. I'd like to get this one right.'

Her smile was quizzical. 'How slow is slow?'

'Layer by layer, level by level, it can be quite sexy that

way.' I leaned over and kissed her. And she returned my kiss with a passion that said we were already beyond that level.

I liked the taste of her lips. I liked the softness of her skin on my face, the small kisses she placed on my eyelids and cheeks, the warm breath on my neck.

Minutes later I liked the shape of her breasts, the round firmness of her nipples, and the way her body arched and moved under my touch. I wanted more than I could give. I wanted all of her, the wetness that had become us and the tenderness of giving.

Although I was alone in my room that night, the bed didn't seem so empty. For the first time I felt a person had entered my life who might actually remain there.

CHAPTER 24

BRIAN HATED WAITING ROOMS. THERE was a boring similarity about them all – the chairs around the wall, the coffee table in the middle and the out-of-date women's magazines. This one was no more exciting except for the aquarium of tropical fish. He felt so sorry for them swimming around in their little home, bumping up against the glass. They must have been so bored facing the same plastic castle and imitation coral every day. It was no wonder they went slightly barmy and nibbled at each other, nipping at tail fins with their silly little mouths, or maybe that was simply a type of oral sex for fish and they were having far more fun than anybody realised.

He wondered how much longer Laura would be. He had promised to come as support but his patience was running out fast. He had never expected her to react so quickly. They had only really discussed the matter less than a week ago and here he was sitting in the waiting room watching a fish orgy.

He picked up the pamphlet sitting on the table beside the magazines. *Facing the Future* – it was an irritating title, too smarmy and clever. Inside there were short explanations of all the treatments, from facelifts to nose jobs, accompanied by highly imaginative prices. The doctor had a list of letters after his name that seemed to contain the whole alphabet. He was probably some forty-three-year-old from Florida with a perfect smile and no wrinkles.

The longer he waited, the more Brian found himself repulsed by the whole idea. It wasn't natural to alter the appearance beyond the creator's pen. It would be like painting over the Mona Lisa's nose to give her the perfect face. She was the most photographed woman in the world and over five hundred years old. He understood the need for plastic surgery for victims of burns and illnesses but those poor unfortunates were only trying to gain back their original looks, not trying to create a totally different appearance. Modern society's aim for perfection was just wrong. It was the inside that made the person not just the outer shell. He could feel a Buddha moment coming over him. He had flirted with Eastern philosophy in college. He had even worn the sandals and the beads around his neck for a whole year, until he realised that no one in the late 1980s Dublin understood what he was talking about and he didn't want to be a vegetarian any more.

The door of the waiting room opened and Laura stood there flushed and flustered. 'I missed the Dart by a minute. I'm sorry.'

'I told you I'd pick you up from work.'

'I know,' she replied, 'but it didn't make sense. You were just around the corner, Brian. Anyway I'm just glad you're here. Thank you for coming to support me. I know how you feel about all this.' She gave him one of her best smiles and sat down beside him. She must have been nervous because she took his hand and held it tightly.

'You don't have to do this you know.'

'Brian, we've talked about this. I want to.'

A voice from a speaker on the wall disturbed them. It was one of those extremely polite voices common in airport lounges and shopping centres. 'Mrs Matthews, you can go through to the doctor's office now. Thank you.'

The office was large and plush. The doctor was small and Asian.

'How do you do? I'm Dr Randhani. You must be Mr and Mrs Matthews. Do come in and sit down.'

The doctor was wearing a ridiculous bow tie and waistcoat, and his accent was colonial Raj. He could have stepped out of the *Gandhi* film set, so precise was his intonation. On the wall behind him were his degrees displayed in ornate frames, all of them from Oxford.

'As you may know, Mrs Matthews, I have worked extensively in this area, six years in America.'

Brian didn't like him already. He couldn't say why and it didn't matter why.

'Irish people are starting to realise that there are enormous psychological benefits to having the body to match the mind. If we look good, we feel good. It's a simple matter really.'

He smiled to reveal a perfect set of teeth. Brian wondered whether his teeth were naturally perfect or created by an orthodontist.

'So how can I help you, Mrs Matthews?'

It was difficult not to answer for his wife, but he knew that his interference would be aggressive and totally unappreciated by them both. He had to say quiet.

Laura sounded slightly nervous. 'Well, really, Mr Randhani, I was hoping for your advice. I just feel my eyes are looking baggy and old and my face doesn't fit me anymore.'

Randhani stood up from his leather chair and walked around to where Laura was sitting. With delicate hands, he held her face and pushed up the skin around her eyes, then played with the small folds under her neck.

'You would be a very easy patient to help, Mrs Matthews. You have good bone structure and you'd benefit from some work around the eyes and chin. It wouldn't be a difficult procedure.' He gave a sympathetic smile and sat back down on his chair.

Brian Matthews couldn't resist scratching the itch of a question that had been there since he had arrived in the waiting room. 'There's obviously some risk with all this?'

'Ah, Mr Matthews, a good question!'

Brian hated being patronised.

'As you both know there is a slight risk with every operation conducted under anaesthetic but the risk is negligible with a healthy young woman such as your wife.'

'But there is a risk?'

'Brian!' Laura shot him a dirty look.

'Mr Matthews, I understand your concern. There is a risk sitting in the sun for too long, but we all do it; or eating the wrong foods, smoking, drinking. Most of life contains an element of risk. We just have to choose which risks we are willing to take. We don't stop taking them.'

'I totally understand, Doctor, and I'm willing to take the risk. Brian, it's a ridiculously small risk.'

That was the end of the meeting as far as Brian was concerned. There were more things said, dates of admission discussed, but the decision was already made in Laura's mind. Even over lunch, she spoke about it as if it was a fait accompli. 'I didn't think the appointment would be so soon. I thought it would take months.' Her voice was happy, enthusiastic.

'Laura, don't you think we should discuss this again before we make the decision?'

'Brian, what are you so negative about? Are you afraid that other men will find me attractive and that I'll run off with someone else?'

'Don't be inane, Laura. I'm sure other men already find you attractive. It's the risk I'm not happy about.'

'That's rubbish, Brian. When we first talked about this you never mentioned the risk, because we both knew it was tiny. You kept ranting on about growing old gracefully, not touching God's work of art and all that stuff.'

Whatever Brian said, it wasn't going to make any difference. He decided on the last resort. 'I love you just the way you are.'

She gave him a sardonic look. 'And that's why I think you're so selfish, Brian.'

'How can I be selfish for loving you?'

'If you loved me you'd let me change, be who I want to be.'

It was another one of those blasted emotional arguments that he was destined to lose. Her eyes had adopted a harsher look now and her lips were pursed. She was mentally ready. Her defence was all thought out and lined up. It was probably why she hadn't wanted the lift. She had been rethinking her arguments.

'Brian, I know you love me just the way I am. But loving someone also means letting them be who they want to be and supporting them.'

'Not if it's dangerous for them.'

'Oh, Brian, change the record. Do I stop you going for a pint? Do I tell you not to smoke cigars every time we celebrate anything? If that's what you want to do, I let you do it. I'm not in this life to live for you, Brian, I'm here to live with you. And if you don't want me in whatever package I decide to be, then you should let me go. I'm not your appendage. I'm a person in my own right.'

There didn't seem to be any counter arguments left. In some ways, he even felt that she was right. He wished he were one of those stupid fish in the waiting room, with nothing to think about except feeding time. He did feel selfish. It was her body and her choice to make.

'Brian, what are you thinking about? You've gone too quiet.'

He thought it was better to be honest. 'I was thinking that you're actually right, Laura, and I'm sorry.'

'Yeah, thanks.'

'I mean it, honey. I've no right to tell you what to do with your life.'

A smile was appearing. She had a nice smile. He hoped it wouldn't change with the operation and become too wide and false.

'Really, Brian? Do you really mean it?'

'Yes, I do.'

'Thank you, then, and thanks for coming this morning.'

He felt guilty. He had only come in the hope of finding some information to avert the whole procedure.

'Let's leave the subject of my face. Have you heard back from the brother in Athlone?'

'No, but it's only been four days.' Brian wasn't sure if he cared any more. It was becoming too complicated. He had other work to do and there were too many barriers in the way of *The Olive Tree* making it to the shelves.

'I'd love to know what happened, Brian. I hope he gets back to you.'

'Well, I'm not sure if I'll follow it up anyway.'

'God, you must. Aren't you curious as to how she died and how the other brother caused it?'

The McLoughlin family were becoming characters in their own soap opera, with Laura driving the plot.

'Of course I'm curious but I have other fish to fry and it's taking up too much time.' His mind was back on the poor fish again.

'But I wonder where he went to live. He could be abroad. I'd come with you if you found him.'

'Laura, if he's skipped the country, I'll send him a letter.'

'That's no good. If he's running from the past, he'll hardly reply. No, you have to go and see him in person. Joe McLoughlin holds the key to this whole story.'

'If he's running from his past, don't you think he should be left in peace to enjoy his future?'

'No! Anyway, that's naïve, Brian. You can't run from the past. It'll be there with him somewhere. And he might need some help in dealing with it.'

This was typical of Laura. She always saw things through the heart and not the mind. She claimed it was because she was a Piscean. But he knew it was because she was a woman. She was far more emotional. It was why she liked watching soaps and he preferred his news and sports, practical programmes. He had no doubt that such preferences were predominantly gender-based.

'Well, I don't want to help Joe McLoughlin deal with anything. I just want to find out if he can help me get the rights to publish the book. His brother intimated that he might.'

'You've no heart, Brian.'

'And you've no sense.'

'Yes, but that's why you love me so much. It's so you can feel superior.'

If she hadn't smiled as she said it, he would have been annoyed. But there was a truth in her words, although he would never admit it.

CHAPTER 25

SOPHIA HELD THE CLOTHES PEG out to her mother and watched as the old woman pinned the shirt up on the line. 'I wish you'd let me do this for you.'

'I wish you'd leave me alone. It's a pity teachers have the whole weekend off.'

Irascible was the word that sprang to mind.

'I came back here to help you, Mum.'

'Yes, I know, but I didn't ask you to. I can cope fine on my own.'

Sophia couldn't afford to feel hurt; she had nowhere else to live and no one else to love. She didn't want to go back to the city.

'If you can manage on your own, why were you always complaining on the phone to Martin?'

Marta Warner shook her head and held her hand out for another peg.

'You're a woman, Sophia, work it out. I wanted him back home, but I got you instead.'

There was no point in Sophia sounding aggrieved. She knew the old woman would just smile and tell her to stop being so sensitive.

'Mum, I've met someone.'

Sophia didn't know where the words came from. They just seemed a good way of changing the subject. But there was always a difficulty feeding her mother such information, she would automatically envisage wedding bells and grandchildren. It was the problem with being the only daughter and single.

'Why are you telling me? It's not like you.'

'I don't really know. I suppose I want you to talk me out of it. You'll go on about wedding bells, I'll get angry and I'll dump him to avoid your pestering.'

Marta laughed. 'I always thought you were a schemer. Do you like him?'

'I do, strangely enough'

'Doesn't sound like it,' her mother said as she put another piece of clothing on the line.

'I'm just worried.'

Her mother let out a small snort. 'What? Worried in case you fall for him and it gets too serious?'

Sophia picked a sock out of the laundry basket and pegged it on the line. She did it to annoy her mother. She looked out of the corner of her eye at the elderly woman. It was a silly thing to do. The old woman couldn't see her glance. Her eyes were fixed, staring into nowhere, waiting for the day when she could see again. The silly old woman had strange notions. She believed that her sight would be restored in heaven. It was why she went to the church every day, to light a candle and thank God for the abilities that would be returned to her in death. She had lost her sight as a young woman: a drunk in a pub, a broken bottle and flailing arms. The glass had cut straight through both lenses, damaging the cornea and retina. The blood had poured from the gash; the scars of the sickening attack continuing down her cheek. The shock of her scream had silenced the pub. She had held her hands to the wound while others watched the flow redden her fingers. It had happened so quickly that no one had responded at first. They just stood and stared while the drunk dropped the bottle to the floor and fell to his knees. Many said that she was lucky that she was already married, as she was no beauty to begin with. The problem was that the attack had not just scarred her face. Her temper was scarred too. There was no bright day that didn't contain a dark mood.

'What's his name? And I told you I could hang my own clothes, Sophia.'

'Joe.'

The old woman put her hands on her hips and frowned. 'The new owner of the café?'

'How do you know about the new café?' Sophia was irritated at her mother's knowledge, and surprised. Except for her frequent visits to the church her mother didn't go out often and she wasn't one for gossip.

'How do you know him?'

'I may be blind but I'm not stupid.'

'That's no answer.'

Marta smiled cheekily. 'Well, postmen see everything.'

'Peadar told you?'

Marta turned to face her daughter. It was a matter of impact and drama. 'Peadar had a letter one day. It was addressed to the cottage. But it wasn't for your Mr Joe White. It was for a Rachel McLoughlin, whoever she may be. Peadar said that he knocked at the door, as he saw no point delivering it to the wrong address.' The old woman picked up the basket and headed down the path to the house.

'So, what happened, was it a wrong address?'

Marta pushed the door to one side and ignored the

question. 'Put the kettle on, Sophia. It's colder out in the wind than you'd think.'

'Come on, quit playing games with me, Mother!' There was more than a hint of impatience in Sophia's voice.

Marta spoke slowly and deliberately. 'He's not the one for you, my love.'

Only a mother could deliver such an irritating line.

'And why?'

'Your friend, Joe, told Peadar it was his sister, but Peadar said that he was decidedly uncomfortable.'

Sophia shook her head as if this was hardly surprising. 'Of course he was uncomfortable – his sister's dead. It must have been disturbing to receive mail for her.'

The kettle was wheezing in the corner and Marta felt for two cups in the cupboard, her hands steady and sure.

'Sophia, I'll tell you what I think. It's not his sister.'

It was irritating the way her mother did it; she would conjure a whole new scenario out of the facts. She always did. It was as if her imagination over-compensated for her loss of sight and was now seeing things that didn't even exist.

'And what do you base this on, Mother? A postman who has to cycle everywhere because he's lost his licence?'

Her mother stirred milk into the coffee and wagged the dripping spoon at her daughter. 'Sophia, I feel it in my waters, something's up with Joe White.'

'God, Mother, I wish I hadn't said anything to you at all.'

Marta turned around. 'You do like this Joe, then?'

'I'd like to know how you jumped to your ridiculous conclusion.'

Her mother didn't see the need to answer the question;

there were more important things to say. 'Look I'm just saying be careful, Sophia. He's new around here. Most people come here to escape something. He's no different. Why don't you ask him about his past and see what he says?'

'I know what he'll say. He had a sister. She died and he received a letter for her.'

'Dead people only get letters to where they once lived!'

'It could have been redirected to him.'

Her mother raised a cynical eyebrow.

Sophia was getting angry now. 'Mum, you've never met Joe. You've no reason to doubt him.'

'I'm not the only one who goes to church, Sophia.'

'What's that supposed to mean?'

'I met someone there recently with the same initials as your friend Joe's supposed sister, but the person I met had a voice like no woman I've ever met.'

Sophia eyed her mother suspiciously.

'I don't understand what you're trying to say, Mother.'

'I'm not saying any more, Sophia. I'm old and I may be wrong in what I'm thinking, but I just think you should keep Joe at arm's length. His life is too complicated, and that's not what you need.'

CHAPTER 26

IT WAS AN ARTICLE IN the newspaper that gave Brian the ammunition he needed, the story of an untimely death. It had appeared to him as a gift from above, perfectly presented in *The Sunday Times*. He had read it, at first, just out of interest, but the striking relevance of the cause of death replaced any random curiosity. His breakfast had even gone cold as he forgot everything that was in front of him except the printed word. If Laura had been in his situation, she would have called the article a matter of fate. She didn't believe in coincidences; everything came with a purpose that couldn't be ignored or it would be tempting fate. He believed in a more haphazard universe where the Big Bang was an accidental explosion not the pre-ordained beginning of creation.

Laura was out.

Coincidence or luck, he wondered? If she had been at home, his attack would have started immediately. But she was visiting her grandmother in the nursing home. He had never felt the desire to accompany her. He hated the smell – a mixture of stale urine and disinfectant – and the lost souls who stood by the door, watching everyone come and go, tilting their heads to one side as they peered through vacant eyes. Even the goldfish at the reception desk, swimming around in their small bowl, seemed luckier as they looked out on the monotony beyond the glass. Brian smiled, his mind seemed to be preoccupied with little scaly friends. He could never have worked in a nursing home among such decaying minds; it would have left him with a permanent fear of ageing, a fear he presumed persecuted Laura.

But Laura obviously hid it well from her grandmother. She sat and talked, brought flowers and boxes of jellies. She listened with patience, was less selfish with her time. She had the same conversation, listened to the demands for more tissues, the pleading for more visits, the constant repetition of last week's news, and yet she continued to visit.

He felt ashamed of his absence. It was his fear that kept him away, the fear of being alone, with no one to visit him as he sat in the corner waiting for the final call. He had once told Laura of his fears and she had laughed, sat on the edge of the bed and allowed her shoulders to shake. He couldn't see anything funny. He had been sincere.

'Do you really think you'll outlive me, Brian?' she had asked.

He looked at the newspaper spread out on the table before him. She wouldn't laugh when she saw this. If she went ahead with the operation, he might well outlive her. There was no better example of the risks than the story he was looking at. Such a waste!

His mind wandered to the McLoughlins and their small terraced house. At least they would have Kenneth to visit them, the mild-mannered electrician with his overalls and sharpened pencil. He didn't seem like the type of son who would neglect to visit his mother or father in a home. On reflection, the father seemed the more likely survivor. He was tall and unwrinkled. The mother seemed so petite and fragile. It must have removed her lust for life to lose her only daughter.

Brian very rarely felt depressed but he could feel a gloom descending and with it a song, some words and even a tune in his head. 'Better to have loved and lost than never to have loved at all.' He knew why it was there - the christening robe in the attic, the empty cot. If Laura was scared about having a child, he was more scared of not trying, of not experiencing that love. At least poor Mrs McLoughlin had enjoyed her daughter and had memories to cherish.

The random thoughts made him wish that the McLoughlins had replied to his request and sent him the address. He wanted to find Joe and solve the puzzle of Rachel's death. He wanted to know what could split a family with such aggression. Incest, suicide, pregnancy, the answers kept changing in his head. Laura had given him other possibilities to think about – an illness that Rachel had found too terrifying to face, and good old sensitive Joe had helped her out of her misery.

He stood up from the table, leaving the paper open. He needed a smoke. The house was out of bounds. He would have to take refuge in the garden. He had told Laura that he had given up ages ago, but every now and then the lure of the taste and smell would bring him down the bottom of the garden. There was a wooden bench by the wall, perfectly placed by a shrub in a barrel. He had idly thought he should replace the poor hyacinth with a tobacco plant, such was the number of butts littering the earth in the barrel, but that would have meant a visit to a garden centre and he hated them more than any other shop. His fingers weren't green, they were poisonous.

Brian cleared the bench of fallen leaves and took the packet of cigarettes from his pocket. He had always smoked French cigarettes, ever since he had opened his bedroom door as a young boy and seen the tall girl smiling at him from the landing. It's strange the impact a person can have during a brief crossing of paths. The foreign student had stayed with them for such a short time. Her breasts were beautifully captured in her thin T-shirt and his adolescence was evident in his awkward stare. She spoke French to him and he spent a month trying to fashion a reply. It was the first time in his life that he had wished he was older, the first time he had experienced the damp patch in his bed in the morning.

He struggled to remember her name. It annoyed him to be so forgetful. It was a name that had occupied most of his teenage fantasies. He played with the alternatives in his mind – Claudia, Veronique, Maria, Pascalle, Mimi. Maybe he should start fantasising again.

'Comfortable?'

He could tell from the tone that she wasn't happy. Laura hated him smoking.

'Oh, you're back already. I didn't expect you so soon, honey.'

'Obviously. It was bath morning so I couldn't stay long.'

'How's your grandmother?'

The change of subject rarely worked; she was like a dog with a bone when she saw the opportunity to berate him.

'She's not well.'

An escape route; he could be sympathetic now. She would forget about the cigarette he had just stubbed out on the patio and take comfort from his words.

'What's wrong with her, darling?'

'It's difficult to explain. She's just not herself. She seemed more addled, less coherent, greyer.'

'Greyer?'

'Yes, no colour in her cheeks, no vibrancy.'

'She's ninety-three, Laura.' It was probably less than sensitive to state the obvious but he felt she needed reminding.

'I know, Brian. I know I should be thankful that she's lived so long. It's just frightening to see someone being consumed by death while still alive.'

He patted to the bench beside him and she sat down and allowed him to put his arm around her.

'Do you want to go out tonight, instead of cooking?' He thought if he asked it would help her to continue ignoring the cigarette butts. He wished he hadn't left the paper open now; it wasn't the right time to introduce the article. She could turn the tables on him so easily. The risk of cancer was much higher than the chance of a reaction to an anaesthetic.

'Yeah, dinner out would be nice. Oh and by the way, your post is still unopened on the hall table, and there's quite a lot of it.'

He winced.

'I didn't want to spoil the weekend. It's probably bills.' He wasn't interested in his post. He would look at it first thing in the morning over breakfast. He was capable of doing that; it drove Laura mad. She had to open hers straight away. It was a natural curiosity, she said. It was the same with the answering machine, that drove her insane too. She didn't understand how he could ignore the messages. It was why she never used the recording facility when she rang home. It was safer to text him.

'How can you leave them unopened, Brian?'

'Oh, don't start, honey. It's just me, okay?'

She shrugged her shoulders and looked at him questioningly.

'Okay, if I get them and open some, will you stop giving me a hard time?'

She smiled and kissed him on the cheek. He had been wound up perfectly again.

'You sit there. I'll get them,' she offered. 'And how about a coffee?'

It was too much to hope that she hadn't seen the newspaper on her way to the kitchen. He wished he hadn't been so clever. It was not the way of his world to manipulate Laura. It was his role to be the manipulated.

'Not very subtle, Brian.' She was holding the coffee cup out to him, almost threatening to pour it over him.

He wondered whether to feign innocence but he was too tired.

'Does it not worry you, Laura, when you see things like that?'

She sat down on the bench and looked straight ahead of her.

'I woke up the other day, Brian, and I got dressed for work. When I looked in the mirror, I expected to look a mess, everyone does in the morning. But you put on the make-up, have the coffee and toast and head off thinking that as the day unfolds your face will wake up too.'

She turned to face him. 'But at lunchtime, I went for

a sandwich to the café near the bridge and as I walked past a shop, I caught a reflection of myself in the window. It frightened me, Brian, it didn't look like the person I thought I was; it was an old face with wrinkles and extra chins. It didn't look like me.'

He held her hand and squeezed it gently.

'So, my love, you're growing older. We'll do it together. I love you. I want to live my life out with you. I don't want a newer model.'

She laughed but it wasn't a happy sound.

CHAPTER 27

I HAD NEVER BEEN FISHING. It was not a pastime that had ever appealed to me and now I knew why. The scenery was beautiful, the lapping of the water against the boat was peaceful but the time spent preparing for the expedition was tedious. John Muckian was the man responsible for my initiation. It had come about from a chat in the pub and too many beers. It was not something I would have agreed to, sober. I had assumed we would have been sea fishing but a long drive in his jeep brought us to the lake.

With most Irish lakes, the other side of the shore is clearly visible, but with Lough Corrib the water stretched to the horizon; small islands dotted around here and there, uninhabited except for trees. Ours was not the only boat out here; others trawled the water hoping for a bite.

'Try to keep the fly on the surface, don't drown her.'

I smiled and lifted the rod slightly higher. The fly lifted and took off in the wind, landing further from the boat.

'It's a good day for fishing. We should take something home.'

John was an optimist, the type of man who always had a smile but never had much to say unless it was about the weather or the time of day. He'd worked most of his life in Dublin but the city had never warmed to him. His pace was too slow.

I had watched him fill the boat from the boot of his jeep. He had carefully boxed bait, spare reels and rods, knives to cut line, a cudgel to kill the fish and cushions made from foam covered with plastic to sit on during the long hours ahead. He packed most of them under the wooden seats with great care and consideration. He even had a spare hat for me in case the breeze stiffened.

'So where's your family from, Joe?'

'Dublin.'

'Oh, whereabouts? I was up there myself for a long time.'

It was easy to lie. I talked of the pier and Sunday afternoon walks. I mentioned the places I had seen when I had worked there.

'You have brothers or sisters?'

'Just a brother.'

'You're lucky. I'm one of eight. There was always a rush for the bathroom in our house.'

The day passed like that, idle conversation, affixing bait and turning around the boat to drift with the wind along the shoreline. I found it difficult to see the interest the sport engendered. I was bored with the rod and its lack of excitement. The fish didn't bite, the scenery didn't change and my companion seemed happy enough with his own thoughts.

A place can often invoke a memory and one particular part of the lake summoned one for me. It was where the trees met the water's edge and the rocky shore turned to sand. In my mind, I saw a man, his shoulders bare and drops of perspiration visible. He had been running towards the beach, his eyes frantically searching the water. And in the water was the boy, his arms flailing at the surface, his face ashen, almost white. He was bobbing up and down beneath the waves like a cork, appearing and disappearing, shouting and then silent. And the man reacted quickly, his shoes on the sand, his muscular arms pulling the water to one side, fighting with the lake to reach his son. But then the bobbing stopped and the water gathered around its victim, hiding him from the desperate searcher.

But in the end the lake lost.

With his arms straining to take the weight, the man emerged from the blues and greens, with the limp little body still breathing. Laying him flat on the soft shingle, he opened the boy's airways, rubbed the body furiously and waited for the vomit to wretch from the grey lips. It came in spurts, the lake slow to release the boy from its watery fingers.

'You're drowning that poor fly again, Joe.'

'Oh sorry, my mind drifted.'

'Thinking of a cold pint, I guess.'

'No actually, I was thinking of my dad.'

A curious mind would have asked, but John Muckian just nodded and turned the boat back towards the jetty. Three hours had passed and we hadn't landed anything big enough to keep.

If Kenneth had drowned that day, my life would have been different. I would have been their only son and they might have forgiven me for Rachel.

I did enjoy the pint when it eventually came. It took as long to empty the boat as it did to fill it. We sat in a bar in the nearest village and I paid for the Guinness as a grateful guest should.

'Thanks, Joe, but I don't really think you liked it out there.'

I had hoped he wouldn't notice. 'I don't think I'm patient enough, John. Probably more stressed than I realised. It would take a very relaxed mind to be happy fishing.'

It was only when I said the words that I realised the truth in them. I was still not totally relaxed in my life. There was still some unfinished business hanging over me. The memory of the lake was part of it.

'You're settling in well, though, aren't you? You like our village.'

'Oh, yeah, I'm happy with my move. It's been a good start for me.'

'And you seem to like one of our women, too.'

I eyed him suspiciously. He had a grin on his face, and to add to the humour of his remark, he slapped me between my shoulders and toasted me with his pint.

'Good luck to you, I say. I tried with Sophia, but she's not the easiest woman in the world.'

'What? You and Sophia?'

'Don't look so surprised. When you're single, there's not a great deal of choice around these parts. Not referring to her of course, but to me.'

I didn't really know what to say. He seemed so much older than me, so different. I couldn't see how he would have interested her.

'She likes the drink, you know. Falls asleep, though. I think she'll make a man happy enough if she loosens up a bit. How long have you been seeing her?'

'I haven't, really. It's only just starting. So how the hell did you know?'

He took a large gulp from his pint. 'The dance, Joe. You were seen leaving the dance together.'

'And what about you, John? With her for long?'

He shook his head almost in regret. 'No, not long

enough, if you know what I mean? I did get to first base though.'

This was definitely not what I had expected. It wasn't fishing or the weather. I was sitting in a bar with a man who had dated Sophia. I felt naïve. Sophia was too good-looking a woman to not have a past, but the one I would have expected would have been somewhere else and with other types – teachers from school, bank managers. The man sitting alongside me had sideburns, a woolly jumper and thick boots. And what did he mean by first base?

'Another pint, Joe?'

'No, thanks, I need to get back, if you don't mind.'

The conversation on the way back was more to my liking. He kept to the biggest catch he had ever made and the secrets of fly-fishing, and I sat and looked interested while watching the green of the valleys turn to rock and bracken. But I couldn't help thinking of his hands on her body and his rough lips on hers. I found my preoccupation with the image irritating and stupid. I was a grown man and jealousy was controlling my emotions.

The cottage was cold when I opened the door and walked in. The sun had dropped below the horizon and left a pinkish glow as a faint reminder. I wished I was seeing Sophia that evening. I needed to touch her, lay claim to her.

Although things had gone too fast in many ways, I had not expected to fall so quickly. I was like a boy in a sweet shop for the first time. I didn't know what I wanted, and I had grabbed greedily for the first thing that had come my way. Although there was shallowness in that thought,

I had always been attracted to women with dark hair and dark eyes, women who looked like Sophia. But Rachel had stopped them all.

I picked up the photograph from the shelf and ran a sleeve across the dust. Would my father have really loved me if Kenneth had not been there to be his perfect son? I doubted it. My father had looked at me with loathing. Only Kenneth and my mother had found some understanding for my behaviour. Even Kenneth changed his tune when he saw how everything affected our mother's health.

I went to bed with the photograph in my hand. I loved Rachel far more now than I did when she was here. I could see her life differently now it was over. The distance gave me a detachment. I could even see some good times among the bad. The time we'd all sat around the table in the ship's lounge, playing cards while waiting for the boat to dock, stuck with each other's company, forced into conversation and familiarity. And I'd not even lost my temper upon losing the game.

It was something that I'd always done as a teenager. Kenneth said later that it must have been the pent-up emotions, the feelings I had through having to hide so many things, things that were a lot harder to deal with than even the pregnancy. I'd told Kenneth about all of it. He had been angry with me. I'd expected some aggression but not the reaction he gave. I felt ashamed. He made me feel ashamed. And I wanted to kill her then, kill her for my part in her life. But I never thought *she'd* ask *me*.

CHAPTER 28

SOPHIA STOOD ON THE DOORSTEP and wondered whether it was too soon to be calling. Joe had asked could they take things slowly, but how slow was slowly? Anyway, she had her own misgivings; she was still unsure about her feelings for him. And her mother's idle prattling hadn't helped. And to make things worse, the bistro had been closed for a week. There was a small notice on the door and no explanation. Joe had been curiously absent. She hadn't seen him in the shop, in the pub or on the street.

She had decided he was sick – the cold or the flu. There were lots of bugs around. She would visit, offer some help, stay to make him soup or a pot of tea. She would even bring scones. Her mother had made them. It seemed silly now as she stood outside his house like a latter-day Red Riding Hood.

'If you don't knock, you can't come in!'

Joe was standing behind her, a smile on his face and a bag of compost in his hands. He looked far too healthy.

'So you're not sick then?'

She knew her voice sounded scolding but she couldn't help it. She felt hoodwinked. Why couldn't he have given a reason for the closed restaurant?

He looked perplexed, mystified by her appearance and show of aggression. 'Why did you think I was sick?'

'The restaurant's shut.'

'Oh, I see. No, I just needed some time off. Business is slow at the moment. I can make you coffee here, though.'

She should have smiled but she could still feel the frown on her face. He read her frown.

'I'll take that as a no, then, Sophia.'

'I'm sorry. Was my look that obvious?'

'I've seen worse, but not by much.'

She did smile this time. 'Sorry, it's just that I came to see if I could help. I even brought scones. I suppose I feel stupid now. You looking so well and all.'

'I look well, do I?'

'That doesn't mean good.'

He feigned disappointment. She handed him the scones.

'I've never had someone bake scones for me before.'

'Actually, my mother made them. I'm useless in the kitchen. I suppose it's also a bit silly, a bit like bringing ice to an Eskimo. I'm sure you bake better scones than my mother.'

'Well, tell your mother thanks and I'm available if she wants me.' He opened the door with one hand and placed the bag of compost on the hall floor.

'Come in. I'll put the kettle on.'

The house was spotless. She liked that about him. He was such a tidy person. The windows to the front of the house were open and a fresh breeze was billowing through the curtains. She could see the islands clear against the blue sky, more definite than in the haze of a summer's day. He had chosen a good place to live; the view from his cottage was amongst the best in the area. She wondered how much he had paid.

'How much was this place, Joe?'

She wasn't sure whether he had heard her. He was in the kitchen. She could see him leaning over the sink, the kettle in his hand. She heard him humming a tune. Maybe she shouldn't be asking him that question anyway. It could be seen as rude. She raised her voice.

'Can I use your bathroom, Joe?'

'Yeah, sure. Mind the lock though, it sticks slightly. Just lift the door up when you're opening it. The hinges are loose.'

It was a cute old bathroom, not much space to manoeuvre but beautifully decorated. The walls were thick like the rest of the cottage and the shower occupied an alcove that was decorated with seashells and painted a sandy yellow. Along the side of the window was an old-fashioned bath, fitted with chrome taps and containing a plastic duck. To the side was a sink sitting below a mirror. There were no streaks of toothpaste on the surface, no grime around the plughole, no shaved hairs on the sides. You are a meticulous man, she thought, maybe too tidy to be real.

She'd always had a curious side to her nature and it was bubbling to the surface now. There was a cupboard under the sink. Made of old wood and painted green, it begged to be opened.

It was just as tidy as the rest of the place: an unused bar of soap, a clean jar of hair gel and a Tupperware box. She knew she was going too far with the box but that didn't stop her. She prised off the lid, almost expecting drugs or something illicit. She closed it again and realised that Joe had no hidden ghosts – these were just the boring items of any household: plasters, ointment and a scissors. He had them all in a plastic container.

She washed her hands and looked at her teeth in the mirror. She grimaced to see if they were clean.

'Your bathroom's lovely. Did you decorate it yourself?'

He was sitting at the window in one of a pair of armchairs facing out to sea.

'Yes. I love doing things myself. It makes it feel more like home.'

'There's a woman's touch about it.'

He didn't seem to mind her comment. 'My mother was good at decorating, made her own curtains and everything. You learn.'

'Have your parents visited you?'

He seemed to mind now. He picked up his coffee and looked thoughtful.

'Since Rachel's death, my family haven't talked. We all feel responsible. We all blame ourselves.'

'I always seem to get it wrong, I'm sorry.'

'You have nothing to feel sorry about. It's just my family. We're not very easy to understand and better left alone. After the coffee, would you like a walk along the beach?'

It was said with enthusiasm, so she didn't feel he was just trying to avoid the conversation. 'Yes, I'd love one.'

It was only five minutes from the house to the nearest beach. The road was a dirt track and dotted with puddles from yesterday's rain. He held her hand and she was pleased. She liked the protection it gave and the possessiveness it showed. He had lent her a jacket, a warm fleece and she realised that she liked the way it smelled, the odour of him.

The beach was not just an arc of sand overlooking the

ocean, it was a causeway to an island, which was covered with water twice daily. There were still some locals living on Inishcairn, but mostly it was just holiday cottages, empty all winter, giving a desolate feel to the island. They walked to the back of the island where there were fewer houses and even less vegetation. The westerly wind drove furiously into this shoreline and the rocks were jagged and the beach without sand.

'This is my favourite spot,' said Joe.

He was standing on a rock looking out to sea, the Atlantic stretching before him all the way to America.

'There's nothing in the way, you know,' he said. 'I looked it up in an atlas. You can draw a line right across to the States without hitting one piece of land.'

She stood on the rock behind him and stared at the same open water. She knew why he liked it. It was a view with possibilities. One could imagine anything out there.

'It makes me think of all the people who have stood here before and seen the same view. Over thousands of years it hasn't changed.'

She felt drawn to him, standing so close. She could see his dark hair curl over the top of his collar; she noticed the small details that she had never seen before. He had a birthmark on the side of his neck, raspberry coloured but flat and unobtrusive. She felt the strange desire to touch it, kiss it as if that would make it go away, like a mother kissing a child's wounds.

He turned to face her. 'You're very quiet.'

It was a romantic place to kiss but she hadn't expected to be the instigator. He was simply there, his blue eyes looking into hers, his lips alluringly close. She had forgotten all her questions, all her mother's words.

The walk back to the house was quicker.

He didn't say anything, just took her hand again. He didn't let it go until she was in the bedroom, the clothes falling to the floor, his hands running over her body. She tried to take his shirt off but he moved away and gave her a smile. Then he came back to her again but with more passion, his lips on her breasts, his hands touching her wetness, his body moving in rhythm to his own inner beat.

'Joe, please take me.'

She wished she had said nothing. His pulsating stopped. He opened his eyes and she saw fear. It scared her for an instant. It was so out of place with the previous moments. She thought there were tears in his eyes but it could have been the half-light in the room.

'I need to go to the bathroom, Sophia. I'll be back in a minute.'

His voice was insistent, his smile unconvincing. She couldn't think why he'd moved away so quickly. The bedroom was empty; she was on the duvet alone. There was no obvious reason for his change of heart. He had seemed so aroused. He had touched her so hungrily. This was embarrassing. Then it came to her. He was looking for protection, although she hadn't seen any in the bathroom. They were more likely to be in a bedside locker. She would take it in her own hands to find one for him.

The top drawer was full. Here at last was the real Joe: cheque stubs, driving licence and a handful of letters. She was curious again. She could hear her mother's argument and see Peadar's face peering at the envelope. The letter was probably among these if anywhere.

She was right.

The address was his cottage but the addressee was Rachel McLoughlin. She didn't think about Joe or the time she had to read it. She was far too engrossed in what secrets she might find. The postmark was Athlone. The letter was on a single white sheet of Manila paper, old-fashioned and perfectly written.

Dear Rachel,

I hope you're well. I wasn't going to reply to your letter but your brother called last week. Someone's been looking for you. He told them you were dead. Do you know how much that makes me cry? To think that I'll never see you again, never hold my daughter in my arms. I miss you, Rachel. You were always so special to me. I can't believe all this. If you hadn't lost Paul, I don't think you would have left us. I know I was harsh with you over the pregnancy but I was worried, worried about what your father would say and the neighbours. Are you punishing me for that now? It's just the way I was brought up, the church, the rights and wrongs of the time. It's different now, I know it is.

You must have been so alone in your head to allow Joe. I won't talk to him, Rachel. You can come back, but not him. He can't be my son.

Kenneth and your dad are still angry.

I don't know what else to say. I feel tired with it all these days. I cry a lot and your father loses his temper over every little thing. He doesn't blame me but he's wrong. I am to blame. I gave birth to you and I raised you. It must be my fault but I don't want you to die.

Please don't go through with it, Rachel. Please come home.

Your loving mum

P.S. If it's too late and you're reading this, I hate you Joe, you and your damn needles and lack of love for our feelings. You could have told us earlier and we would have found another way out of this. You gave us no chance to save Rachel. You'll never be welcome here.

She felt spooked now. She could see nothing in the letter to comfort her about Joe. She was miles from the village and in a strange man's house with darkness fast approaching. Her clothes were on the floor. He was still in the bathroom and all she could think to do was run.

CHAPTER 29

I LOOKED IN THE MIRROR. I'd been too long in the bathroom. I hadn't been thinking straight. There were too many problems with having a woman in my bed. I ached to be with Sophia but I couldn't see how it could happen without a terrifying revelation that might drive her away for ever. But she had wanted me. She had asked, so there had to be some hope.

I sat on the toilet lid and stared down at the floor. There was no excuse I could give her for this. If I wanted her friendship, I would have to tell her the truth and tell her about Rachel. There was no hiding this time; I had deluded myself for far too long. Rachel had warned me. It was just so difficult to sit back and do nothing when the temptation was there. I had wanted to show off my new freedom.

There was nothing for it. I had to tell her.

But the bedroom was empty. Sophia's clothes were gone from the floor. On the bed was the letter. It would take more than an explanation now. Sophia must have read it all. Rachel was dead and buried and no one could be allowed to ruin all the planning and the sacrifice, not even Sophia.

I found my car keys and drove off to find her.

CHAPTER 30

LAURA HELD THE PAPER IN her hand and looked down at Brian as he sat on the couch, making him miss the goal he had waited for all afternoon.

'So you want to talk about Olivia Goldsmith?' She knew her tone was too acerbic.

He missed the replay as he turned to answer her.

'Did you read the whole article?'

'Yes.' Of course she had read the whole article. She had worries too. It was not something she had not thought about. Mistakes did happen. But to have the wrinkles removed and the chin brought back to its youthful appearance was too alluring.

'It's a shocker, isn't it?' He was looking at her with his stupid, wide-eyed innocence as if he expected her to agree and back down.

'It's like anything else, Brian, walking on a country road in the dark, eating a burger from a dodgy food stand or travelling by plane on the wrong day. It's a tragedy but not the end of the world.'

She sounded as if she was going to burst into song. Various alternatives ran through his head, but this was a time to be sensible.

'She died from an anaesthetic, Laura. Completely avoidable!'

'Lots of people are killed with needles, Brian, but life goes on, you ride your luck.'

'That's fine for you to say but what would your parents say if you died on the operating table?'

She gave him a smile and sat on his knee provocatively. 'They'd be angry with you for letting me do it, Brian. They'd think that you were having an affair and I was trying to look young again to win you back. They'd bury me with tears in their eyes, their lost daughter.'

'I hate your cynicism, Laura. It's not funny. They *would* blame me – your parents, your friends, even my parents. They'd think I wasn't capable of making you happy.'

Laura pursed her lips and made a soft tutting sound. 'But honey, that's the point. You can't.'

He went to rise from the chair but she pushed him back and straddled his legs, her eyes laughing at him, her groin achingly close to his. 'I love you, Brian. I'm teasing you. Let's go to bed.'

'With the lights on?'

She shook her head. 'No, with the lights off, Brian. But when I have the surgery you can light up the room like the 4th of July, and I'll still come.'

She was in a strange mood. He wasn't sure how to take her; the reference to the 4th of July hadn't helped either. All it brought to mind was a camping holiday in France as a very young child. His family had rented a mobile home overlooking the sea at La Rochelle. They had travelled for a day and a half to get there by boat and car, and by the time they had arrived, he was as sick as a dog. He decorated the mobile home with the contents of the ferry's restaurant. His father had taken the easy option and gone to the beach with his brothers, but his poor mum had rolled up her sleeves and found the stomach to do the hard work. 'Happy 4th of July, Mary!' he had heard her remark sarcastically, as she cleaned the floor. He had felt ashamed that night, lying in the dark, listening to them laugh on the other side of the partition. He knew it was about him. His father kept making retching sounds; his mother kept squealing and begging him to stop. Then they went quiet, all too suddenly, and he lay there in the dark, with his queasiness and embarrassment, listening to his younger brothers sleep.

'Brian, are you coming or are you going to sit there staring into space?'

'Oh, I'll come all right, whether the light's on or off.'

'I'll bring the magazines with me then, in case you come too quickly.'

He was up from the chair and tickling her now. She deserved to be punished for such a comment. He had never left a woman wanting, except for one time on a college trip to London when an alcoholic haze had clouded his judgement and he had slipped out before making an impression. It was not something he had repeated. It was a matter of pride.

Laura stood before him in the bedroom and took off her bra without removing her clothes. It amazed him how she managed it. Then it was all about the speed of the hands, the clothes would be discarded, the duvet would be lifted and she would be under the covers before he had time to make out a familiar feature in the partial darkness.

He was used to the process by now. He had teased her when they were first married, chased her around the bedroom, pulling at the clothes as she hugged them to her breasts. Some days she'd found it funny and allowed herself to be caught; other days she'd head for the bathroom and lock the door, refusing to come out until he was in the bed with the light off and the duvet over his eyes. Maybe it was time for her to have a new lease of confidence, maybe the operations were necessary. But he didn't really believe that. He just wanted her to be happy, as he was happy with the way she looked, the way her smile was naturally warm and welcoming and her eyes lit up when she was excited about something. He remembered the first time she had talked to him about her decision to become a hydrological engineer. They were both fresh-faced young college students. She had sat in the university bar, still wearing her long woollen scarf, and extolled the virtues of the decision. She would build wells in Africa, help people who had no water and make a difference. He could never imagine how anybody could get that passionate about boreholes and springs, water tables and soils. She was still passionate about her work, although she had never made the move to work abroad. Their marriage had put an end to that dream. Maybe that was part of the reason for her unhappiness now. She had let go of many of her dreams while he was still living his.

The thought of waiting in the hospital while she was given an anaesthetic frightened him. The idea of a knife cutting open her flesh made him feel sick. Would she still look like his Laura when the surgeon was finished? Would she be unnatural and stiff? He could not see why anyone would want to face such a process just to look better on the outside. But then his self-image was good. He fell asleep wondering about where they came from, these insecurities of the woman he loved.

*

The orange juice was sharp. He drank it slowly and thought back to last night. Laura was still in bed. The sex had been more passionate than usual. She had kicked off her clothes and allowed the darkness to clothe her, a darkness interrupted by a band of light from the gap in the curtains.

The alarm went off too early. He'd wanted to stay with her, soak up the feeling of being together. And if he was honest with himself, he wanted her again this morning.

He looked at the thick pile of post she'd left for him on the table and gave a groan. He was not in the mood to sort through it. He only wanted toast, coffee and the radio. He always listened to the morning shows. They comforted him that he wasn't the only one with an early start, and at least he didn't have to feign good humour at seven in the morning. Their voices always amused him, so chirpy and south Dublin. There was probably a school somewhere for smarmy disc jockeys. Then there were the cars that passed him on the way to work, the radio station's logo emblazoned on the side; young blonde women with perfect teeth behind the wheel or the male alternative, his low-cut T-shirt showing off a hairless chest and bronzed skin.

The top envelope contained a charity request. There was at least one a month. They always made him cringe with embarrassment, then think of handing over his next pay cheque to some African nation plagued by AIDS and tuberculosis; but the feeling didn't last long when he saw the articles on government corruption. Of course he knew that this was an excuse for being selfish, a delusion to save him from self-induced poverty.

The next envelope was addressed to Laura. She had already opened it. It was one of those office envelopes with the little window in the front for the address to show through. He had always wondered what sad secretary had invented those envelopes - sitting at her desk, typing away furiously and then suddenly seeing the light and dancing around the office in a solitary conga, thrilled with the fact that she would save time in future when addressing envelopes. Laura had left it in his pile on purpose. Whatever it was, he was meant to read it.

He sighed. Dr Randhani. The doctor's face sprang to mind immediately. It all made sense now: her good mood last night, the conversation about the post.

There was a date for the operation. It was as quick as that. No cooling-off period, no second consultancy, a small card with a time and place printed in black ink. There was also a *Facing the Future* pamphlet, a glossy, colour affair with recommendations for an overnight bag and the cost of the procedures on the back in miniscule print. He felt like tearing it all up and throwing it in the bin. He had so little time to accept the decision. The operation was scheduled for Monday week. Nobody was going to go to hospital that day. He was going to make her stay at home. He laughed at his own mind and the way it thought. He definitely wouldn't like Mondays from now on.

He threw the remaining letters onto the middle of the table and picked up his coffee. He felt helpless. There was nothing he could do to alter the situation. It was her body and she had the right to have it whatever way she wanted, even if that meant carving pieces off and stitching pieces together. He would still love her. She would still be the same person, even if she went ahead with the procedure knowing his reservations. It just meant that their values weren't the same.

The programmes on the television he'd seen hadn't helped: the old women with their poodles, sitting in armchairs, staring at the camera, two black eyes, dried blood under their chin, stitches clearly visible, afraid to smile in case their faces tore apart. They were all in their sixties, pitiful. But Laura was only thirty-six; there was no need for the knife. If she started the process now, what would she be like when she was older? And would he, with his middle-aged spread, galloping body hair and certain baldness, be exchanged for a younger model to go with her new self-image? He had to question his survival in their relationship if she had ideas of permanent youth. He would not be going for any physical remoulding.

Brian stood up from the table and walked into the hallway. The mirror they were given as a wedding present stared back at him with disapproval. 'I remember you when you were thin,' it said. 'I remember you when you could bend down and do your shoelaces up without a chair.'

Insulting piece of wood and glass, he thought. He had a good mind to replace it with a hat stand. On the other hand, it reflected his smile quite favourably, gave his face a good report. He hadn't lost his looks in that department. He could still turn a few heads if they looked from the chin upwards.

It was time for work.

CHAPTER 31

'Do you have a crystal ball, mother?'

'Your father always said I did, God rest his soul.'

Sophia sat down on the chair by the fire and held her hands out to the warmth.

'What's wrong, Sophia?'

'You were right about Joe.'

The old woman put the knitting needles down on her lap, offering her full attention. 'So, go on, tell me what made you change your mind.'

'I went to see him. I thought he was sick because the restaurant's been closed. But he was there, gardening, full of smiles, asked me in for a coffee.'

'Did it stop there?'

'No, we went for a walk, down by the beach. He was fine, in fact very charming.' She felt stupid telling her mother all the details of the day. She was a woman, not a girl straight out of school. She didn't have to continue the story, she could leave it there, have an early night, make an excuse.

'He doesn't have a sister does he?' Marta asked.

'According to the letter he does.'

'You read the letter? The one that Peadar delivered?'

'Yes.'

'How?'

'It doesn't matter.'

'What did it say?'

She wasn't doing well at keeping her counsel. Her mother was unlikely to let the story escape her now.

'It was a letter to his sister. Her name was Rachel. Joe helped her to die.'

Marta didn't register the news. She just sat quietly, hands folded, face expressionless. 'What makes you say that?' she asked.

'Partly the letter, partly something Joe had said before.'

Marta shook her head. 'Well it wasn't euthanasia, I can tell you that much, Laura. I have a feeling it's not even murder. For a smart woman, I think you are missing the obvious.'

Sophia's voice rose. 'Mum, I don't know what it was. It just scares me. There are too many questions.' She didn't really know what she thought. Joe had told her about his sister. He hadn't concealed the photograph and lied to her. It was there on the fireplace, the girl in the cap and gown, the proud parents standing behind her shoulder. Surely if he had killed her, he would have covered up her existence, not boasted about her intelligence and left her writing out on the table. None of it made any sense.

'She might have been mentally ill, Sophia. It might have been a mercy killing to help her to pass over to a better life. Also, he needed a life on his own, I feel.'

'How can you say that? You don't believe in such things. You're devout, Mum.'

'Compassion, Sophia, it's called compassion. Don't you remember your Uncle Amos? Your father helped him.'

Sophia shot her mother another wasted look.

'You can't equate the two things. Amos was almost

eighty-four when he died. He'd suffered from a stroke. His life was just a slow death.'

'Your father still did it, Sophia. He gave him more than he needed.'

She knew her mother was right. They had all visited Amos: her mother, her father and Martin. He'd been sent home from hospital, there was no more they could do for him. He had taken up residence in a wheelchair in the kitchen, his mouth constantly chewing on some non-existent substance, saliva always running down his chin. He frightened her with his lack of life, his vacant eyes and white skin. He looked as though every bit of blood had been drained from his body. He was almost translucent.

'Joe's sister was young. There really is no comparison.'

'Yes, but maybe she was very ill in her own way. Unhappy, depressed. Joe might have had no option but to help her. He might have helped her for good reasons, Sophia. You're like the rest of the world, always seeing things on the surface. I'm probably the least blind person in this village.'

Sophia wanted to believe that Joe was a decent man who had given his sister a way out of her misery. It was just the tone of the letter, the anger in his mother's words, the pleading with her daughter.

'Well something tells me she wasn't ill, Mother. I'm just worried that he's not the nice man I thought he was.'

Marta smiled and rubbed a hand across her scar. 'Are you going to be the psychic one in the family now? Because you're right there, my love. Maybe he's not the man you thought he was at all.'

'No, I'm not being psychic, Mother, but I'm going to be the realist.'

'That's exactly what your father was with Amos. He saw your uncle in practical terms – a man who could do nothing for himself. He knew the man was dead inside. It was just good sense to let his body go the same way as his mind. Amos and your dad believed in heaven. They saw no disrespect in speeding up the journey. Your dad always said that poor Amos was kept alive by modern medicine. In the old days, his stroke would have killed him straight off and he would never have had to suffer the ignominy of sitting in that chair, a nappy between his legs.'

'Why do you keep talking about Amos, Mother? That was ages ago.'

Sophia looked at her mother and felt horribly depressed.

'Does death scare you, Mum?'

'No. I've seen it too many times to worry about it.'

'It scares me.'

'That's because you've lost your faith.'

'Maybe.' Sophia had to think about that. Had she lost her faith?

Her mother's next comment took her by surprise.

'And maybe Joe has faith.'

'What makes you say that? I don't see him that way.'

'And what do you see him as? A heartless murderer?'

She didn't have time to answer. The was a knock at the door. They weren't expecting guests. It was her mother who responded first. 'Did you leave Joe's in a hurry?' It was an astute question.

'Yes.'

'Then that's probably him. Do you want me to answer it?'

'I don't want to talk to him.'

Marta placed her feet inside her slippers and raised herself from the seat. Her jaw was set firm and her eyes were steady. She crossed to the hallway and placed the chain on the hook. Sophia watched her, pleased that she was careful but ashamed that she had allowed her mother to deal with her problem. But that in itself proved something to her; it meant that she really didn't see Joe as a killer. She would never have let her mother face him if she really thought he was dangerous. She just didn't want to talk to him. She felt ridiculous. She had left the letter open on the bed and fled from the house with her clothes barely on straight.

'There's no one here, Sophia. If it was him, he's gone.'

Sophia crossed to the door. It must have been him. Why had he left? 'Shut the door, Mum, it's chilly. I'm tired. I'm going to bed.'

The duvet was cold at first. She pulled it up around her neck and then tucked the bottom edge under her feet. She did this every night. It was her cocoon. The habit had started after a night in her childhood watching a DVD with her brother. She had never felt such fear before; the gruesome deaths of the holidaymakers. Her answer was to tuck the duvet under her legs, as if the fish could come up from the depths of the bed and ravage her. I'm as nuts as my mother, she thought, and I still can't break the habit.

Her bed became warmer. The duvet moulded itself to her shape. She would have preferred another human being to provide her with the same comfort. She had hoped it would be Joe. There was something about him that was endearing. He did have a tender side. She should have stayed and confronted him with the letter. But she had no right to open it in the first place. She had been a nosy cow, looking through his things, searching for something to incriminate him, something to give her a reason to avoid another relationship. She was like Jekyll and Hyde: wanting him one minute, hating him the next.

She was glad there was school tomorrow. She needed an escape from Joe and his secret life. She would shut the classroom door and forget that any other adults existed. Her history book wouldn't alter the facts or change the picture. It was steadfast and loyal.

She didn't need to eat cheese that night. Her nightmares came from reality. She saw a woman, a familiar face, small hands and blue eyes. The woman held a baby in her arms, the little body quiet and limp. It was a scary dream. She recognised the woman's sad smile and tried to run away, but the woman chased her. Sophia usually escaped in her dreams but this end was terrifying. The woman ripped open Sophia's flesh, stuffed the baby into her empty womb and then vanished.

It was safer being awake, placing pleasant thoughts into her mind, giving it alternatives. She tried to think of a summer's day out on the sea, helping her father put down the pots. It wasn't his job; he just did it for a friend. He liked the smell of seawater on his clothes, the saltiness on his lips. He liked the taste of a pint after a thirsty day on the boat.

He'd been dead seven years. Sophia didn't know what dead meant. Was it there or not there? Was there a future or no future? She didn't miss her father. She felt guilty about that. It seemed expected of her. There were other things in her life that she missed, and the most important of these was a child. It was difficult to explain to friends how lucky they were with their children. They only saw nappies and evenings in, sleepless nights and a limited relationship with their husband. She saw something totally different. She saw belonging. The world, as she saw it, was about the bonds made with children. Children would always love their parents but never as much as their parents loved them. And because of that love, human life was guaranteed, cemented.

Joe had changed his life because of his sister. The question was why. He had turned his back on parental acceptance for something else, but she didn't know what.

She knew so little about him and yet she had invested so many thoughts in him. For a brief time, she had visualised him in her future – a house, children, a normal relationship. He had seemed a good opportunity. He owned a business, a place of his own and had no commitments. At least that's what she thought. But now she realised his commitments were to the past. He was caught up in problems that were too hard for her to understand, too awful for her to contemplate. And what had her mother been talking about? Most of what she had said confused Sophia even more.

CHAPTER 32

'BRIAN, IT'S ME. ARE YOU busy?'

He was tempted to be sarcastic. The letter with the appointment date hadn't left him feeling happy. Laura was lucky he had just clinched a deal on a book about lighthouses. It wasn't the type of book he usually accepted – too limited a market, too narrow an appeal. But the writer had made the difference. He had arrived in his office with a carved wooden lighthouse and a captain's hat on his head, his grey hair long and coarse, his beard resembling that of a pirate. Brian knew the author could sell thousands of copies. He was a character from the past, larger than life and brimming with interesting thoughts.

And fact sold these days. Fiction was slow. It was much easier selling a book on the memoirs of a crewman than a literary masterpiece based on a ship. It was crossing over from television: the fly-on-the-wall documentaries in paperback.

'What's up, Laura?' He knew the tone of his voice would upset her.

'You're busy then?'

'No, I'm just raw about the letter in the post.'

'Oh.'

'And I have a meeting in five.' That was a lie; he had no more meetings until after lunch.

'Brian, I wanted to tell you about the appointment myself but I knew you'd be hostile about it.'

'So you thought you'd sleep with me and then leave it with the other letters so I'd read it.'

'It wasn't as calculated as that. I'd tried to get you to look at the post yesterday afternoon. I would have talked to you about it then. But you were more interested in that bloody article.'

'What, the one about the vain woman dying from plastic surgery?'

He knew it was a mistake to have hit so low. Laura didn't reply; she simply hung up. He couldn't say sorry to an engaged tone. She'd taken the phone off the hook. He would probably find no dinner on the table tonight. He contemplated flowers or a bottle of wine but he knew that he had to pay with more than a simple gesture. This would be a grovelling scenario. In fact, she was probably at home right now thinking he'd played into her hands. He had lost the high ground. He wouldn't have the nerve to berate her over the operation now. He'd be on the back foot.

He picked up a pencil, tossed it in the air aggressively and caught it deftly in one hand. Well, she could think again. He wasn't going to let one stray sentence end his campaign to make her change her mind. He had other arguments to deliver. She had to expect more than the odd insult.

He swivelled around in his chair and looked out the window. He had a good view of the quays. There weren't many boats docked today. A Panamanian cargo ship was the nearest. She had a rusty-looking hull and her crew was sitting on the edge of the deck, smoking cigarettes and tossing butts into the river. He wondered where they'd come from and when they were leaving. Part of him wanted to join them – drinking, smoking, a woman in every port, no ties, no decisions, no mortgage to pay. He saw only a small part of the world from his window; they saw the whole world from their boat.

South America was where he wanted to go – high mountains, thunderous waterfalls and huge rivers. It was everything Ireland wasn't. It was the macro to Ireland's micro. His whole life was micro. He had never hit the heights. There were so many things he had wanted to achieve.

Maybe that was the approach he needed to take with Laura. If she wanted her plastic surgery, he wanted his trip of a lifetime. He had asked her to travel with him in the past but she had always said no. She could trade with him: a face-lift for an Amazonian adventure. The idea would terrify her. She hated spiders, snakes, creepy-crawlies and naked people. The jungle had them all. She would point out all the risks, from tropical diseases to cannibalism, and then he could turn around and say that some risks were worth taking. Hopefully she would get the point without too much labouring.

The more he thought about it, the more the idea grew. It was a wonderful idea, flawless in its simplicity. He already envisaged llama rides in the Andes, mountain trekking in Patagonia and diving off Acapulco. He patted his stomach and decided that if he were to be serious about the adventure he would have to visit the gym for some muscle tone. His legs had shrivelled so much that, in shorts, he rather resembled a toffee apple.

He swivelled back to his desk. The dreams could wait.

He had a mountain to climb in his own office first – a postal one. It was amazing how many pieces of junk mail filtered through to his tray. He had given his secretary the job at one stage but he had found her unable to tell the difference between his private post and business. So now she just typed all his replies and handled his calls. She was good at answering the phone – money well spent on elocution lessons. She looked well too. It was part of the reason he had employed her. He didn't see the point in having a secretary who would put off the clients. Or lessen his enjoyment of life.

Not that he would have overstepped the mark. It was just nice to get the chance to flirt or fantasise. He had committed the latter offence on a few occasions. He had gone to bed contemplating her naked body standing before him. He blamed Laura and her ducking and diving. He wanted a woman to look him in the eyes and, button by button, reveal herself.

He didn't feel pathetic or embarrassed about his feelings. He knew they were normal, red-blooded, an important aspect of his life. Mankind would cease to exist without the libido of men like him. He was pleased to be part of the evolutionary chain. He just wished that his part could be more practical than theoretical. The older Laura was becoming, the less practise he was getting. Maybe the surgery would make her feel younger in other ways. It was the one aspect that appealed to him.

As he thought, he worked his way through the mail. An invitation to a charity ball was appealing. He rather liked wearing a dress suit and a bow tie; there were so few occasions to leave the house looking like James Bond. It was possibly a childish reason, but he didn't care. He had all the films on DVD. He was attracted to the macho lifestyle. Laura had once told him that he resembled Sean Connery. It was an image of himself he liked.

The next envelope revealed a brochure for a camp site in the south of France. It looked like every holiday brochure – smiling parents, perfect teeth, happy kids with buckets and spades. It was not the image of the type of holiday he needed. It just reminded him of the children he didn't have.

Laura had wanted them to get a dog last Christmas but he had refused. A dog was an admission that you were a childless couple and intended to remain that way. A dog was a hairy substitute for a child.

A smaller envelope with a handwritten address looked far more interesting. The handwriting was a spidery scrawl, hardly leaving a visible impression. He turned it over. There was no return address, but the postmark on the front caused him to take notice. It was posted from Athlone.

Dear Mr Matthews,

I don't know whether I am making the right decision by writing to you. My son, Kenneth, told me that I should and I have spent the last week thinking about it. Thinking is harder than it used to be. Everything is, since Rachel left. I get confused easily over little things. I have started this letter three times and each time I've thought it too ridiculous to send.

I don't even remember your visit.

And my husband would be angry if he knew I was writing. He's told me to move on, forget about things.

Maybe that's why I've forgotten so much.

But Rachel, I can't forget her. I gave birth to her. I held her hand the first day of school. I took her to the hospital when she fell off the swing and cut her forehead. I stood beside her, my hand on her arm, when they lowered her son's coffin into the grave, my own grandson, little Paulie. These memories I can't forget.

Do you have any children, I wonder? If you do, then you'll know how I feel. You'll know that when they go from you it breaks your heart more than anything else can do.

So I'm sending you the address you want. If you find Joe, give him the photographs I've enclosed. They will remind him of Rachel. Tell him that I don't want him home. He has no place here with us.

Yours sincerely,
Aggie McLoughlin.

Brian held the photographs in his hand. There were about twelve of them, all in colour, some better than others. Each one contained the image of Rachel McLoughlin. Each one showed the little girl whose life had caused such a problem. He felt sad looking at her, knowing she was dead. In one photograph she held a giant lollipop, the red and white psychedelic swirls almost the same size as her face. Her eyes had an impudent look and her grin was devilish as she thrust the lollipop at the camera. In the background was a fairground with a roller coaster, and the sky was dotted with grey clouds. In another she sat on her mother's knee, her hands clutching a rabbit, her face full of excitement. Her mother was smiling.

His favourite photograph was of a teenage Rachel sitting at a table, sucking the top of a biro. In front of her was a wad of papers, and he could imagine that it was her first attempt at writing, maybe the story of *The Olive Tree* in its earliest form. Her hair was short and dark, and she looked thoughtful and reflective.

But this photograph didn't stir him the most. The most moving photograph was taken in a hospital room, the white walls cold and clinical. Sitting up in a bed was a different Rachel, her face slightly puffy, her smile tired but happy, a newborn baby in her arms. On the back were the words *Rachel with Paul*. This was the saddest photograph of them all. He looked at the face in the photograph and then at the address at the bottom of the letter.

'I'm going to find out your story, Rachel. And I'm going to find out what happened to Paul. And this may sound selfish but, if writers and not words sell books, your tragic life might make us a small fortune. Well, enough for some plastic surgery and a new car.'

CHAPTER 33

I sat on the grass and watched the waves breaking over the beach. The tide was coming in and the anchor was still visible. There was a whole story behind the anchor. It came from a British cargo vessel that had sunk off the coast, losing all its crewmembers on 31 December 1940. The ship had been carrying goods for the North but was blown off course. A German U-boat came fast on her heels, hoping to sink another target, not caring to pick up the survivors. It was said that the locals saw the ship go down and put out in their boats, but being a very Republican area, they saved the goods, not the crew.

It was a date that always resonated – New Year's Eve. The crew was probably looking forward to a midnight celebration: drinks in the canteen, music on the wireless, pictures of loved ones passed around. Instead they found the water flooding through their vessel, trapping some inside and washing away their lives and past.

The anchor sat and looked at me. I wanted to heave it out of the sand with my bare hands and throw it back in the water. It would have been quite a feat. It weighed at least half a ton and was twice the height of a man.

I took my phone out of my pocket and scrolled through the list of contacts. There were so many people who no longer factored in my life. They were mostly Rachel's friends and not mine. I didn't know why I had kept their numbers. I suppose it was just a way to hold on to the best of the bad times.

I stopped scrolling at the name Ken. I wouldn't have made the call if I had really thought about it.

'Hi, Ken, it's me.'

'Sorry, who's this?'

'Kenneth, it's Joe.'

The phone went dead. What had I expected? I sat and wondered why, after all this time, I had rung his number. It was probably the letter and Sophia. It was probably the fact that I felt my new life unravelling and I had no one to ask for advice.

I hit the redial button.

'Hello?'

'Please don't hang up. I need to talk to you. You're my brother. That has to mean something.' I waited for a response but he said nothing. 'I know you're angry but I need you to understand.'

I could hear him breathing. I could hear him sighing.

'It's difficult without my family, Kenneth.'

'That was your choice.'

I was being so stupid. He didn't want to know. 'No, it wasn't my choice. I'd no support. I had to leave.'

'Jesus, I don't know who you are any more. I didn't even recognise your voice just now, it's so deep. I don't want to talk to you.'

It had been a mistake to phone. I felt stupid having betrayed myself. There had been nothing to gain. Rachel wouldn't have phoned. She would have had more staying power than me. She had left and not looked back, knowing she would never see them again.

'Is Rachel gone?'

His voice sounded slightly upset. It surprised me.

'Yes.'

'Then fuck you. How could you do it? How could you break Mum's heart? She loved you. Was it because of Paul? Oh what the hell, do you know, I don't fucking care! I'm their only child now and I will take care of them. You just bugger off and live that new life you've always wanted.'

My brother was not one to use bad language and I didn't get a chance to reply. He didn't even wait for my answers. I was left listening to a sharp dial tone. I put the phone back in my pocket.

The anchor was struggling now to keep its head above water. Seagulls were squawking away as they sat on its flat-handled top. The view was beginning to irritate me and I stood up from the grass and took the path to the village. The coffee shop was supposed to reopen tomorrow and I had done very little in preparation.

The path was stony and narrow. It wound around the coast like a snake clinging to a tree, perilously close to the edge. From its highest point it passed the graveyard, where Rosemary Frances Benson was buried. I couldn't resist seeking out the plot where they had placed her remains. It was in the far corner under a row of small trees. The place was dark and wet. A good spot would not have been given to a foreigner who had no relatives to visit. It wasn't a matter of unkindness; it was simply practical. At least they had given her a headstone. It was a chunk of granite. On a card attached to flowers, someone had written a small inscription: *No man is an island.* I thought it was a strange epitaph; she had been sent to her grave in a foreign land with no family or friends to mourn her passing. She was an island in our midst.

A horrible thought crept through me. I could see my grave placed beside hers. A village standing around the plot, looking down at the freshly dug hole but not shedding tears; Fran and her brothers and father standing side by side, whispering and shaking their heads; Sophia not even in attendance. There was even the same granite block for my name and the inscription *God has claimed another of his children.*

A silly pair of dead heads – Rosemary Benson and Joe White! From another grave, I picked two flowers from an overflowing pot and laid them over Rosemary's resting place. I didn't want to lie in death beside her. I didn't want it to be my future. I had to talk to Sophia. I had to tell her the truth. There was no point facing the future with the past holding me back. I had to give her the respect of the truth, give her the opportunity to love me with all my failings. I stood up from the grave and looked out at the sea. It wasn't the worst place to be buried.

The road to the café was quiet. I had expected the odd car to pass by, but it was Wednesday and most of the locals were at a special Mass. It was one of the reasons I had ventured out. I knew I'd be alone in the village.

The café was cold. I switched on the heating and opened the blinds in the kitchen. There was no movement on the pier. The boats were nestled together in the harbour. The paint flaked from the walls of the ice plant and the crane was a rusty red. And yet there was an attractiveness to it all – it reflected a community's hard existence as it strove to survive against the odds.

I flicked the switch on the oven, then flicked it off just as quickly. My mind wasn't ready to cook food and bake bread. I took my jacket from the back of the chair and headed for the pub. It would be quiet and I could drink my pint alone.

'A pint of Guinness please, Peggy.'

'Haven't seen you for a while, Joe.'

'I've been doing some work on my garden.'

She smiled. 'Not so easy around here making plants grow.'

'Yeah, so I'm finding out. I think it'll be a few shrubs and a lot of hope.'

I took the pint and sat in the corner. I was not planning on standing by the bar discussing the futility of gardening.

'Hi, Peggy, can I have a Coke please?'

Recognising the voice didn't make me happy. I was not ready for honesty just yet. Sophia was obviously not ready either. She saw me and blushed, not a bright red blush that others would notice but a blush nonetheless.

We stared at each other for a moment and I saw that Peggy was watching us, curious about the distance between us.

'You're not at the Mass, then, Sophia?' Peggy asked, holding out the glass.

'No. I was in Galway.'

'Shopping?'

'No, visiting my friend, Josie. You know, the one who married the Turkish guy. I needed to escape the village and Josie's always up for a laugh.'

She had raised her voice slightly so that I could hear. Peggy noticed but didn't react.

'Oh we all need that. It can be too quiet here sometimes.

A bit isolated without the odd day out.'

Sophia sat up on a bar stool and smiled at Peggy.

'To tell you the truth, Peggy, it can be a bit lonely if you don't have someone to share it with.'

Peggy nodded and wiped the counter as if the bar had been full of customers all day and needed a good cleaning. 'I know what you mean. Since Jack passed away, I've often wished he'd lasted longer and yet, when he was alive, I often wished him dead.' Peggy laughed.

Sophia looked at her and shook her head. 'You're an awful storyteller. You know that's not true.'

I watched them talking. I wanted to be elsewhere but I would have felt ridiculous leaving a full pint. There was also the problem that I liked looking at Sophia. I liked being in her presence. It made me feel certain that I had to tell her the truth. But how to tell her was the issue. It couldn't be in a pub or the café. It had to be somewhere even quieter. And how would I get her on her own? She had read the letter. I had found it on the bed. She must have looked at it and made some kind of dreadful assumption. She had left so quickly.

'Joe, do you need anything else?' Peggy asked. 'I need to slip in the back for a minute and put on the tea.'

I looked up at Peggy. Sophia was staring at her glass, ignoring the fact that I was there.

'No, I'm fine, thanks.'

Peggy disappeared through the door into her house and Sophia waited until she was gone and then left. She hadn't been able to look me in the eye. I suppose it was naïve of me to think that she would have wanted to talk to me. I had shown her a strange time recently. Maybe I was wrong to think that I could make her a part of my life.

There were bound to be other women, other opportunities. Maybe Rachel had been right: deciding to choose the first woman who looked my way had been ridiculous. Sophia was not the only woman in the West of Ireland and I was not the worst-looking man in the area.

'Is Sophia gone, Joe?'

I didn't know why she was asking, as the glass was empty and so was the stool.

'Yes, Peggy.'

'Did I detect a bit of unease between the pair of you?'

Her honesty amazed me. I didn't really know Peggy that well and it would have been more normal for her to ignore me. I looked back at her but didn't say a thing.

'She's my first cousin, you know. Her dad and my mother were brother and sister. She's a good woman. Talks to me a lot.'

It was a factor I'd forgotten; people were usually related in this bloody village.

'She's had a lot of problems recently with the men in her life. Wouldn't want to see her hurt again.'

'Peggy, I like Sophia. I don't want to hurt her either, but if you don't mind, whether you're related or not, it's none of your business.'

Peggy looked at me from over the counter and shook her head. 'And if you don't mind me saying, Joe, you're a bit new in the village to go making enemies.'

I'd had enough of her advice and her bar. I stood up and put my half-empty glass on the counter. There was no need to say anything. I felt I had lost my first battle and was angry at the encounter.

CHAPTER 34

THE DINNER WAS READY WHEN Brian got home. He was surprised. He had presumed Laura would have eaten a salad and retired to bed to watch television. But she was standing in the kitchen listening to the radio, arguing back to some announcer about the merits of social housing. She hadn't even heard him enter the house. She had laid the kitchen table with candles and a bottle of red wine and was putting the finishing touches to dessert.

'Laura.'

She jumped nervously and turned to him.

'I didn't hear you come in. How was your day?'

'I thought you weren't going to talk to me.'

'I don't want us to argue, Brian. I'm sorry I didn't tell you about next Monday. I was wrong.'

'It just seems so soon.'

'I know. It took me by surprise too, but seemingly he's always that quick.'

'In case the patient changes their mind, probably.' Brian knew it wasn't the right thing to say. She had made an effort. 'Sorry, I didn't mean that.'

The apology seemed to work; she smiled and pointed to the table. 'I thought we'd have a nice meal and talk.'

'Okay. I'll just go upstairs and change. I've something to tell you too.'

The bedroom was tidy. She'd been cleaning again. These days she was continually cleaning. He sat on the bed and undid his tie. He hated wearing ties. It was a hatred he had picked up in school, the Brothers always fixing the knot with their clammy fingers, their eyes sharp and silent. In fact it wasn't just the wearing of ties that he hated. He hated school, and ties were a reminder of those days, the stultifying boredom of classrooms, rows of chairs and desks, the teacher standing at the top, suspicious of anybody at the back, his friend pelting his head with paper bullets, the queues at lunchtime for a meal of beans and sausages. He had always thought it was the worst combination to feed adolescent boys. The first class after lunch was the worst, with all the noxious fumes.

He pulled off his shirt and reached for a T-shirt from the cupboard. The wedding picture sitting on top of the cupboard caught his eye.

'I was looking at our wedding photograph on the cupboard upstairs. We really haven't changed much.'

'You have such a rose-coloured view of everything, Brian.'

She sat down at the table and poured them each a glass of wine.

'What if I don't like the change this Dr Randhani makes?'

'Brian, please don't start. I've made the meal. Let's enjoy it.'

He picked up his fork and realised it was useless for eating crab claws. 'Laura, you mean everything to me. I don't want you to change. I don't want a wife whose face looks back at me with a permanently surprised expression.

And will you stop at one operation if it goes well? I doubt it. You'll be back for more in another five years and it will continue after that until he has all our spare cash and you have a plastic face.'

She was up from the table and staring down at him menacingly. 'You can't let it go, can you? You're like a spoilt child who thinks everything revolves around how he feels. This is not for you, Brian. It's for me. And if it makes me feel better, then I will do it again and again and again if I think it's necessary. This is becoming more in terms of being myself, and if that means being myself without your permission, then so be it.'

She stopped and looked at him for a response. He didn't feel like giving any. She sat down and started eating her dinner.

'Eat, Brian. It annoys me that I've gone to so much trouble and you're ruining it.'

The food was good but he couldn't really taste it. He wanted to leave, go down to the pub and sit in front of a pint. Sitting with her felt empty and sad, she was so stubborn, so difficult to talk to when her mind was decided.

'I want to go on a holiday.'

She looked at him, puzzled.

'Where?'

'I want to go to South America.'

'Are you taking the proverbial, Brian?'

'No, I'm being serious. I want us to go trekking down the Amazon. I've told you before about it and I want to go before I'm too old.'

She rose from the table and brought over the food from the oven. She had made his favourite dish – chicken chasseur. She had even added extra mushrooms and red peppers. It made him feel like softening but the cause was too important.

'South America, the Amazon? Are you really serious, Brian?'

He was amazed that she hadn't worked out his ploy. 'I've always wanted to see the place and I think this summer would be the right time.'

She put a fork of food into her mouth and chewed it slowly. She was thinking. He could see the cogs whirring. She was planning her answer carefully. She was wondering how to make her escape.

'Do you think it's a good idea with your father in and out of hospital?'

'As you said yourself, it's the same as usual. He's always going to suffer. I don't think I should wait around in case anything worse befalls him.'

He could see her struggle. There was no escape from the truth.

'Brian, I can't go there. You know I hate spiders, snakes and all that kind of stuff. Isn't there somewhere else you want to go?'

He smiled. The victory was his. 'But didn't you say that in a marriage we had to understand the needs of the partner, be willing to accept what they needed.'

The penny had dropped now. She was up from the table and moving to the sink.

'You stupid, childish bastard.'

He smiled again.

'Don't smile at me. Is that what all this is about? Me and my surgery, you and your jungle? They're not the same, Brian. You really are a selfish shit. I want to change the way I see myself, you want to go on a bloody holiday.'

Suddenly he was feeling small. His mood changed completely.

The box room was cold. The sofa bed was uncomfortable. He wasn't inebriated enough to fall asleep under the spare quilt. He hadn't been given the chance to apologise. She had stormed out of the kitchen, strode upstairs and locked the bedroom door. He had thought of knocking and asking for forgiveness but the thought was transitory; she was too angry.

He picked a book from the shelf and opened the first page. It was one Laura had bought. The title was enough to make him want to burn it. He could never understand what she saw in romantic fiction. The women were always desperate and shy and the men were always quiet and moody. How they ever got together was a mystery and not a romance. The only positive thing that the books had going for them was that they were truly an anaesthetic.

He closed his eyes and allowed the book to fall to the floor. In front of his eyes he could see a hospital bed, a baby and a mother. He hadn't had the opportunity to tell Laura about R. J. McLoughlin. She would have found answers to the puzzle. The baby would have posed no problem to her powers of deduction.

He thought of the work he had planned for tomorrow. Tomorrow was a slow day in the office. He would ring in and tell them he was taking the day off and possibly two. He could travel to Galway and find Joe White and learn all the answers for himself. It would take his mind off Laura and give her the space to calm down. And if he came back with a book deal nearer to signing, then she might even forgive him. It was unlikely but possible. In any case, he would be spared the cold glances for the next two days.

CHAPTER 35

Fran placed the chairs behind the tables and put the broom back in the storeroom.

'I'll be going now, Joe.'

'Okay, thanks.'

'What time do you want me tomorrow?'

'Eleven will be fine.'

I heard the jangle of the bell as she left and was surprised by the same sound two minutes later.

'What did you leave behind?'

'A lot of unanswered questions.'

Sophia. I hadn't expected to hear her voice again. I had given up on the chance of a resolution. I didn't want to end up offending any more cousins. She had entered the kitchen and was standing looking at me.

'I think we should talk.'

She had nothing to lose. I had everything.

'I'd like to understand about your sister.'

The truth had never been a part of my life. Now I thought about my future, realising that nothing had changed. I wanted to lie again, cover the truth in a web of deceit. I couldn't explain thirty years of my life to this woman, no matter how I felt about her.

'You shouldn't have read the letter, Sophia. It was none of your business.'

The best form of defence was attack. Some idiot with a bloodied nose must have written that nugget of wisdom.

'I know I shouldn't have read the letter, but I did, and now I want to ask you what happened to your sister. I thought we had something going between us, Joe, but there can't be if I don't trust you.'

'But I can't trust you either. You looked through my things.'

She sighed and turned to the door.

'Sophia, you don't understand. I do want to explain. I just don't know how to.'

'Joe, I want to be with you. I don't know why, but I do. If we can just sort this out, then maybe there's something to work with.'

'Do you want a cup of coffee?'

'Yes, please.'

There was no point letting her leave. I wanted her in my life too. I had recognised that the first moment she had walked into the restaurant.

How strange life is when you think you have all the answers but then it finds more questions for you to answer again. I thought I could make a new life, leave the past behind me, but here it was following me like a pathetic dog wanting a home.

'You take milk and no sugar, don't you?'

'It's good that you remember.'

'I run a café. I have to pay attention to details.'

'You don't have to be so defensive.'

'You don't know what I'm about to tell you.'

She shrugged her shoulders and looked at me with a faint smile. 'The truth is always the best.'

I envisaged a juggler in the circus trying to keep all

his balls in the air at the one time, practising for hours in the loneliness of his caravan, hoping nobody would see through his fear of failure. I was like that juggler with no practise time. I had all the balls in the air at one time and no hands to catch them. My hands were tied, tied by the past.

We sat at a table. I liked my Bare Bones Café – the seats were comfortable and the lines clean, the atmosphere pleasant, even when empty.

'Are you sure you want to know?'

'Are you sure you want a relationship with me?' she said.

I looked into her eyes and I saw what I wanted. It was comforting.

She said nothing. We sat for a few moments in silence. I was desperately trying to find the words. We all do that. We don't just spew the truth out onto the floor; we cloak it, wrap it up in softness.

'Rachel and I were twins.' The words came. They surprised me. I wasn't expecting them.

'She was born two minutes before. It was how our lives existed from that moment on – she led and I followed. We were inseparable. I couldn't live without her, and although she hated me trailing after her, she loved me too.'

Sophia said nothing. She held my hand across the table. Her fingers were warm.

'My parents loved Rachel. My mother loved her little girl, dressed her in flowery patterns and put ribbons in her hair. They didn't need me. They already had Kenneth. At least that's the way I felt at the time.' When I said the words, they sounded pathetic. They sounded like a long moan forced despairingly from a tube, the hollowness of the tube all that's left behind.

She squeezed my hand. I hadn't lost her yet. She was still on my side.

'Go on, don't stop.'

Her voice was soothing. I was happy to have her attention.

'Our togetherness was on every level. It was emotional, spiritual and physical.'

I could feel her hand recoil slightly.

'You slept with your own sister?'

'That would be too hard a way to see it. We were just very close.'

'How close?'

'Close enough for me to die when she slept with him.'

'Who's "him"?'

'Her boyfriend. I didn't want him around. I hated it when he touched her. I wanted to shout and hit out but I couldn't. And she hated it too. I know she did. She wanted me.'

'Joe, what are you saying?'

I wasn't prepared to stop and answer questions.

'But then it all went so badly wrong. She got pregnant. He dumped her.' The lies just kept coming now. Once I had started, they poured out easily, covering the cracks in my new life. 'She felt used. She couldn't face me with her bump, showing me how much she had been with him. It was there all the time, a sign of his intrusion into our life together.'

I rose from the table. She wouldn't hold my hand any more. Hundreds of thoughts were crashing around my mind, aching to escape, claim a place in the spotlight. I wanted to secure them. I wanted to hold them in check, preserve myself, but it was becoming too late to salvage self-respect.

'I did kill her, Sophia.'

'Jesus, Joe, what are you saying? I want to go. You're scaring me.'

'But only after she'd lost Paul. It's what we agreed to do. I injected her knowing that it would be the end. But it's what she wanted. She asked to die. Her only reason for living was Paul and she felt that God had taken him away from her because of me. It was too much to face life without him.'

I turned to face her. She was holding the coffee cup with both hands, her knuckles white. I knew I had to soften the blow, dress it in a cloak. Its nakedness was abhorrent.

'Sophia, I am not as bad as you think. I loved Rachel. I miss her. But she was ill. She had contracted it from him and then he left her with the illness and a baby. She didn't want a slow death. She was full-blown. It would have only been a matter of time. She couldn't tell our parents. She didn't want them to know.'

'Are you saying she had AIDS?'

I nodded.

What was I doing? What had I left my old life for? I needed to be honest but I didn't have the guts to open myself up. I was scared that everything I had done would be rejected, so it was better to tell the lies and not hear that rejection.

'But Joe, there are powerful new drugs now. There was no need for such drastic action. This makes no sense. I really can't take all this in. I'm sorry, I know this is not what you want to hear but I need to go home.'

I couldn't reply. I felt numb. I had cast the lies out and they had landed on my victim; but I didn't know where they would take root, and whether they would grow into something good or die where they sat. A knot was forming in my stomach and I felt sick. I felt the world was chasing me into a corner again. There was nowhere to hide and there was no comfort zone.

I heard the door of the café shut. I felt the coldness of the air that rushed in and I looked out at the harbour with its boats and rusting wreckage. The village no longer looked like home. It was tarnished with my story. I could feel every curtain twitch and every eye stare and I knew that the gamble I had taken might have all been in vain. Why hadn't I told her everything? Why had I cloaked it in even more lies?

I cleared the coffee cups from the table, closed the blinds and headed for the door. I wanted to be back in the cottage. I needed to feel secure.

The evening was fine. The sea was calm, with no white waves or flashes of sunlight on rising spray. The walk improved my mood. Maybe I could persuade her that I was basically a good man. I wanted her to accept me. I wanted a woman to accept me.

CHAPTER 36

'Are you awake, Brian?'

'That depends. Are you here to give out to me?'

'No. Can I have a hug?'

Brian pulled back the duvet on the small sofa bed and wriggled over to make space for his wife. He didn't know what to say. He didn't know why she was there. He just liked the feel of her body in his arms. It always made him feel good. It was as if his arms had a purpose greater than the ordinary everyday things they did. He squeezed her gently; she didn't pull away. He was afraid to say anything in case he said the wrong thing. He didn't want her to leave as quickly as she came.

'Brian?'

'Hmm?'

'I don't know what it is with me. I don't want it to come between us. I don't know why I feel this way.'

'What way, Laura?' He wouldn't presume to know. He had done that before and been horribly inaccurate.

'Remember when we were in college and you dumped me for that girl in First Med?'

He didn't know whether it was wise to remember, but he was tired and couldn't play games all night.

'Yes, I remember, but I was foolish and it was only for a short time.'

'But it happened.' She was looking up at him now, her eyes soft and thoughtful. 'And it happened again, two years later, with a different girl.'

He didn't like the path this conversation was taking. It spelled trouble.

'I know but I was young, we both were. I met you before I had time to experience things. I had to get it out of my system.'

'I wasn't enough for you, Brian. You left me and went looking.'

'But I came back.'

'Part of me wishes you hadn't.'

He hadn't expected that. He felt arrogant and stupid. He had always thought that she loved him.

'I love you, Laura.'

'I think that's the problem, Brian. I don't think that I've ever really trusted that. I think I believe that you just came back to me because I was available and wanted you.'

He turned on his side and looked at her, puzzled. 'You can't really believe that. You're just going through some sort of crisis at the moment.'

Her angry scream came from deep within. 'The crisis is you, Brian. I'm afraid of losing you.'

She had never hit him before in all their years together. Her hand caught him on the shoulder and again on the cheek. It smarted but it didn't hurt as much as the words had.

'Stop, Laura. Please stop and think sensibly about all this.'

Her eyes were misting.

'I know I left you twice but I came back, and not because you were available but because I missed you, I loved you. I was just too damn stupid and immature to realise it. I thought college was meant to be about girls and lots of them, not one girl for the whole four years. I loved you but I was too stupid to know that straight away. I wanted to have my own time first. I was selfish.'

She was crying. He held her in his arms but he couldn't stop her tears.

'I wish you'd known how much it hurt, Brian. I was so pleased when you chose me as your girlfriend. You were so popular, so good-looking. I would have done anything for you. I feel stupid even saying this.'

'Why didn't you tell me back then? Why did you hold it inside all these years?'

She shrugged her shoulders and wiped a hand across her cheek. 'I suppose I was too grateful that you came back to me. And that's my lack of confidence. But now I'm scared Brian, I'm really scared.' She had left the comfort of his arms and was standing by the window.

'Scared of what, Laura? Scared of what?'

'Scared that as we get older, you'll not want me anymore, that you'll look at my baggy eyes and sagging breasts and want someone else, just like you wanted someone else before.'

He stood up from the sofa and walked towards her. He felt so stupid. He hadn't seen this coming. He had thought they were happy. Except for the recent arguments over surgery, he had thought they were a good couple. He had never thought that he was the reason for her insecurities.

'Please, Brian, don't touch me. I feel foolish.'

'Laura, I do love you. I'm sorry I've made you feel this way but it was all such a long time ago. Don't you think I would have left you before this if I wasn't happy with you? I don't want anybody else. I'm looking forward to us growing old together.'

'Growing old, Brian, that's the problem. Maybe I will grow old before my time, maybe my hands will be gnarled and useless before I'm sixty. Maybe I don't want to be older.'

She put her face in her hands and rubbed her eyes furiously as if she was trying to make the whole scene disappear.

'I know this is probably silly in your eyes. You're standing there now wondering what kind of idiot you married, wishing you'd picked one of the other girls instead.'

He had to interrupt. He hated the insult of it all. 'You're so wrong, Laura. I'm standing here wishing you'd come back to bed and lie in my arms and believe that I love you. That's the truth.'

She was tempted by his offer. He could see it in her eyes. But she shook her head and folded her arms against any approach.

'I can't, Brian. I need to feel secure with you and I don't.'

'Please, Laura, let's go back to our bed and talk.'

'I don't want you to hug me. We'll just talk.'

'Okay.'

The room was strangely tidy. The bedspread was perfectly in place and the pillows plump and unused.

'I thought you'd gone to bed.'

She looked at him and shook her head. 'I didn't want to. I sat on the floor and waited for you to come.'

'Laura, you slammed the door and left me in the kitchen. I thought you wanted space.'

'No, Brian, you didn't want the bother of a fight. You didn't care enough about me to come after me.'

'Maybe I was just tired, Laura.'

'Maybe you don't know how to talk to me.'

There were no answers springing to mind that he felt she would accept. She had that look on her face he had seen before. She believed in her own worthlessness. It would take a miracle to convince her tonight. But she was right in one small way – had he cared enough to try?

'Laura, marry me?'

'What? Don't be stupid, we're already married. I don't need your inane sense of humour now.'

'I mean it, Laura. This isn't a joke. Marry me again. Let's exchange vows for a second time, with flowers and music and anything you want.'

'Are you serious?'

'Yes. You don't think I love you. I'm saying that I would marry you again without any hesitation.'

She was laughing and crying. He couldn't understand the response but it was better than another slap across the face.

'God, Brian, that's the most romantic thing you've ever said to me, but not because I want to marry you again. I've always thought the people who do it are ridiculous. But it means a lot to me that you'd go through it again just for me.'

'Yeah, I would. But you've just hurt my feelings. I would have loved to exchange vows again.'

His smirk gave him away. She dug him playfully in the ribs and he knew he had broken the ice between them. She was in his arms now, the duvet pulled up to her neck, her face resting on his shoulder.

'Laura?'

'Yes.'

'I know you don't want to exchange vows but maybe we could go away on a second honeymoon or something.'

'What? Like the Amazon?'

He was pleased that she was teasing him but he wanted her to understand that it was a serious suggestion. 'No, maybe the States, something for both of us.'

'Can we afford to?'

'Things aren't that bad. We could stretch to it. And maybe I'll be handling a bestseller soon.'

'What do you mean? Did something else come in that you really like?'

'No. I heard from the mother in Athlone. She sent me an address for the brother, for Joe.'

'Oh, God, are you going to go and talk to him.'

'Why not? It's a mystery I'd like to solve.'

'He might be a dangerous man.'

'I don't think so. I think you were right before. It was probably a helping hand in her suicide, something he had to do. Look, why don't you come with me. We'll spend the next few days together. It could be good for us. We haven't had time away for a while.'

She tightened slightly. He could feel it in her shoulders.

'I'm still going to the appointment on Monday, Brian.'

'I know. That's not what I was trying to do. Tomorrow's Thursday. We could drive to Galway, visit this guy Joe and spend Friday and Saturday just the two of us, with nothing to do. I'll bring you home on Sunday.'

He waited for a reply but she said nothing.

'Laura, I haven't forgotten what you said earlier. I hate the fact that you don't trust me. I want to spend time with you, convince you that I love you.'

'You must think I'm so silly.'

'No, actually, I don't. I just wish you had said all this a long time ago. I thought when you married me that you realised I wanted you above anyone else.'

'I thought I was still just a passing phase. Loads of married men have affairs.'

'You thought wrong. I love you, Laura. Maybe I don't say it often enough but I do.'

'Do you really want me to come?'

'Yes.'

'What about my work?'

'Ring up and make an excuse. Or even better, come clean and say that you need a few days away. They owe you some in that place.'

She hugged him. He hoped that it was the first of many. He didn't like the thought that she doubted him, but at least he understood now why she wanted the surgery. She felt she had to compete with younger women – the women he was foolish enough to look at when they walked past or sat at a nearby table. He had presumed that Laura knew he had no desire to be with them. He wasn't arrogant. He knew they would look at his expanding stomach and hairy chest and pass him over for a younger man. Looking at other women was like walking around an art gallery – there were some you liked and others that bemused you, but you didn't want to buy them or take them home. She had no right to mistrust him for looking. Women did the same, they noticed men too. Laura had said it herself.

The problem all came down to lack of confidence. He knew that. He also worried that the plastic surgery wouldn't cure the problem.

CHAPTER 37

MARTA FOLDED HER HANDS ON her lap and waited patiently for the adverts to end.

'Do you think *The Late Late Show* will ever end?'

'Oh God I hope so.'

Marta shook her head and frowned.

'Sophia, your tongue's too sharp. I happen to like it and I don't want it to end.'

'Well, don't worry, it probably won't, Mother. I read somewhere that it's the world's longest-running show.'

'That's good. They won't want to lose the record then.'

Sophia looked at her mother and smiled. 'I'm sorry I was so negative. Why do you like it so much?'

'Because I can listen to the interviews and hear the music. I don't need to see it to enjoy it. It's radio on the box.'

The fire was down for the evening and her mother was sitting on the armchair, moving her feet around in her slippers to stop them from stiffening.

'Sophia, where were you earlier? You never said you were going out.'

'I went to the village. We needed milk.'

'You were always the same as a child, a terrible liar.'

'And you've always been too difficult.'

'I could be hurt by that,' her mother said.

'I could be annoyed with your interference in my life.'

'So where were you? Visiting Joe?'

It was easier to leave the room. Her mother could sit and listen to the television on her own. Sophia wasn't prepared to be badgered into submission. She wanted her thoughts to herself. It wasn't much to ask for at her age.

Her bedroom was cold. She had left the window open and the evening was entering like an unwanted guest. She closed the metal clasp and looked out at the night. The air was still. There was nothing moving outside. It was eerily calm. She could imagine the world refusing to turn, tired of all the misery it had to carry. Miserable people like Joe's sister, like Rachel.

She hadn't asked half of the questions that had entered her head in the café. She had sat there and listened, empty from the thought of Joe's actions. But now she wanted to know; she needed to know how exactly Rachel's baby had died, if she and Joe had consummated their relationship, and how he had helped her to die. She wanted to understand how he could have given her the injections if he really loved her. It all seemed too strange. Had he really admitted to incest or was she confused by his words and her feelings for him?

She didn't like the thought that she had stripped to her flesh and waited for him in his bed. She had allowed him to kiss her. His lips might have kissed Rachel's. He might have kissed them before he had ended her life. It all seemed so unreal; she could have shared a bed with a cold, calculating man.

She didn't know him that well. She shouldn't have trusted her emotions.

Sophia sat on the bed and curled her legs underneath

her. It was a strange way to feel, the way she felt now. She had gone to bed only last week thinking of his body next to hers, breathing in his maleness, allowing him to make love to her. The mere thoughts had brought her close to satisfaction. It had been a long time since she had been with a man.

And it had been Joe who had given her those feelings. Tonight she wanted to wash him off her skin as if their near intimacy in his bed had not been so close. And the only difference between then and now was the letter she had read and his revelation of a life she couldn't understand. It would have been so easy not to have opened that letter, to have left it unread. It would have been so easy to have given herself to him.

The thought made her scared. The world was full of people she didn't understand and they all had so many secrets. She wanted to feel safe, but that required trust, and she didn't feel very trusting tonight. If she hadn't read that letter, would he have told her anything?

She swung her legs from the bed to the floor and slipped her feet into her shoes. She had seen a film once where the woman had left her house in the middle of the night and visited the murderer. The whole audience had begged the naïve woman to stay at home. They had foreseen the calamitous ending of the film just as the director had wanted, but the heroine still went. She went out of some perverse need to see evil up close and personal, the same need makes drivers slow down as they pass an accident or children stare at a disfigured face.

'Mum, I'm going out for a while. I won't be long. I just need some fresh air.'

The small figure in the chair waved a hand over her

head and said nothing. She was concentrating on the words from the television, an agreeable smile on her lips.

There was a veil of clouds across the moon. They added to the mystery of the evening. They made Sophia laugh at herself. She was creating tension and drama to replace the monotony of her everyday life. She was walking down the road to Joe's house to feed her need for excitement.

It was a strange thing to do, given all the reasonable arguments against such a visit. If he was a dangerous man, she had no way to protect herself. She hadn't brought a knife from the kitchen or any other weapon. She hadn't even considered how she was going to approach him. He had seemed calm and rational in the café. He'd not appeared like a cold-blooded killer. He'd told his story quietly and humbly as if he knew it might jeopardise their future, but also in the knowledge that the truth had to have its place in their lives.

A car passed her too closely. It caused the hem of her skirt to lift slightly. She watched as its lights disappeared around the corner. An ironic thought occurred to her. It could have been the same car that killed the American tourist. She felt guilty because she couldn't remember her name. It was there on the tip of her tongue but it refused to come. It began with a *b* or an *r* or something similar. She wished it would come to her. It made her feel uncaring. The poor woman was lying in a cold plot of earth. She shivered slightly. It was a dark night. The car could have hit her. It could have left her on the side of the road, waiting for someone to notice the crumpled mess.

Turning back was an option. She didn't want to be in

danger at all. There was the desire to be in front of the television listening to her mother's criticisms and dealing with the boredom.

The road dipped. She could see Joe's house on the hill. She convinced herself that her thoughts were getting the better of her. There would be no danger. He would open the door in his dressing gown and slippers and offer her a coffee. He would not hold any malice; he would be tired and accommodating.

Her mother would have called it intuition. Sophia called it deduction. But as she stood outside his house, the door shut and the lights out, she knew there was something wrong. A wind chime was clanging in the wind. It was discordant, annoying. She put her ear to the door and listened as if the house was going to tell her something. It didn't make a noise; it didn't give away any occupant, it merely groaned, as old houses are prone to do. Then she felt silly because if he opened the door, she would look ridiculous, like an amateur sleuth on a bad day.

She stood in front of the oak door. It was large, almost impenetrable, and there was no doorbell. It was something she hadn't noticed before. She had always arrived with Joe or when he was out in the garden. It was a well-kept garden. That was part of the problem – his profile didn't really scream threatening, although sometimes she felt his tidiness might border on obsession.

She turned to go home. She felt stupid standing in the dark. She wished that she had listened to her inner voice, the one that had told her to ignore Joe and find someone less complicated, more suitable. The only problem was that she couldn't listen; she was receiving interference from other inner voices, voices that disagreed, that saw a chance of a relationship with someone deeper and more thoughtful.

Maybe she'd just walk around the house and look in the front windows. She could see if there were any lights on. Although that was stupid too, it was better just to knock on the door and wait. She'd seen his car in the driveway. He was probably at home.

Having knocked, she expected him to answer. She was irritated when he didn't. She knocked again, louder this time, almost impertinently. The oak door remained defiantly closed, and walking around the house became more of an option.

There was nothing to see. It was dark. She nearly fell, stumbling over the tufts of grass. And it was all in vain. The curtains were drawn and only a sliver of moonlight showed her the path back to the driveway and the safety of the gravel. She was angry with Joe now. He had no right to be out when she needed questions answered. She rummaged in her coat pocket for a piece of paper and a pen. She could leave a note. It would make her feel that her visit hadn't been worthless. But she had no paper, only a red biro. It was obviously not meant to be. This was one of those days when her sun sign was in juxtaposition with everything. Not that she believed in any of that rubbish; it was just that there were days when it seemed that the whole solar system was against her and she was fighting it alone.

CHAPTER 38

I LOOKED IN THE MIRROR. My face looked well. There was no point in shaving. I wasn't going anywhere. I'd stopped in the pub on the way home. It was rare for me to drink more than the limit but I really didn't care. Although I felt guilty when I thought of other potential Rosemary Bensons that could have been out there, with me swerving past them, and I was glad when I was home in my cottage without having injured another human being. I'd done enough damage, hurt too many people. I was drunk and self-indulgent. Morose feelings were pouring out. The mirror in the bathroom sighed at my reflection.

Strange places, bathrooms. They can give so much pleasure: the hot, steamy bath, the invigorating shower, the quiet time spent alone with book and a candle. But then there's the starkness as well, the emptiness of nudity, the self-image shattered by reality.

I kept thinking of Sophia and the look on her face.

Things hadn't changed. I had only swapped one lie for another. I had stood in the restaurant with her eyes watching me and told another fiction. Why had I thought that I could hide the past? There was no escape from it. In order to be close to someone else I had to be honest. I had to give them the whole story, otherwise I would be living a different lie for the rest of my life.

I liked Sophia. There had been a promise in the way we talked, something beyond the usual. Her initial cagey approach broke into warmer moments and gave them more resonance. She was quirky, interesting, and I found her attractive. And she found me attractive too. I had seen it in her look and loved seeing it there, as if my new life had been vindicated. But I had been naïve. I had been foolish to think I could live without Rachel and keep her death a secret.

I slammed my fist into the mocking glass. The mirror fractured; blood from my knuckles dripped into the sink. This was not the way I had seen the story ending. I was meant to find love, get married and have children. I was meant to cheat the odds and make sense of the imperfection that was me.

My face looked odd now in the splintered reflection. It looked like two people trying to form into one. There was no togetherness, no cohesion. I could see Rachel in my eyes and I wished that she were with me in the bathroom.

As a child I had sat on a beach and refused to take part in a holiday. I was thirteen and I was going through puberty. It had been a shock to my world, my understanding of life. Rachel had developed breasts, was bleeding once a month and becoming moody. I couldn't stand it. I didn't want anything to change. I didn't want to grow up with her. I wanted to do things my way.

We live in such a visual world. We are what others see. I didn't want them to see me on that beach. I sat on the sand and covered my body. Kenneth helped me. He used a spade and heaped sand over my arms and legs until eventually I was just a head, sticking out of the sand, with a straw hat to protect me from the sun. I stayed there happily, the grains of the beach settling into my clothes, the dampness from the percolating sea cooling my temper. I was Joe and I would live my life my way – the Joe who liked football, climbing trees and helping my father in his shop. I would sit for hours watching him fixing kettles and televisions, irons and toasters. He had such patience, his hands nimble with the fiddly screws. Every now and then he would let me replace the cover on a piece, telling me to be careful with the threading. Kenneth was given more complicated jobs when he came. He finished school later and was always greeted with a big smile and a cup of coffee. The conversation would change too. They would discuss fishing and the future of the electrical trade. They would sit side by side and my father would teach him all he knew.

I missed Kenneth. He had always been caring towards me when we were younger. I had fallen once and broken my nose and he had held the cut tight with his hand and stemmed the flow of blood. The pain that day had been horrible but my tears had only come when I realised that I'd ripped my new football shirt. I had bought it with my pocket money, saved for months, walked proudly into the clothes shop on the high street and walked out with the large white bag. It was a shirt I rarely took off after that. It had the club name emblazoned on the front and the number ten on the back. It drove my mother mad when she found me sleeping in it. She would take it when I was in school and for three days I would have to wait until it went through the washing and drying process.

My bedroom wall was my shrine to all my football idols. I had hundreds of images, small folded pieces of Sellotape carefully placed on the back of them to stick them to the wall. If I closed my eyes I could name them from left to right, beginning at the jamb of the door all the way to the window. They were mostly forwards. Like most, I found the defenders boring; they were never in the limelight and rarely scored goals. When the lights went out and my parents were downstairs watching television, I would close my eyes and pretend I was the Cup Final goal scorer, thumping the air with my clenched fist and taking the adulation from the crowd. I had girlfriends too, the type that footballers attracted. They were my fantasy women, the women that all boys wanted in bed at night.

It was time for a bath. I had spent enough idle moments looking in the mirror and seeing the past. The hot water spluttered from the tap. The steam filled the room and the mirror fogged over. As I stripped from my clothes, I rubbed my hands over the scars: self-inflicted worthless attacks, meaningless since my lies to Sophia.

I don't know why I did what I did next. It just happened. I took the razor from the shelf and, lying in the hot water, I began shaving: legs at first, from knee to ankle, and then my arms. Large clumps of hair floated in the water, the blade struggling with the thickness, the volume and my haste. In places the thin stainless steel cut my skin and speckles of blood dotted my arms. I scrapped at my chest and watched the flow of red mix with the bath water. It was becoming more than a purge of hair and the heat of the bath was masking the pain.

I didn't want to stop. There was a sense of release, of justification.

But then, oddly, in the middle of it all there was a moment of clarity, and I felt ashamed of the picture I was creating, the nakedness and the distress. I felt I was being watched. It was Rachel; she was there with me. I had helped her to die but she was there, talking to me, rebuking me.

'Jesus, Joe, what are you doing?'

'I'm just angry. Leave me alone.'

'You're angry!' Her voice was shaky, almost unrecognisable. 'I'm bloody furious, Joe. I lost Paul. I don't want to lose you too.'

'I'm sorry.'

'You're pathetic. This is meant to be the start of your new life and you fall at the first hurdle.'

'There's always going to be hurdles. I was stupid to think that there wouldn't be.'

'Do you remember when Paul was born?'

'Yes.'

'You stood there and looked into the cot and you were afraid to pick him up in case you dropped him.'

'I wanted to be his dad.'

'You knew that wasn't possible. I was his mum. I had to look after him. Not you.' She went quiet then. Her voice became a harsh whisper in my ear. 'But I didn't, did I? I let him die. I allowed those dammed creatures to sting him to death. And then there seemed no point in pretending, in going on the way we were. I needed to die with him. I had failed as a mother.'

The water in the bath was cooling. I allowed the razor to fall into the water. I didn't want to move. I was stuck in a place I had been to before. I was in the darkness that was me.

'Don't do this, Joe. We can make this work.'

'There is no us, Rachel. There is only me. Don't you remember? You're dead.'

CHAPTER 39

BRIAN MATTHEWS PLACED THE SMALL case into the boot of his car and patted the side pocket where he'd hidden the new ring. It seemed like the best way to start their weekend. He had purchased it from a jeweller that morning. The same shop where they had found her engagement ring, but this time he had the money and the ring could be special. No small chips or false stones, but a twist of gold around two large diamonds. He liked the ring. He thought it represented them. He had wanted to leave early and beat the traffic out of town. He was worried that he might lose the book and not discover the truth about Rachel and her brother. But Laura had to finish off some work before she left for the weekend, so he hadn't wasted the time waiting. He had bought her the ring.

He would buy champagne in the hotel and hand her the ring over dinner. Part of him worried that she wouldn't like it. Part of him knew she would. It depended on the moment, on the food and on her mood. It was always so easy to upset her these days, but at least now he knew why. She had lived in doubt for too long and lacked the trust their relationship needed. It was a stupid situation as far as he was concerned. The other women had been before their marriage. He had never fooled around. Most men were mistrusted because of affairs or messages found on phones but he was in trouble for long-forgotten dates from his youth. Although there was one girl he remembered, who had made him smile – Vanessa Murphy. They had found each other in second year, on a college trip with the football club. She had been the coach's daughter; he had been the worst player in the club, never turning up on time, often without his gear and usually half shot. Sitting on the side of the pitch for his sins, they had started talking. But the talking turned to more when the game was in progress and the changing rooms were empty. She had not been like Laura. She had allowed her clothes to fall to the floor and her nakedness to drip over him. He knew that when she took his hand and guided it that he wasn't the first and wouldn't be the last. It was strange that he thought of her now. He hadn't thought of her for years, and usually it was when he'd had too much to drink and was watching football on the television.

Laura appeared at the hall door and gave him a wide smile. 'I've finished. We can go.'

'Wonderful! I've locked everything up and I'm ready. If we leave now, we can hit Jackson's for lunch.'

'And we can sit outside in the beer garden. It's a lovely day.' She smiled.

'And I can eat one of their thick-crust pies and you can forget about how unhealthy they are for a while, wifey.'

She smiled at him again and opened the car door. 'Okay, that's a deal as long as we can listen to my music in the car.'

A meat pie for wishy-washy love songs. He shrugged and decided it was worth it.

The traffic was horrible. Brian's foot stiffened from the constant effort of keeping the car just above stalling. And Laura was dozing, using the boredom to catch up on the previous night's broken sleep. He couldn't even switch the music, as he knew a change in the rhythm would wake her.

It was two hours before they reached Athlone as the traffic was bumper to bumper. He felt fit to curse. He had almost cried with frustration when he passed the sign informing him that he would have reached Galway less than an hour ago if he'd gone by plane. It was the best advert for air travel he had ever seen. It summed up the whole futility of driving across Ireland.

By the time they stopped at Jackson's, he was moody.

'Are you all right, Brian? I'm sorry for falling asleep.'

'It's no problem. I'm just tired from the bumper-to-bumper driving.'

She took his hand and placed it to her lips.

'Poor you. Never mind, we'll be in a hotel tonight with no work to worry about and I'll give you a massage.'

Laura was in an extraordinary mood. It was as if telling him her fears had removed the burden from her thoughts. She was smiling and suggestive and flirtatious.

'I'd better have two pies for energy then.' He grinned.

'Oh no you won't. I'm not having you peg out with a heart attack just when I'm about to look better than I've done for years. I want you around to admire me.'

He shook his head and blew her a kiss. 'I've always fancied you, so that won't change.'

'Well maybe my extra input into our sex life will.'

The lunch was good. It always was in Jackson's. While most places were still serving carvery roasts and sandwiches, Jackson's offered paninis, tortillas and risottos. They deserved their full car park and the queue for tables. Today, thankfully, there wasn't too long a wait.

Laura ordered a quarter bottle of wine and it liberated her conversation. 'What do you think he'll look like, our Mr Joe McLoughlin?'

'I don't know. I've never thought about it.'

'Oh you must have some image. I see him as tall and mousy, a bit of a nervous type with very long fingers.'

Her description made him smile. He hadn't a clue where she got it from but he was sure she wasn't correct. He had seen the pictures on the mantelpiece, the pictures of Kenneth and Rachel. They weren't anything like that, and they were his siblings.

'No, he won't be like that. He'll be smallish and dark, almost swarthy, with nice eyes and a good smile.'

It was Laura's turn to smile. 'How can you know that?'

'I've seen his family. I've seen Rachel's photograph. He must be something similar.'

'Well, he sounds quite good-looking in that case. A man I might fancy myself.'

'Except he could be a cold-blooded murderer and you couldn't sleep with him without the fear of not waking up in the morning.'

'Jesus, Brian, that's a jump to make. I said he might be fanciable not that I'd like to go to bed with him.'

He laughed at the look of disgust on her face.

'Mind you, a cold-blooded murderer could be very attractive simply by the nature of the beast. He might appeal to the bad side of me.'

Brian burst out laughing. 'What bad side? You have trouble making love with the light on.'

She pretended to take umbrage but he wasn't fooled. He put his hand on her knee and squeezed it gently, and she put her hand on his thigh and ran her fingers up his leg. He really liked the new Laura and she hadn't even had the surgery yet.

The rest of the journey was interesting and enjoyable. They listened to his music, sang to all the loud songs and discussed their best moments together. It was good to listen to how many she remembered. The past wasn't all bad times.

'I love you, Laura.'

He realised as he said the words that he hadn't told her often enough. She was looking at him, watching him drive, her face looking content. It was driving him crazy, the change in her attitude. He thought he had worked it out but he needed to ask her. Yet there was a danger in asking. It might burst the bubble.

'Why are you so much happier today, Laura? What's changed?'

She pursed her lips and eyed him suspiciously. 'Are you complaining?'

'No, I'm delighted. I just want to know why.'

'Curiosity killed the cat.'

'And saved the rat,' he said.

She looked at him even more askance. 'And you are the biggest rat of all, Brian Matthews.'

He nodded in agreement and waited for more of a reply. 'I'm happier because I told you how I felt, if you must know. I'm happier because you now know that I'm worried about losing you and you would be a shit to leave me after finding out.'

He shook his head and smiled. 'You're such a funny

bunny. I have no intention of leaving you. I'm happy with you. You're my partner and I want to keep it that way.'

They travelled in silence for a while, his hand resting on her hand and her smile reassuring him. They passed through Galway quicker than he expected and then they were into the final stage of the journey. They had rarely been past Oughterard before, and the high mountains and dark lakes created a beautiful view as the sun was setting on the horizon.

'I'm glad I came with you,' she finally said.

'Why's that?' he asked.

'It's the countryside. I'd forgotten how amazing it is out here. It's like another world. You can almost sense the past deprivation of the people and their reliance on the land for their existence. Can't you feel it all around us, as if those days are still here? It's almost spooky.'

He knew what she meant. He could feel it himself. There were few houses to break the isolation and the few cars belied the modern world. It was as if with each mile they were driving back in time, back to the Famine times and even earlier.

'I'm going to have a long bath when we get to the hotel,' Laura said.

'And I'm going to have a shower.'

'Don't you want a bath with me?'

Brian smiled. He would never refuse such an offer.

CHAPTER 40

I WAS CALMER THAN THE day before. The stupidity of the shaving had ended my temper. I'd lain on the floor of my living room and looked up at the oak-beamed ceiling, counting the knots to distract myself from uglier thoughts. There were two hundred and forty-nine knots in one section, no more and no less.

I'd slept in the nude, trying to understand the person I'd become. Rachel had been right as always; I had run too fast, thrown myself headlong into a relationship I was not prepared for. The mental bruises caused by meeting Sophia were self-inflicted. I should have stayed alone for longer and given myself the time to understand the new life I'd made. If only Sophia had not walked into my café that day.

I was cold. There was a warm day brewing outside, but as I lay on the rug with my body pale and bruised, I felt colder than ever before. It wasn't the lack of clothes. It was the lack of self-respect. It was a problem I'd developed as a child, standing outside school, all the other girls walking up to Rachel, trying to make friends, cringing at her attempts to converse, longing to run off and play football with the boys and leave her behind. But she would always come too and then the boys would laugh.

Rachel and Joe – inseparable.

It was time to get dressed and rectify the situation. I couldn't lie on the rug for ever. Maybe I needed to write it all down just for me, in stark black and white. Then at last it might all make sense.

I am Jo. It was the name I always preferred when I looked at my birth certificate. The other names weren't me. It's strange when your youngest memories as a child are of not belonging. Most children remember birthdays and Christmas, summer holidays and sandcastles; all I can remember is a constant battle of trying to be me. Standing in the corner and refusing to wear the clothes, using my fists on my brother when the words were inadequate, not even knowing what I was fighting against.

I hated Rachel sometimes. It wasn't all the time. In national school it was easy to play with the boys, concentrate on schoolwork and ignore the future. A child doesn't think beyond the everyday. The world doesn't define them rigidly until they reach their teens. As a child I could escape, most of the time, with my head in the clouds and no thought for my deeper feelings.

It was the growing up that mattered. The defining moment of sexuality, when the body changes shape and the horrible reality of the future is rammed down your throat, almost choking you. I looked in the mirror and wanted something else, as if through all my early years, I had secretly thought I was going to change from a caterpillar into a butterfly. I hated the growth of my breasts, the onset of periods and the swelling of my hips. My body was developing into a person that

I could never be. It wasn't me. I was Jo, not Rachel Joanna.

I gave Rachel my best effort. I tried to save her life. I did all the things expected of me. I had boyfriends, I grew my hair long, I tried to look feminine, but underneath there was just turmoil. To cope, I cut off my inner feelings, concentrated on my exams and practical living. I became a clever, successful person but I had no warmth. There was nothing emotional I cared to express to anyone. My emotions were locked away as they belonged to a different me. The me that came out at night in my dreams and woke hoping to find a different world, one where I was a man and my body was masculine.

And then came Paul. My son. I hadn't planned for him. I hadn't wanted children. They were a product of a man and woman having sex. Children were born to women. How could I have a child?

So I blamed myself for his death. I saw it as a punishment from God. Now I see that that notion was ridiculous. I didn't ask to be born with this body and this mind – their incompatibility. I was not born a man and I was not born a woman. I was born a strange mix of both, as if it was a Friday at five o'clock and God had some leftover pieces and threw them together in a haphazard fashion.

I am an oddity in the polarised society in which I live, and my ideal life will never be possible because I can't go back into the womb and reprogram myself. I can't change my body to suit my mind and then stand in front of the world and claim to be a man. I have tried and failed.

INSIDE OUT

I have just become a spare-part person. I have no functioning sexual organ, but I have scars on my chest and a lie on my lips every time I look into a woman's eyes and refuse to tell her my story. How can I tell the truth? I am still Rachel and she is still Jo/Joe. I will always be Rachel Joanna McLoughlin, the gender dysphoric person. I was born inside out and that's the way I should have stayed. It was the real me, the bit of both, the mistake of nature.

Don't get me wrong, I like my new body. It reflects my inner thoughts perfectly. And now when I look in the mirror I can see the man who I have always been inside. When I walk into a bar, no one makes me wince anymore by calling me madam or treating me as a female. I can relax and be me. Before I changed, I was a woman with a butch attitude, a woman sometimes labelled lesbian because the feminine side was so subdued.

It would have been easier to be a lesbian. To have walked into a relationship with another woman and enjoyed the companionship I needed. But I couldn't do that. I couldn't be with a woman and allow her to touch my femininity. In my mind I was male and my self-image would be shattered if a woman touched my body. And it was the same with men; it was like taking part in a weird homosexual relationship in order to gain any pleasure at all.

I suppose none of this makes sense.

Sometimes I'm not sure it does to me.

But does it have to make sense? The duck-billed platypus looks like no other creature on earth but it exists and has a purpose. Nature does not relegate the platypus to the refuse heap because it looks different. It still belongs. But with humans, it's different. Humans demand perfection. Image is everything. You can't look one way and behave another and expect to be respected. You have to be male or female, don't you? You have to make a choice. Have the bloody sex change and became the man inside or bury the man inside and live as a woman, unseen and misunderstood. What kind of alternatives are those?

The problem is that I do miss my family. They were my stability as I grew up. They protected me and gave me a name, albeit the wrong one. And now I dislike Christmas and my birthday. There is no one to send me cards and care. I want someone to visit in hospital and look after when they're older. But they didn't want me in my altered state. They only wanted Rachel and I needed them to love me as Jo too. Because I am Joe too.

I remember the first person I told about Joe. I talked and talked for hours. It was as if, for twenty-eight years, Joe had been dumb and was suddenly given the right to speak. He had so much to say.

My friend listened and then walked away. They hugged me and sympathised but then left my life, refusing to be there for me, making me feel ashamed to be me.

But I have nothing to feel ashamed of; I am no murderer or sexual deviant or embezzler or thief or abuser. I am just a person who just wants the space to exist as my true self, the space to live my life in whatever form it takes.

INSIDE OUT

I am Joe but I am also Rachel. Gender identity disordered, as the psychiatrist would have it.

But please don't call me that. It's just a label. And it's a label that is negative and limiting. I'm not disordered. Is a penguin not still a bird just because he prefers swimming to flying? It is time we learned from Darwin and looked at people like me differently. Evolution occurs, the world moves forward, new types of species come to our attention. I am not disordered. I am perfectly ordered. I'm just another variation of an order.

I am Rachel but I am also Joe.

CHAPTER 41

Marta Warner sliced her toast in two and waited for her daughter to sit and join her. Sophia had come back late the previous night and she had not heard the important finale of the story.

'Would you like more tea, Mum?'

'No thanks, just sit down and join me. Your breakfast is going cold.'

'I've told you I'm not really hungry.'

'Yes, I know, and I ignored you because breakfast is the most important meal of the day.'

'Will you ever let me grow up, Mother?'

'I'm not sure if I can afford to, especially after your little excursion last night.'

Sophia sat down at the table and spread marmalade on her toast.

'It wasn't an excursion.'

'Where did you go?'

'You wouldn't believe me if I told you.'

'So you went back to Joe's. Did you talk to him?'

It was irritating that her mother was always right. Blind as she was, she still knew most of what happened around her.

'He wasn't there.'

'How do you know? He could have been in and avoiding you.'

'Yes, he could have, but I don't know why you think he would.'

'He's got too many issues, that boy. He doesn't know if he's coming or going.'

'What makes you say that? You've never met him.'

'Oh, you don't know that. I meet a lot of people at that church of mine.'

'You've met Joe there?'

'Possibly, and I tried to tell you that yesterday but I knew that you weren't listening. I might have met him. That's if he was sitting on his own, refusing to be very talkative.'

'Stop playing games, Mum. You either have or you haven't.'

The old woman picked up her toast and took a large bite. She made her daughter wait as she chewed slowly. 'Well, I might have and I might not have because he didn't say his name. But I think it was him.'

'Why didn't you tell me before?'

'Because there's not much to tell. He was there when I went to light a candle and he left before I got to ask him anything. But I can smell distress at a hundred yards and he has his troubles.'

Her mother took another bite of toast and Sophia watched her curiously. Her words revealed nothing new. She knew Joe was distressed. The man had helped to kill his sister and his parents had disowned him. He had good reason to be in a church praying for help.

It was strange that her mother had thought that was why he had been in the church, though. He might have been there for another purpose, but she doubted it. His conscience would have brought him there, and the horror of his actions.

'Mum, I'm going to go back after breakfast. I want to talk to him.'

'What about school? You'll be late.'

'No, I have a late start and I won't be long. I just want to clear up a few issues.'

Marta scratched the scar on her face and shook her head slowly. 'I don't think you should go. I have a bad feeling about all this. You're going to get hurt, Sophia. You're too conventional for the likes of Joe.'

It was typical of her mother. She never knew how to discuss things normally. There was always her intuition and her waters.

'I'm going anyway, Mum.'

'All right, suit yourself. Anyway, my bad feeling doesn't include you coming to harm.'

'What does it include?'

Marta rubbed her scar as if it itched intolerably. 'It includes death.'

'Jesus, you're a spooky old woman sometimes.'

Her mother laughed and bit into another slice of toast. 'Spooky but accurate. I wouldn't ignore my warning, Sophia. I'm afraid for Mr White.'

Sophia left the table and picked up the pile of exercise books on the chair in the corner. She would have to be quick at Joe's. She didn't have much time before work.

It was a damp morning. The air was wet, the ground was wet and her car was cold. It didn't start at first and she nearly flooded the engine in her impatience. There was nobody out on the road. The farmers were already in their fields and the early-morning commuters had gone, their cars already pouring into Galway and clogging up the roundabouts.

Sophia approached Joe's cottage as quietly as possible. Nothing had changed from the previous night. The car hadn't moved, the curtains hadn't opened and the house still appeared empty. But there was one big difference – the hall door was wide open and the house was at her mercy.

She called out Joe's name before she entered. She stood in the doorway and shouted it twice. She knew she would get no reply. There was an echo of emptiness about the place. Gingerly she walked into the living room. It was as clean as usual except for a torn sheet of paper on the floor and a wine glass on the table. She tried to pick up the pieces and patch them together, but the pieces were small and the process was difficult. It was easy to tell what the paper had been, though. It was a birth certificate. There was a harp and various other telltale signs she could identify.

She left the pieces on the coffee table and walked into the kitchen. It was empty too. There were no signs of breakfast or dishes from last night's dinner, if he had eaten. The place was spotless. Curiously she opened a cupboard, not knowing what she was looking for. It was a fruitless exercise. It was full of jars of pickles and sauces, no murder weapon or incriminating evidence. Her mind was behaving strangely. This was just Joe's kitchen and the things of his everyday life.

Walking into the bedroom made her wince. She thought of the letter and her sudden departure; she thought of his hands on her breasts and his lips on her nipples. There was an eroticism in the fear of it all. It made her feel uneasy and immoral. For some reason she leant over and picked up the pillow. It smelled of perfume, her perfume. He had obviously not washed the covers since she had left.

The front door banging made her jump. She threw the pillow on to the bed and almost ran to the doorway. There was no one there. A sudden gust of wind was rattling the shutters and clanging the wind chimes. She was overwrought. It was her mother's fault, her mother's stupid premonition of death. She shut her eyes and tried to compose herself. There was only one more room left to check – the bathroom.

There was no certainty in what she saw. The room just left more questions to be answered. And it was shocking and frightening. The mirror was shattered on the wall, jagged pieces hanging over the sink. On the floor there were clothes scattered, no tidy pile on the chair as she would have expected. But it was the bath that made her scream, a tide of blood around the edge and a mess of hair across the surface. There was too much blood for an innocent explanation, too much hair for an obvious answer. Her mind couldn't even conjure up an idea as to what might have occurred. It groped around, then descended into a panic. When, finally, an answer occurred to her, it was not one she could accept easily. This was Rachel's blood. Joe had killed her before and now he had cut up the body to dispose of it. And that meant that he was only out to bury her. He would be back soon to clean up the bath.

Sophia went into the lounge and sat on the leather couch. She was insane. She knew there was no truth to her thoughts. She knew Joe was not capable of such an act. There had to be some other explanation. She was not afraid. She would wait for him to return. She would ask him face-to-face. She thought of his smile that first day in the coffee shop. He wouldn't hurt her.

She felt a coward in the car on the way home. She hadn't had the courage to stay, or maybe she had seen sense and realised that she knew too little of this man to take any risk with her own safety.

Her mind kept racing through the possibilities of what could have happened in that bathroom – the cracked mirror, the hair, the blood. It made no sense, so it had to be something bad. She only knew that she wasn't going to tell her mother yet. She was going to drive around the area and see if she could find him.

CHAPTER 42

BRIAN OPENED THE BEDROOM CURTAINS and looked out over the bay. It was a breathtaking view. The sea stretched in a thin wisp to the fullness of the Atlantic Ocean beyond. He realised how busy he had been lately and how little time they had spent away from the city. It was Laura who had suggested that they waited until the morning to find the mysterious Joe. By the time they had reached Clochan it was already dark and they would have found it difficult to find so remote a place. But Brian was itching to get on the road now and seal a deal. It seemed so close and possible all of a sudden.

Laura was still sleeping. She had made good on her teasing last night. She had behaved like a woman bent on change. And he was still puzzled by her new behaviour. It had arrived so suddenly, come from nowhere. In fact, he was wrong; it had come after a period of absolute negativity towards their sex life. But maybe it was not to be questioned and just to be enjoyed.

'Brian, order breakfast in the room, please.'

Her voice was sleepy.

'Are you sure you want to wake up? You still sound tired. I could go out and find our mystery man.'

She gave him a weak smile and patted the bed beside her. 'I don't want to sleep all day. I want to spend time with you. Just give me a minute and I promise that I'll be dressed.'

His inner voice was nagging at him again. There was something coming; he was being naïve. Laura usually loved having a lie in.

'Laura?'

She looked up at him, waiting for the question. But he couldn't ask it. She would be hurt by his request. She had told him yesterday why her mood had changed – she was happy knowing that he understood her fear. She was happy because he still wanted her. So what made him question it so much? He didn't know the answer. Maybe it was just years of being manipulated, knowing that behind every soft voice lay a giant trap into which he always fell.

He felt guilty now. Here was his wife, smiling up at him, offering him more than he had enjoyed for ages and he was waiting for the catch. There had to be a catch. Maybe she was going to have more surgery than she had told him about. Maybe Monday involved other procedures that she hadn't mentioned. He was saddened by his own cynical thoughts. He wanted to trust the new Laura.

'So will we go to find Joe?' she asked, tucking a clean shirt into tight-fitting jeans.

'A very quick breakfast first,' he replied. 'I just think we might not find anything else to eat around here if we leave without breakfast.'

'You and your food, Brian. You're hilarious.'

'Man cannot live on sex alone.'

The road out to the village wound its way lazily around the coast. It was in no hurry to reach anywhere. Brian was feeling the opposite. His apprehension was rising. Would they find a callous murderer? What was the truth about Joe? Maybe they shouldn't have even been heading out to meet him unprepared. It could be dangerous. They knew nothing about him except the off-putting things that his family had reported. But somewhere at the end of the journey, there was a hope of publishing a good book and finding an exciting story that would sell it to the public. Let's be honest, Brian thought, this was not the usual run-of-the-mill situation.

The car dealt admirably with the potholes and rough patches of replacement gravel. This was not an area near enough to a city to warrant decent roads. The scenery was beautiful but Brian felt glad he didn't live in the country. They had no theatres, no cinemas, no airports nearby and no hospitals. The first three he realised he could live with but the fourth was a matter of life and death. A heart attack victim could die in the ambulance, so far away was the nearest emergency department.

'Brian, what are you thinking about?'

'Hospitals.'

Laura pulled a funny smile. 'Why?'

'Oh, I don't know, I was just thinking how fantastic the scenery is down here but that anyone living here has to compromise on other things.'

'Nowhere's perfect, honey.'

'And no person is either, my love.'

He was worried in case the comment was too sharp but she was ready with her answer.

'Yes, you're right. But we can all make the most of

ourselves in whatever way we can. There's no reason to settle for second best.'

He knew what to say then. 'I promise you, Laura, that I have never settled for second best, especially when I married you. I knew I had hit the jackpot.'

The words had sounded better in his head. He felt a bit of an idiot, a pathetic schoolboy, trying to impress a girl, but her smile meant that she had loved it and was happy to hear more.

But Brian wasn't in the mood to make a total fool of himself. He decided to quit while he was ahead, and Laura was happy to change the subject.

'What are you going to say to him when you find him?'

'I don't know. Play it by ear, I suppose. I'm a bit worried that he may be the man his family says he is.'

'What if he won't talk to you?'

'I'll offer him lots of money for the book and see what happens from there. Nearly everyone talks when you offer money.'

'Not if they're guilty of a crime. He might just blow your head off. There's obviously bad blood between him and his family over his sister, so you've got to be careful. He could be unhinged.'

Brian laughed. 'Maybe if he is a bit whacky I'll let you talk to him. He'd have met his match then.'

She shot him a fake-offended glance. 'It's quite exciting, this, isn't it, driving across the country to solve a mystery?'

Laura was right. This chase across the country was a boost to the system. A huge part of him was hoping that Joe McLoughlin would turn out to be a callous murderer and a vicious maniac. It would give him a rush of excitement that would last for years. A tasty murder story would also sell the book. It would ensure amazing publicity.

'Brian?'

'Yeah.'

'Thanks for supporting me now, with the plastic surgery. It means a lot.'

'It's okay. It just took a long while to get my head around it.'

'I'll be all right, you know.'

'Laura, you'd better be or I'll kill you myself.'

She smiled at him and they were silent for a while. The scenery was changing. There were fewer houses and the stone-walled fields seemed even smaller. Around every corner another island appeared off the coast, each one more beautiful than the last. It was easy not to talk; there was so much to take in.

'You've missed the turn, Brian. We've passed the signpost.'

'Are you sure? This looks like the main road.'

'Brian, I saw it myself. Why do you always think you're right and I'm wrong?'

'Years of being proven right I suppose.'

Her look was more than threatening.

'Only joking, I'll turn around and go back, my love.'

'We should ask in the village, where he lives. Everyone knows everyone in the country.'

The village was nestled in a dip in the headland. There was only one road in and one road out, with houses on both sides, and the houses were small. Most were well kept and picture perfect but there were no thatched cottages. It was a strange feature about the West. Even though the Gaeltacht dominated part of the area, it was devoid of the typical Irish housing that reflected the past. It was all bungalows with slate or tiled roofs.

Brian stopped his car outside Joyce's pub. There were more pubs than shops in the village. Brian counted four. This was his kind of place, he thought.

Laura had pulled down the passenger's mirror and was fixing her make-up.

'You look lovely,' Brian said.

'I will soon,' she replied.

The pub was empty, but then it was only eleven-thirty on a Friday. There wasn't anyone behind the counter. Brian pulled a stool out for Laura and looked around the pub. It was a barn of a room: chairs all around the walls and small tables in front of them. A large wooden dance floor dominated three-quarters of the space, and at the back in the corner, there was a keyboard.

Laura nudged Brian and gave a schoolgirl giggle. 'Look, there's someone asleep in the corner.'

Brian's eyes adjusted to the darkness of the room and spotted the figure, snoring away blissfully.

'Don't mind Peadar. He's left over from last night. Couldn't make it home, the daft bugger.'

A large woman had appeared through a door behind the bar. She smiled and took a glass from the shelf.

'What can I get you folks?'

Laura replied first. She wanted coffee. Brian longed for a cold beer and ordered one.

'It's a nice day. Are you in the area for long?'

'No, actually we're looking for someone. Maybe you could help us?'

'I'll try my best,' she answered, placing his pint on the

bar and sitting down on a seat across the counter from them.

'We're looking for a Joe McLoughlin.'

The woman looked at him thoughtfully and then shook her head.

'Don't know anyone by the name of McLoughlin around here. Are you sure it's in Clochan he lives? There's loads of little villages scattered about.'

'Yeah, I have his address.'

Brian considered reading it out, but he handed the piece of paper across the counter and waited for another shake of the head.

'Well, I know where this house is, but wait until I ask Dan in the back to be sure. He might be more certain than me. But you've the wrong name anyhow. This house belongs to Joe White.'

She disappeared through the door into the house behind.

Laura placed a hand on Brian's arm.

'Jesus, Brian, we're stupid. It's him. He would have changed his name if he was hiding from the past.'

'It's a possibility, and if he did, it makes him more suspicious in my eyes.'

Laura looked apprehensive. 'Do you think we should call the local garda?'

'And say what exactly, Laura, that I'm a publisher and Joe has killed the author of a book, who happens to be his sister?'

She huffed at him slightly. 'Why not?'

'Because if Joe's parents didn't even report the crime, there's probably no way they'll believe us. Anyway, it's only a supposition we have, based on a frail old woman and an angry old man.'

The large woman appeared again.

'Well I was right. That house is Joe White's, not Joe McLoughlin's. Funny the first name being the same, though, isn't it? Are you looking for a friend?'

Brian took back the piece of paper with the address and put it in his shirt pocket. 'No, it's business.'

'Well if you want to talk to Joe and solve your mystery, he owns the café near the harbour, but it's been closed the last week, so you'll probably not find him there. But maybe you should look just in case. The house is another two miles out of the village.'

The curious woman gave them directions. Brian knew he had just started a trail of rumours for poor Joe White, if that was his real name.

They left their car outside the pub and walked towards the harbour. They found the cleanly painted café around the corner on the way to the pier. The door was locked and inside a closed sign hung limply from a plastic hook

'Do you want to walk down the pier while we're here?' Brian suggested.

Laura shook her head. 'No, let's go and find him. I don't know about you but I'm dying to know the full story.'

Brian looked at his wife. 'I was joking, dear. I suppose I am a bit worried about taking us both into trouble. I'm not sure you should come. As you said yourself, he might be dangerous.'

'No way, Brian, no bloody way. I'm coming with you.'

There was no point arguing. She was a stubborn woman when it suited her.

'Okay, back to the car, then.'

The house wasn't two miles from the village. It was nearer to four. Brian wondered if he should have insisted on Laura staying in the village. But they were getting on so well that he had no desire for an argument.

There was a car in the driveway. It wasn't that new and the bumper was loose. Brian smiled when he saw the house. It was a cottage, and thatched. There was a name carved into the stone gate pillar – CHIMERA. It was a word he had seen before but he couldn't remember its meaning. It was some type of mythological animal created from spare parts but which parts he didn't know.

'That's a strange name.' Laura had seen it too.

He looked at her face. She knew what the word meant and was waiting for him to ask. He decided to spoil her moment of glory and tell her first.

'It's a mythological animal,' he said, expecting her face to register surprise.

'Yes, but it also has other meanings. It can be something wished for but impossible to achieve.' She was smiling now, knowing she'd won.

'Oh, aren't you smart?'

'Don't be a condescending pig, Brian, or your next time in bed with me will be a chimera!'

He decided to leave her with the last word.

He told her to stay in the car, but Laura insisted on coming to the door. There was no need to knock; the door was open, but when Brian called out, no one answered.

'We'll come back later. He's out.'

'No, Brian, let's go in and have a look. There's a car here. He can't have gone far.'

'We can't. It's trespassing.'

'Rubbish! He could be deaf and sitting in his house unaware that we're here.'

Laura didn't wait for his reply. She walked through the open door. He had no option but to follow her. There was nobody in the living room, and Laura had disappeared through another door.

When Brian found her, she was standing in the bathroom, her face ashen. He put a hand on her shoulder and they both stood and looked at the chaos around them.

'What the hell do you think has happened, Brian?'

'I don't know, love. I really don't.'

'There's so much blood in the bath, but it's the hair that makes it even worse.'

'Yeah, it's a bit macabre.'

'Come on, Laura, let's leave it. Let's go. Maybe we should go to the police now.'

'No, let's search the rest of the house. There could be someone bleeding to death in here.'

Brian saw the determined expression on her face. 'Okay, but let's do it together. Maybe this Joe was a fruitcake and maybe he did murder his sister.'

Brian closed the bathroom door behind them and together they went into the bedroom. There was no sign of any blood or a hacked up body. His mind was working overtime. A few items of clothing were scattered on the floor and a wet towel lay across the back of a chair. The bed was made and cushions were placed carefully on the duvet. Laura was busy opening drawers and looking in envelopes.

'I really don't think you should be doing that, honey. What if there has been a murder? You're contaminating the scene.'

INSIDE OUT

She threw him a disparaging look. 'Don't be so boring, Brian, you could have a book by a murdered writer in your office. This is far too fascinating to back away from.'

Brian felt uneasy about their snooping. He wanted to leave.

'Brian, I have something here. Look at this.'

Laura held two sheets of paper in her hand. Together they sat on the bed to read them. The first page began with the words *I am Joe*. Laura was reading quicker than him, her lips mouthing the words.

'Jesus, Brian, neither of us came anywhere near to this!'

Brian couldn't reply. Thoughts were crashing around his mind. He couldn't believe that there was no sister. Although even that belief was foolish; in reality there was no Joe. *He* was the sister. He was Rachel. It was like the movie *Psycho* when the son turned out to be the mother. There was an air of horror about it all but there was also an overwhelming sadness for the person who had put their words to paper. But it was a sadness drowned immediately by a contradictory feeling. It was niggling at him, making him feel narrow-minded and conservative. Laura didn't give him time to voice it. She was up from the bed and speaking decisively.

'He's unstable, Brian. I bet that's his blood in the bath, and his hair.'

Brian was still taking in the information. 'But why?'

'I think he's regretting what he's done. He's shaved off his hair in anger.'

'But why would he regret it if it's what he's wanted all his life?'

Laura was slightly exasperated with his slowness. 'Oh, Brian, he said it in the letter. He's not good enough now,

– 289 –

either. He feels no matter how many changes he has made that he'll never be a real man.'

'You mean he's some kind of adult Pinocchio?'

She put the sheets of paper in her pocket and emitted a deep sigh. 'Don't, Brian. We have to find him. He needs protecting from himself.'

'We could call the police.'

Laura shrugged. 'And tell them what, that you were looking for a woman writer and found a man?'

Brian knew she was right but he didn't know if he wanted to pursue it any further. This was not his idea of being a publisher. He didn't even know whether he wanted to save someone like Joe. His whole understanding of the last two months was changing. His sympathies lay more with the poor parents and the brother now. Joe, or Rachel, had given them a terrible time, killing off their daughter and claiming to be a man.

'I don't know, Laura. Let's just go back to the hotel and think about this one.'

She shook her head. 'No, we're going back to the pub. Someone in there might have spotted him since.'

'Okay, I give in. I could do with a pint, anyway, and a sandwich.'

'You could do with a sharp smack on the head, Brian. Don't you think it's sad? This person has lived all their life in what they consider the wrong body, only to change it and realise that they felt no better. It was still all a lie.'

Laura was shaking her head now and almost angrily pushing her hair back off her forehead. 'It makes me feel stupid. What the hell am I worrying about? My body might not be perfect but at least it is me.'

Brian looked at his wife. Maybe there was something

positive in this after all. Maybe he should try to publish the book and give the whole strange story an airing. There was definitely something bizarre about it, and readers like bizarre.

CHAPTER 43

SOPHIA STOOD ON THE PIER and watched the water swell over the moorings. There was a wind whipping across the bay, making mischief with the boats, turning them this way and that, threatening to tear them from safety. And yet the sky was calm – no clouds, all blue and almost flawless.

Her eyes were looking out to sea but her mind was elsewhere. All she could think of was the bathroom, the blood and the mess. It was disturbing. She needed to talk to Joe and find out what had happened.

Joe – that irritating man who was always causing her problems and never making her feel at ease. Since she had met him, she didn't know whether to hug him or walk away. He evoked a strange mixture of feelings, not all of them positive. He was like an itch that she constantly needed to scratch, an itch with nice eyes.

She had been looking for him for the past half hour. He had not turned up at the café, where Fran was waiting. He had not been at home, and there was no sign of him in the village. He had disappeared. In some ways, she felt rather stupid in her quest. There was probably an innocent explanation for what she had seen. He was probably away visiting relatives in Galway or picking up supplies for the café or meeting old friends. Her last hypothesis she found difficult to imagine. Joe didn't seem to be the type of man who had many friends. He was quiet, considerate and fond of his own company. Anyway, she had work to do and she couldn't waste the whole morning looking for him. She had asked Fran where he was, but found the young girl showing quite a depth of concern herself for the whereabouts of her boss. Her face was drawn with worry. He had given her a week off work but she was supposed to start again on Friday, and there had been no notice on the door or contact from him. She had even called to the house and left a note. It was all Sophia could do to stop Fran from ringing the gardaí and filing a missing person's report.

Sophia sat down on a lobster pot and frowned. It was difficult to know why Joe mattered at all. From the moment she had arrived at school that morning, she had taught with one eye on the blackboard and the other firmly fixed on the window. It wasn't that Joe would walk past; it was just the notion that somewhere out there was a life beyond teaching. And Joe might have been a part of that life. He was the offer of something different.

The boats were making a clanging sound with their masts and rigging. The life rafts on the anchored ferries were swaying from side to side. The wind was still rising. A stormy evening lay ahead. Sophia felt it coming. It was time to leave the pier. She wasn't going to wait around for Joe at his cottage. There was no reason. He had obviously made a decision to leave the area for the day, and she would be silly to wait on his doorstep like a reception committee. Besides, this was her half day from work. She would have a quiet lunch in the village. It was a bad idea to rush home to her mother's questioning. Before she could decide on which direction to take, a friendly voice interrupted her musings.

'Hi, Sophia. No school today?'

'No, it's my early finish, Brendan. How are things with you?' Sophia could never understand why they allowed overweight gardaí. Brendan was a good man but there was no way that he could chase anyone anywhere, with his stomach hanging over his trousers.

'We're busy at the minute, you know? Still haven't found the driver from the hit and run. That's why I'm here. We had a tip that the car might be over on the island. So I'm taking the boat out at two.'

'So it's someone local then?'

'Well now, I didn't say that, so don't go quoting me. We're still investigating.'

Sophia thought it was funny the use of the word *investigating*. He was taking a boat trip for the afternoon, not down at forensics with a sample of blood or a strand of fibre. She could never imagine any of the local guards performing high-powered police work. It always seemed to be crowd control at markets and speed traps on the back roads. If Brendan only knew about the mess in Joe's bathroom, she thought. But he was still thinking about the hit-and-run case.

'A person arrived looking for her, you know?'

'Looking for who?' Sophia asked.

Brendan took a deep breath and sighed at his own thoughts. 'That poor tourist, Rosemary Benson.'

'Oh, God love them! That must have been hard for them.'

He scratched the back of his ear and nodded. 'Tough,

all right. She wasn't even family, so there was nothing we could do for her.'

'What do you mean?' Sophia was only mildly interested.

The ferry had arrived and Micilín, one of the crew, threw Brendan a rope to catch. The garda moved away to tie it firmly around the mooring. He didn't come back to finish the conversation; he was too busy chatting and helping lower the gangplank.

Sophia was hungry. It was time for lunch. It was a pity the café wasn't open. She liked the food there. She turned from the pier and looked at the café with its closed door and pulled blinds. As soon as Joe had finished painting it, the building had added charm to the village. Joe was not a man to allow the grass to grow under his feet. He had whitewashed the walls, planted window-boxes and hammered a name above the door. She looked at the dark lettering and wondered why he had chosen the name. It had never entered her thoughts before. She was amazed that she hadn't noticed. The Bare Bones. He might have skinned someone down to the bare bones, such was the mess in his bathroom. She shuddered at the thought. Although she knew what she had seen was a self-inflicted attack.

She wondered again where he was. Talking to him would be awkward but comforting. She needed to know that he was safe even though his behaviour was bizarre.

The pub was nearly empty. A backpacker with a map sat on a barstool planning his journey. One hand held a map while the other was holding a pint of Guinness. The only others in the room were a couple occupying the corner seat, eating sandwiches.

'Hi, Peggy. A half and a bag of crisps.'

'I hope that's not your lunch, Sophia.'

'I'm not really hungry. How's your mother?' Sophia thought it better to change the subject than to have a lecture from her cousin on her eating habits.

'Oh, she's not too bad. A bit stiff at times, but then she's no spring chicken.'

Peggy was wiping the counter with a damp cloth and rubbing furiously at marks that Sophia knew had been there for ages. They were scratches in the wood rather than dirt. She stopped rubbing and looked up at Sophia. 'See those people in the corner? They were here earlier and asked after your friend Joe, except they had a different surname for him. They weren't looking for a Joe White. They called him something else but I can't for the life of me remember what it was now.'

Sophia glanced around at the couple in the corner. They didn't look like tourists. They were dressed casually and were probably in their thirties.

'How do you know it was Joe they were looking for?'

'They showed me his address but, as I said, it wasn't his surname they gave.'

Sophia took a drink from her Guinness and wondered what it meant. They were probably old friends, possibly relatives.

'It's a bit mysterious isn't it?' Peggy continued. 'Do you think your Joe has a secret past, a hidden life?'

'Don't be silly, Peggy. And he's not my Joe,' she said, raising her voice more than she meant to.

But Peggy wasn't to be dissuaded. 'Do you think he's done a runner? The café's been closed for a week now. Folk have been asking about the reasons for that, you see. Not that I would have asked. I'm not one to prattle on about the lives of others. But he was questioned about the poor Benson woman because of his red car. But I think Brendan's off to the island about that today. So it can't have been Joe. Mind you, that pair could be plain-clothes police. He might be guilty of a crime, your innocent-looking Joe.'

Sophia gave Peggy a faint smile. 'You're not in the dark about anything around here. I know nothing compared to you, Peggy.' But all she could think of were Joe's words. He had admitted that he had helped his sister to die, a punishable crime. Peggy might have been closer to the truth than she realised.

Sophia looked at the couple again. They didn't seem to be gardaí. They looked too comfortable with each other. They were more of a couple, a man and wife on their holidays; possibly old friends of Joe's who just happened to be in the area and decided to look for him and pay a visit. She decided to find out the answer for herself rather than sit and speculate.

'Hi, I'm sorry to bother you, but I heard you were looking for Joe.'

The man broke into a friendly smile and thrust out a hand. 'Yes, how are you? My name is Brian Matthews and this is my wife, Laura.'

Laura smiled, acknowledging his introduction. A good-looking woman, Sophia thought, well-dressed and conscious of her appearance. He was slightly overweight but open-faced and charming.

'Do you know Joe?' the man continued.

'Yes, he's a friend. Did you find him?'

'Actually no. We've been to the house and the coffee shop but had no luck at either. Is he away?'

Sophia smiled. 'That's the big question. I've been looking for him too. Are you friends of his?'

The woman answered this time. Her voice was clipped and she spoke fast. 'No, Brian's a publisher and we were looking for Joe concerning his sister's book.'

Brian Matthews seemed perturbed. 'Yes, it would be nice to make contact with him, but I suppose we'll have to wait and go back to the house later.'

Sophia looked at the couple earnestly. 'So you've been to the house already?'

'Yes.' It was the wife who answered again. 'And the door was open so we went in.'

Sophia knew what Laura Matthews was trying to say. She could read it in her eyes and in the tone of her voice. They had been into the house and they had seen the bathroom.

'Well, I'm worried for his safety,' Sophia admitted.

'We are too,' the wife said. 'Maybe we could help you look for him?'

'I've tried already, but there are too many places to cover.'

It was all worked out within ten minutes. Sophia liked the publisher's wife. She was straight and proactive. They made a list of all the places and they divided it up between them.

It was on the way out of the pub Laura Matthews handed Sophia two sheets of paper and told her to keep them safe. 'Here, we found these in Joe's house. I think you should keep them. It doesn't seem right for a complete stranger to have them.'

As Sophia read, tears began to pour down her cheeks.

CHAPTER 44

THE PATH WAS QUIET. THE small spade was tucked under my arm. There was purpose in my stride. I needed to go back and see her. I was so lost in my own thoughts that I nearly knocked over the small, bent figure that came out from behind a yew tree.

'I'm really sorry,' I said as she took a sharp intake of breath.

'You nearly flattened me,' she replied, still breathing heavily. 'I heard the footsteps but couldn't get out of the way in time.'

'Again, I'm sorry.'

The old woman pushed her scarf back from her face and revealed a deep red scar. She held out her hand and I took hold of it while she stepped gently across a small grouping of stones on the path.

'How did you know they were there?' I asked.

'Well unlike you, Mr White, I've lived here all my life and I don't need to see something to know it's there.'

I was taken aback by her recognition of my voice, but then I realised that must be her best way of recognising people – their voice.

'Oh, it's not just the voice that's the giveaway.'

Was this strange old woman psychic too?

'It's the scent of a person also, Mr White. It's very

distinctive. Yours is quite pleasant, I might add – a mix of aftershave and baked bread. so your profession gives your identity away. And your accent has the same lilt as the day I met you in the church. I'd say you're from the midlands somewhere.'

I let go of her hand and thought about leaving her there. Miss Marple couldn't have been more deductive and I was in a rush.

'Are you going to run again, Mr White? I don't think you should, you know.'

'I'm afraid I don't know what you're talking about. You don't know me at all.'

The old lady sighed and rubbed the scar on her cheek. 'Oh, I think I know you better than you think. And my daughter knows you even better. Sophia knows you very well. But I didn't tell her the truth. I thought it best all along if you did.'

I was finding her more than irritating now. She had no right to stand on the path, in my way, and lecture me about how I should deal with people. Life was never that simple. And how could she possibly think she knew my truth?

'I have told you before, Mr White, in the church, that when you don't have the eyes to see, you have to rely on other senses to understand things. I listen carefully, pick up things from here and there, and I put things together quick enough. But I must admit it was mostly to do with the postman and his letter for you. Or should I say the old you. I can understand why you didn't tell my daughter the truth. I don't think she would have taken it well. I love her, of course, but she's a conservative girl. She never really left the village behind when she went to Dublin. Its old-fashioned morality stayed with her. But I wasn't born here, Mr White. I am the product of a different place.'

The conversation was surreal. For over a year I had been carefully keeping any signs of my former life out of my new world, and here was a blind old lady who had somehow understood it all before anyone else.

'Will you tell Sophia?' she asked.

'I'm sorry. I know you probably mean well but I really don't feel like talking now. I have things to do.'

'Yes, I can imagine.' Her head bowed slightly and she took a small St Christopher's cross out of her skirt pocket. Without a word, she reached out, grabbed my hand and pressed it into my palm, closing my fingers around it.

'What's this for?'

She smiled a rather crooked smile and looked through me with her blind eyes. 'It's for safe passage, Mr White. It's to help you make the right decision about where you intend to travel next. I hope it's somewhere in this world. Someone could have loved you for yourself, you know? It all seems so sad, changing your appearance to find acceptance.'

I don't know why it hurt me, but tears came to my eyes and I felt hostility towards this meddling old woman, although I knew that she was trying to be kind. 'I don't need your cross,' I said tersely.

'That's the answer of a hurt child, Mr White.'

'Who gives you the right to lecture me? Just because you're blind doesn't mean that you can get away with interfering in someone else's life. It doesn't excuse you from social etiquette.' I said, brushing tears from my cheek.

'I suppose you're right, Joe, if I can call you that. But

sometimes I get irritated by a lack of truth. People saying one thing and meaning another. I like to get to the truth, don't you?'

I was running then. I don't know why but I was running away from her and down the path towards the beach, the small cross held tightly in one hand and the spade in the other. I needed to get Rachel back. She was my truth. I needed to be together again and whole.

The beach was quiet. I took the spade from the plastic bag and started to dig into the soft sand. The tide was out but the waves were rising. A steady wind stirred up an irritating dust. My eyes were sore but I was sure that the task wouldn't take long. I had an idea as to where the box was buried. Three weeks had passed, but I felt sure I had buried it opposite the anchor.

I was glad the beach was empty. I didn't want to look so manic in front of local dog walkers or joggers. I had a mission and I wanted to complete it without interruption. Somewhere under the sand was Rachel, and I wanted her back.

I began to panic when the hole revealed nothing. There was no point in digging deeper; water was already seeping in. I was in the wrong place. But where was the right place, two feet to the left, two to the right or farther back? There were too many possibilities and every part of the beach looked the same. Maybe I had remembered wrongly.

I soon had the beach looking like a minefield. The sweat poured from my face, the heaps of discarded sand keeping count of my failed attempts to unearth my past. When I eventually hit the metal tin, the tears poured from my eyes and I sat like a child among the sand piles and held the box in my arms.

Then I laughed. I laughed at myself, the Mad Hatter at his own tea party, the lunatic from the asylum. I was losing the plot a little. I was making all the years of suffering I had gone through a waste of time. I was behaving like a woman.

It was difficult to open the box. The salt in the seawater had rusted the lock. I took the penknife from my pocket and carefully levered the lid open. I half expected it to be empty. I don't know why.

The pictures were in perfect condition. The plastic envelope had served its purpose. As I looked through them, I realised that all these memories were of unhappy moments. There were none that gave me a good feeling. It was a terrible realisation, as I knew there had been good times. I had just been selective in my choice of photographs, wiping out the good times so that I could move on and embrace the future without regret. My choices had protected me.

The wind was much stronger now. A series of fishing boats were making their way back to the harbour for shelter. The tide was turning. The water was steadily creeping towards me. Soon the beach would be nothing but water.

I turned the penknife over in my hand. I had thought about suicide before. I had thought about it many times as Rachel, before I had ever allowed Joe to exist – the thinness of the skin, the ease with which a vein would open. Death is not a difficult thing to contemplate. It is merely an acceptance that life offers no further reason for living. And I wasn't scared of nothingness.

My thoughts were so negative that I didn't hear her approaching. She had come down from the embankment of grass behind the beach and was standing over me.

'Are you Joe White?'

I didn't recognise her voice, so I didn't turn to face her. 'Who's asking?'

'My name's Laura. We've been looking for you.'

'Why are you looking for me? I don't even know you.'

'I've been to your house. The door was open.'

'That was careless of me.'

I didn't want to talk to her. I didn't care anymore why she had come. I just wanted her off my beach.

'Do you mind if I sit down?'

'Yes I do. I want to be here alone.'

'Well, my husband's coming, and your friend Sophia.'

It was too much to ignore now. I had to know what she wanted, especially if it involved Sophia. 'Okay, sit down if you must, but tell me why you're here.'

'Sophia was worried about you. We said we'd help her find you. She saw the mess in your bathroom and it scared her.'

I thought about the mess I had left and this total stranger knowing that it existed. She didn't really matter, but Sophia did. 'She has nothing to be scared of. I wouldn't hurt her.'

The woman looked at me and smiled sympathetically, her bow-shaped mouth growing wider. 'She wasn't scared for herself. She was scared for you.'

'There's no need for her to worry about me.'

'When someone cares for you, they always worry.'

'So I cut myself shaving, that's all!'

'Why did you do it, though? Were you looking for Rachel?'

My pulse quickened and my limbs froze. 'How dare

you ask me that? Who the hell are you?'

'I'm sorry,' she said, 'that was unfair of me. But I read your note and I know what you've been through.'

'What note?'

'The one you left on your bedside locker.'

If I could have moved my legs I would have run and kept running, but they seemed unable to respond. 'You had no business in my home. What kind of a person are you, prying into someone's life?'

She didn't answer immediately. She scooped some sand in her hands and allowed the grains to slip through her fingers. When her reply came it was delivered apologetically. 'My husband's a publisher. He loves your book. He wants to publish it. He's been looking for you for ages. But he's been looking for Rachel.'

I wanted to cry. The book that I had written to take my mind off Paul's death had found a reader. With all the changes, I had forgotten it was out there. 'But I posted that over a year or more ago.'

She shrugged her shoulders and smiled. 'What can I say? My husband's a slow reader, but he thinks it's really good.'

It was ironic. Rachel's book had unearthed me. With all the effort I had made to bury her, I had left a large chunk of her on the surface.

But there was more to consider than the novel. Suddenly I realised that I had missed the obvious. 'Does Sophia know?'

'What do you mean, about the book or about you?'

'About me.'

'Haven't you told her about you?' She didn't wait for a reply because she already knew the answer. 'I'm afraid I might have inadvertently told her. I gave her the note you wrote. I'm sorry.'

That was it, then, no more pretence, no more lies. Sophia would look at me and see the horror of it all, the spare-parts person underneath.

'I'm sorry, Joe.'

I appreciated that she called me Joe. I softened slightly. 'It's okay. Things haven't been going too smoothly anyway.'

'I'm sure she'll understand.'

It was a reasonable comment to make but it was naïve. I turned to face the woman. Now I really wanted to make her leave. 'You have no idea what you're talking about. No idea at all. How can you understand? You sit there, interrupting my life and you have a face and a body that matches your identity. It doesn't scream at you when you look in the mirror or leave you feeling terrified for the future. Your face fits. It's the face of a woman. It's who you are.' I was on a tirade and I couldn't stop. 'My face used to anger me. It was soft and feminine and shouted "woman" while my mind shouted "man". And my body was an even bigger insult. It grew tits when all I wanted was muscles. It embarrassed me at every opportunity. So I hated it. I cut it with a knife, hid it in thick jumpers, hoped that it would go away. But it didn't until I made it. I went to a doctor and he hacked off parts and gave me hormones so that Rachel would never come back again.' I took a breath but didn't give her time to respond. 'And was it worth it? No. It was just a sham, an attempt to fit in. Look at me now! Do I look like a man?'

I think she was afraid to answer. She gave me a sympathetic look. 'You look like a man to me. I would never have guessed you weren't.'

'Then look closer. It's only window dressing.'

I don't know now why I did what I did next. I suppose it was a mixture of anger and frustration, but it was cruel. I took her hand and I shoved it firmly between my legs. She pulled it away and slapped me hard across the face.

'You shit.'

'Yes I am, but you act as if you know me. Well, you know more now, don't you? There was nothing there, was there? You didn't feel a man. I haven't got that part done yet. It was next on my list.'

I could see her looking at me, sizing up the situation. I didn't want sympathy from her, so I kept talking. It was easy now the topic was out there. 'It was all a waste of effort. I fell for the image in my head instead of living with the reality. I can never be a true man. I wasn't born that way. I should have learned to find a way to live with the body God gave me.'

It surprised me that she was still sitting and listening.

'I'm sorry I slapped you,' she said, staring down at the sand.

'No, don't be, I deserved it. I'm sorry. What I did was childish.'

'I find it really hard to believe that you were once a woman. It's all a bit surreal. You look so perfectly male.'

'Looks can be deceiving. I've created the image my mind desired. Sad, isn't it? I was told that I was in the wrong body when I went for counselling. I was gender disorientated and looking for help. I believed that there was no other option for someone like me but to have a sex change. I was never introduced to anyone who had successfully lived in their birth body. I thought, felt and wanted the same things as most men, so they turned me into a man. The medical profession is very good at that. If you complain about how you look, they'll just change it – a snip here, a tuck there, a sex change. And that appealed to me because all I had ever wanted was for my outside to represent my inside. But now it's not good enough. Rachel was, and is, a part of me. I can't bury her. She'll always be with me. She was how I looked to the world. And although changing my appearance made me feel happier, it didn't solve the underlying problem. I wasn't born a man. Physically, I'll never be a complete man. This is all just a sham.'

She placed her hand on mine. Her touch was comforting.

'So what's the answer?'

'I don't know. Maybe there isn't one.'

She looked at the photographs that lay at my feet on the sand. 'Can I look?' she asked.

'Yes, sure.'

She picked up a few and looked through them. 'You were a good-looking woman.'

'Maybe, but I didn't like being one.'

'Can what you've done be reversed?'

I had never thought of reversing the process. It was something I could never do. I liked the way I looked now, even if it had meant killing off the original me. 'I wouldn't want to do that.' I said. 'But maybe bringing Rachel back is important, too. I can't hide her. If I want a woman to love me she has to know the truth. Rachel has to be there. But will any woman hang around after she finds out I'm an incomplete man? Somehow I don't think so. Women want to be with men. And they want children, don't they?'

'Maybe we all need to learn to love the whole person, not just the body.'

She was right, of course.

'What about your family, Joe?'

'Oh, they don't want to know me. They can't deal with it.'

'My husband has met them, you know. They never mentioned your condition.'

Condition. It was an odd word to use. It sounded like I had a curable disease rather than the physical deformity that I perceived.

'They told him that Rachel was dead, that Joe had killed her. We didn't know who we were coming to meet. We actually thought you were two people.'

'That's a funny coincidence. It's what I told Sophia when she asked me.'

I was almost warming to this woman who refused to leave me alone on the beach. She seemed to understand.

'It's a terrible lie to hide behind,' she continued.

'It was all I could think of at the time.'

We sat for a few moments, neither of us saying anything. I wondered what she was thinking. I wondered whether Sophia would listen to my story as sympathetically.

'Does your husband really want to publish *The Olive Tree*?'

'Yes, he does, and he's right, it's very good. I've read it too, and I agree.'

'Really?'

She was smiling now. I liked this woman. She was a curious mix of forcefulness and empathy.

'Yes, really! It's a good story, very well told.'

'It would be amazing to see it in print. It would be one

way of being the real me. I wrote it before I even thought of changing.'

'Well, you might get your wish. And then you can write an autobiography.'

'I don't think so. It would be too painful and embarrassing.'

It was getting cold and I was about to suggest that we left the beach, but she had already begun to rise to her feet. She had seen something that I had missed. Walking towards us was a tall man in a leather jacket.

'My husband's coming. You can ask him for a contract.'

CHAPTER 45

BRIAN HATED THE SAND IN his shoes. He loved building sandcastles, but sand in his shoes was a pet peeve. He considered taking them off and leaving them in the car. But there was something odd about meeting a person for the first time barefoot. He had spotted them from the road as he was driving back to the village. He hadn't realised it was them at first. They were sitting too close, looking like a couple.

It irritated him that Laura had found Rachel first. He couldn't think why but the feeling was there. They had split up in the village, Laura choosing to walk down to the beach and the woman, Sophia, heading off to the graveyard in her car. He had been assigned the local pubs to check.

By the time he had crossed the sand to where they had been sitting, they were both standing waiting for him.

'Brian, this is Joe, Joe White.'

Joe thrust out a hand towards him but Brian was loath to accept it. The look of irritation on Laura's face made him respond, though. He gingerly shook Joe's hand and felt the strength of a man behind it.

'Your wife says you're a publisher.'

'Yes, that's right.'

Laura was giving him the evil eye again. She had

perceived his reticence and didn't approve. 'I told Joe that you were interested in publishing *The Olive Tree*, Brian.'

She had told Joe. Why did she use his pseudonym so freely? A man was more than a few hormone injections and a deep voice.

'We could possibly do a deal, Mr. White. We'd need to talk first, make sure you have a marketable profile.'

He knew he was being rude. He was surprised at his feelings. He didn't think his reaction appropriate but he couldn't seem to change it either. The person standing in front of him, dressed as a man, was causing him distinct problems.

Joe White stared at him with a penetrating look that made him feel embarrassed.

'How about coffee?' It was Laura trying to rescue the situation. Brian knew she was angry with him but he found his mood impossible to control.

'I don't think your husband really wants to talk to me, Mrs Matthews.'

Brian felt forced to respond in a friendlier tone. 'No, we should go for coffee. There are things to say.'

'I have a café in the village. We could sit there. Do you know where it is? I can meet you there in half an hour.'

CHAPTER 46

LAURA SAT BESIDE HIM IN the car and said nothing. Brian knew she was festering. He knew she would launch an attack sooner or later. She had found his manner on the beach unacceptable. And even he didn't know where it had come from.

They were nearly back in the village before Laura spoke. 'You could have offered him a lift.'

'She said that she wanted to walk.'

'She, Brian? Really? What's wrong with you? He is not a she, Brian. Why were you so bloody odd back there? Are you threatened by him?'

'Don't be so stupid. There's no threat.'

'You behave like there is. You were like a Neanderthal, the way you grunted at him.'

Maybe that was the answer to his feelings. Maybe she had hit the proverbial nail on the head – he was responding from a primeval subconsciousness to the artificially created Joe who did not belong in his world. In his world, there were only men and women and he didn't want his male domination threatened by a hybrid. He didn't like the idea of a creation that he couldn't compete with on an equal footing. He was being true to his sex. He was protecting their survival from an interloper.

'Don't you think he has gone through enough, Brian?'

He agreed on one level. He had read the pages too, seen the blood and hair in the bath. Rationally, his first response had been positive. He'd gone out to find the woman, but when she was standing in front of him, posing as a man, he couldn't fight his reaction.

'Look, Laura, I'm sorry I'm annoying you, but I can't help the way I feel.'

'And how do you feel, Brian?' There was an edge to her voice.

'I feel that Rachel was born a woman and should have stayed that way. And I'm obviously right, because she isn't happy, is she? Changing the way she looked didn't make things perfect, Laura.'

'Oh, very good, Brian, who are we talking about now, Joe or me?'

She was right of course. He had seen the opportunity for a victory in the surgery debate and couldn't bring himself to pass it up. He wasn't going to stop either. He was going to finish the matter. 'We're talking about accepting the reality of who we are, Laura, whether we're male or female, young or old. I'm sorry but it's the way I see things.'

She was shaking her head now, her face flushed and angry. 'No, Brian, you're not hitting me with that one. This situation is totally different and I'm not surprised that you've totally missed the point. You're so close-minded.'

He bristled at that. He was as liberal in his views as the next man. But his annoyance would have to wait. Laura hadn't finished in her diatribe.

'Joe had a sex change in order to be the person he wanted to be. He didn't want to be the person the world saw. But, my dearest husband, I want plastic surgery to become the best I can be. I don't want to change who I am. I just want to improve it.'

'Then why is Rachel unhappy as Joe? Isn't that the best he can be?'

'No, Brian, because she, or he, is not Joe either! I think that's the whole nub of the problem. I think that's what he's discovered. He wasn't born male and he wasn't born totally female either. He is a mix of both. And living with that knowledge won't be easy, but at least it will be true.'

She was crying now. It made him feel terrible.

'What's wrong, Laura?'

'I just feel sad, Brian. Here am I worried about being a better looking me and poor Joe can't even find a way to exist in the world. He's something that this world hasn't even accepted yet. Maybe we've accepted transsexuals on some level, but what about those who don't want to change? How do they get to be who they are if every time they talk about their feelings they are offered a sex change so that they'll fit into our gender stereotypes? Are there just two sexes, Brian? We haven't even skimmed the surface of this issue. What about hermaphrodites?'

There was nothing he could say. Her argument made sense. It was why he found Joe so difficult to acknowledge. Brian Matthews was less empathetic than he cared to admit. He was happy with the rationale of two sexes. He didn't want to cope with a third or a fourth. He wanted to walk into a bar and know the sexuality of the person he was addressing. There were important differences between being male and female, differences that he wanted delineated.

However, there was also a bloody good book that could

be published out of all this, and not just *The Olive Tree*. There was the possibility of a novel, backed by a memoir if he could persuade Joe to write it. Brian smiled, he had used the name Joe. Maybe he had been looking at the situation the wrong way. He should have been responding as a businessman. After all, Joe seemed willing to consider the idea of publishing his novel, and Brian already knew that it could be a bestseller.

'I'm sorry, Laura, you could be right about all this. Maybe Joe does need a helping hand and a good Samaritan.'

But Laura wasn't listening to him. Her mind was elsewhere and she looked perturbed.

'Jesus, Brian, we forgot about Sophia? We need to tell her we've found him.'

CHAPTER 47

SOPHIA SAT ON THE GRAVEYARD wall, holding the two sheets of paper in her hand. Her mind was all over the place. She went from believing to disbelieving with alarming speed. She thought back to the dance and Joe's hand holding hers. She remembered his touch and his breath on her cheek. Then she cried and shivered in disgust at the thought. How could she have not known? How could a woman have duped her? Because that's what the words meant – Joe was not a man. Joe was a woman who had chopped off her breasts and cheated reality.

And she had undressed in front of him. She had waited in his bed, hoping to be loved. She hated him now. She hated not being able to think of him as him. Joe was Rachel. Joe was her. Jesus, so much for her instincts! How could she have been so foolish?

It wasn't right. She had dined on a plate of lies.

They had kissed. Even that thought made her feel sick. She had kissed another woman. It wasn't that she was homophobic. She was accepting of lesbians and homosexuals, but she had no wish to be turned into one herself. She wanted sex with a man. A real one. And what about children? Someone like Joe, if she could call him that, was never going to give her children. It was all too ridiculous.

Mother. It suddenly dawned on her. Had she known? The things she had said. No, she couldn't have known. No one in the village knew. They had all been taken in by Mr Joe Bloody White. Even the name! What a lie!

She thought of the film *Meeting Joe Black* and the fact that Joe Black hadn't been who he had said he was either. Sophia wondered had Joe taken the name White out of some ridiculous reference to the film.

Drops of rain started to fall. She didn't want to move. She didn't want to go home and face her mother, and nowhere else was safe from Joe. He might be in the village. He might be anywhere.

She looked at the note again. The rain was making the words run down the page. Joe's sordid revelation was being washed away. She tore the paper angrily. She wanted to tear him, tear open the skin and reveal the shallowness of his masculinity. But that was wrong too. Underneath, Joe claimed to be a man.

Nothing really made sense. She needed someone to explain to her how it had all happened. Of course she had seen the programmes on TV. She knew the stark facts about how it was done, all the procedures. She had even felt a modicum of sympathy for people like Joe. But to be taken in like that, to be denied the truth and made a fool of, to be told all the lies. It was unbearable.

Marta was standing by the sink washing her clothes. Even though they had a washing machine, she insisted on doing them herself. She didn't trust the machine.

'If you're wet, you should change your clothes.'

Sophia was happy to hear her mother's orders. They

gave the day a sense of much-needed normality.

'Tea is nearly ready. I've made a stew. Where've you been all afternoon? It's been raining this last hour.'

Sophia was tempted to lie. Her mother was old-fashioned and probably wouldn't understand. But she needed to talk and needed someone to listen.

'I've found out about Joe.'

'You've talked to him?'

'No. I was handed his story on two sheets of paper.'

Marta turned from the sink and walked to the kitchen table. 'I think we'd better sit down, my love. I know by your voice that you're upset.'

'I'm all right.'

It was a blatant lie and they both knew it.

'So what did you read and who gave it to you?'

'It was Joe's life story, I suppose, an admission of who he was and who he is.'

'And who is that? Not who you thought, I suppose.'

'Oh, I don't know about that. He was a murderer. He murdered the truth. He made me think he was a man.'

Marta's facial expression didn't change. She just calmly waited for the next revelation as if it was expected.

'Mum, Joe's not a man. He's a woman, for Christ's sake, a bloody woman.'

Sophia hadn't meant to blurt it out so baldly but there didn't seem any better way of doing it. The truth was stark no matter which why it was clothed. The lack of immediate response from her mother disappointed her. She wanted shock; she wanted horror and she needed sympathy.

'I had guessed that, Sophia. The poor man, don't you think? A hard way to live in the world, never feeling like you belong.'

'What do you mean, poor man? What do you mean you already guessed? Did you hear what I said? Joe's a woman. His name was Rachel. How could you have guessed that? Was that what you were hinting at yesterday when we were talking? Why didn't you bloody tell me straight out? Why is nothing ever straight with you, Mother?'

Marta gave a sigh and nodded. 'Because you're straight-laced enough for both of us, Sophia. You're too hard on yourself and you're too hard on life. I couldn't tell you what I thought. It was up to Joe to do that. But I did try to protect you from yourself. I did try to tell you that he wasn't the one for you. That he had issues. I can understand that you're upset, my love, but he must have been so unhappy to have gone through what he did.'

Sophia wanted the sympathy for herself. She didn't want to know how difficult life had been for Joe. Joe was a liar by the name of Rachel. He did not deserve sympathy.

The reaction was typical of her mother, always looking at the other side of the argument, playing devil's advocate. Sophia had grown up with it. Her emotional upheavals were always met with the axiom that there was someone out there whose problems were worse.

'Sophia, I am sorry, my dear. I know you liked him, otherwise you wouldn't be so upset.'

'He lied to me, Mum, a very big lie about who he was.'

'Oh, I don't know if he really did.'

'How can you say that?'

'Because he didn't lie as such. He told you he was Joe, and that's who he is inside and always has been. Surgery didn't change that; it just gave him permission to live his life more easily. It allowed him to reveal a hidden part of himself. He's probably never been Rachel, really.'

'Well if that's true, why is he lying to everybody now? Why is he so upset and angry?' Sophia knew the answer herself. She had read it in his words, but she needed confirmation.

Her mother folded her apron on her lap. 'He's still lying because he thinks, or maybe knows, that people won't accept him no matter what changes he makes.'

'But transsexuals are accepted, Mother. They have a place in society now.'

'You don't accept him.'

'I don't accept that he lied to me. And not just once but loads of times.'

'Sophia, the man is confused. He's doubting everything about himself.'

It didn't matter what her mother said. Sophia couldn't forgive him. She had invested in him. She had thought about marriage and children and all the things that were missing from her life. At least she hadn't known him for that long. She hadn't wasted too many hours pinning her dreams of a future on him. She didn't have time for empty relationships.

'You should go and talk to him, Sophia. He must be hurting.'

'What about my hurt? You're supposed to be my mother.'

'I am, my love, but he didn't want to hurt you. He only wanted to love you.'

'No, mother, he didn't want to love me. He only wanted someone to love him, to love what he created. I've never met the real Joe.'

Marta rose from the table and walked to the mirror on the wall. 'I can't see what I look like on the outside,

Sophia. But people treat me differently because I'm blind. They see me and make decisions about my intelligence and capabilities without even getting to know me. They judge me purely on my appearance. And Joe has suffered the same. All his life he's been treated like a woman because of what people see. The sad thing, Sophia, is that those with eyes are often blind. They can't see that it's what's on the inside that counts; they can't see that the body is merely a shell, a vehicle to carry us through this life. Our body is purely the car, the chassis. It is not the driver. That is our soul, our spirit.'

Marta turned away from the mirror and faced her daughter. 'There is something else you should consider. If I found an operation to return my sight, you would support me, I know you would, and the village would raise funds for me and people would be delighted. But for Joe, his physical problems will earn him no sympathy. No one will give him money to be what he needs. In fact they'll find out about him and probably treat him with distain.'

'Oh Mother, that's only true down here in our village. In the cities it's different. And they're probably given the money by health services for their operations.'

'Then why can't you accept Joe now, Sophia? Are you not supposed to be a liberal thinker? Did you not leave me and this little village because you wanted to grow and find a bigger world? You've returned more closed off than most of us who stayed here.'

Sophia looked at her mother and felt irritatingly proud of her.

Marta sat back down at the table and reached for Sophia's hand. 'Sophia, you liked Joe and not for his looks alone, you liked him for his personality and his masculinity. If he were really just a woman dressed in men's clothing, you wouldn't have fallen for him. You would have objected to the femininity, a femininity that he never fully possessed.'

'I understand, Mum. I think it's more that he lied to me.' There was sense to her mother's argument, though. She had fallen for Joe and it wasn't just his looks, although they mattered too. 'I do hear what you're saying but I'm still angry.'

'I know, and it's because you feel he was fooling you, when really he has been fooling himself.'

'Look, if you don't mind, I'm going to lie down for a while. I'm tired.'

'That's a good idea. A sleep would help.'

Sophia closed the curtains of her bedroom and took off her shoes. As she curled up on the bed, she thought of Joe. She didn't want Rachel to exist. She wanted her mother to be right. There had never been a complete Rachel; there had always been a hidden Joe. People had never seen the truth, only recognised the surface on view. She had been lucky enough to meet Joe, but she knew now that she had also met Rachel.

Because Rachel did exist. She was Joe's physicality, his softness, his empathy and his understanding of women. Rachel had been a living, breathing woman who had experienced something that Sophia herself had yearned to experience. Rachel, or Joe, had given birth. How much of a definition of womanhood was bound up in that one act of creation! And in giving birth, she had acknowledged another fact; she had acknowledged the coupling of her body with a man's.

Sophia strangled a scream. It had never happened

to her before. She was plagued with a million awful questions, each one more perverse than the last. Her head was bursting and the feeling was leaving her angry.

You're dead to me, Joe, she thought. You might have buried Rachel, but now I have to bury you. I can't look past the lie that you sold me when you attempted to suck me into your peculiar world.

She pulled the duvet up to her chin. She felt mean. She felt selfish and hard.

A NEW BEGINNING

I CAN'T GO INTO THE café just yet. I'm not ready to meet these people and discuss my book or my life. They sit in the car waiting. I stand at the end of the pier, bracing myself. The ferry has arrived from the island and the pier is suddenly crowded with good humour and noisy conversation. I look at the stream of colourful humanity. I no longer feel alien to these wanderers. They are just like me, all of them. They have their own fears, misgivings and hopes. They are struggling through life, all hoping to find someone to love them, when what they really need to do is to learn to love themselves first. When you look at it like that, aren't we all the same underneath?

I will get my book published. I will sign with the irascible Mr Matthews. I liked his wife. He may be prickly towards me but I can see past that if it means I can finally see my book in print.

It was the only thing, except Paul, that I really loved as Rachel. I wrote for hours, putting down in pen and ink the lives I would have led if I had been born a man. They were my escape. I invested my spirit into those words. I was every character in *The Olive Tree*, from the thoughtful Yanni to the playful Adam. Every facet of me was written into their mannerisms and insecurities.

A fisherman who frequents The Bare Bones tips his cap at me as he walks past. 'Evening, Joe.'

I smile at him, thinking that if he knew he might not be as friendly. I lied to them all, not just Sophia. I came to this remote little village to build a new life, and yet here I was building it all on lies. How ridiculous that now seemed.

All my early life I played a part, took on a false role. I acted as a woman, had boyfriends, gave birth to a child and even breastfed, but it was all an act. It wasn't the real me in that life. But now I am still acting: 'Hello, I'm Joe White. I'm a real man, can't you see? I've taken hormones to give me a deeper voice and bigger biceps.' But I'm not Joe White. He's not real either.

So I will walk back into my café and make the deal with this publisher from Dublin. I will publish my past, the Walter Mitty me, and then I will write another book. And this time I will own it all. I will tell the world exactly who I am, in vibrant colour, and it may not be as simple as being gender identity disordered or transsexual. It may not be simple at all. And it may challenge people in their perception of gender and who we all really are, but the truth needs to be told. And I have avoided that for so long.

I don't know if my family will ever forgive me or take me back. Someday I hope they will. I cannot give them their daughter back. They didn't really have a complete daughter in the first place. They had me, a curious mix. The label *daughter* only applied to my shell. I wanted so much for them to see the real me, the me inside. Maybe if I had told them how I had felt as a teenager, they could have treated me differently. They could have given me more freedom to be me.

And who is me? Isn't that the problem that I have

been battling all my life?

I am not Joe and I am not Rachel. Those two labels are only one way of looking at me. And those two labels have brought me nothing but trouble and pain. And I am never going to be fully either.

I am a mind and a soul and a body – three in one, indivisible and unalterable. I am a male brain in a female body with a genderless spirit. I didn't ask to be born this way, but it isn't wrong. There is nothing wrong with me. I am perfect in every way. It is just a perfection that exists outside the accepted norm.

A cold wind blows across the harbour, bringing sea spray onto the pier. With a new purpose, I turn up my coat collar and head back to my café. I have a new future to create. But this time, Rachel is coming too. We will go as we were born – together.